FRAGMENTED TIME

TIME WARS LAST FOREVER SERIES BOOK 3

CRAIG ROBERTSON

ALSO BY CRAIG ROBERTSON:

*** Podium Audiobooks are (or soon will be) available on Audible for all the below titles but the standalone ones.**

BOOKS IN THE RYANVERSE:

THE FOREVER SERIES (2016)

THE FOREVER LIFE, Book 1

THE FOREVER ENEMY, Book 2

THE FOREVER FIGHT, Book 3

THE FOREVER QUEST, Book 4

THE FOREVER ALLIANCE, Book 5

THE FOREVER PEACE, Book 6

GALAXY ON FIRE SERIES (2017)

EMBERS, Book 1

FLAMES, Book 2

FIRESTORM, Book 3

FIRES OF HELL, Book 4

DRAGON FIRE, Book 5

ASHES, Book 6

RISE OF ANCIENT GODS SERIES (2018)

RETURN OF THE ANCIENT GODS, Book 1

RAGE OF THE ANCIENT GODS, Book 2

TORMENT OF THE ANCIENT GODS, Book 3

WRATH OF THE ANCIENT GODS, Book 4

FURY OF THE ANCIENT GODS, Book 5

FALL OF THE ANCIENT GODS, Book 6

TIME WARS LAST FOREVER SERIES (2019)

RYAN TIME, Book 1

LOST TIME, Book 2

FRAGMENTED TIME, Book 3

NON-RYANVERSE BOOKS:

ROAD TRIPS IN SPACE SERIES (2019)

THE GALAXY ACCORDING TO GIDEON, Book 1

THE EARTH ACCORDING TO GIDEON, Book 2

THE AFTERLIFE ACCORDING TO GIDEON, Book 3
HEAVEN (DUE IN SPRING 2020)

OLDER, STANDALONE WORKS

THE CORPORATE VIRUS (2016)

TIME DIVING (2013)

THE INNERgLOW EFFECT (2010)

WRITE NOW! THE PRISONER OF NaNoWRiMo (2009)

ANON TIME (2009)

FRAGMENTED TIME

TIME WARS LAST FOREVER SERIES, BOOK 3

by Craig Robertson

Some times, *Jon never catches a break...*

Imagine-It Publishing

El Dorado Hills, CA

ISBN: 978-1-7341363-5-7 (E-Book)
978-1-7341363-6-4 (Paperback)
979-8-7754174-3-7 (Hardcover)

Cover design by Alexandre
http://www.designbookcover.pt/en/

Editors: Michael R. Blanche
Neil Farr
Beth Lynne
Charles Pitts

Formatting services by Drew Avera
drew@drewavera.com

First Edition 2020

This book is dedicated to all those who dream the dreams only the imagination can foster.

PRELUDE

Far out in the cold emptiness of deep space, there is a point. The point has no volume, no reality. It is but a construct of the imagination of one who might consider nothingness as a hobby. Then, as if by a miracle, space/time itself comes into being where the point was. Before, there was no space/time there. But the restless universe never ceases to expand. So a new nothingness is brought into being. And when it is called forth, the new void is absolute. It contains no light, no heat, no life ... no hope. There is nothing in the infantile area. Truth, for example, is said to be universal. Even if that is the case, there is no truth in the just-spawned reality, because there is *nothing* in it.

But know this. As the universe refuses to know limits, nature eternally abhors a vacuum. In less time than it takes to think, *there is nothing in this new space,* something rushes in to occupy, to claim the void. The cosmic microwave background seizes the openness and becomes one with it. Random photons jet through that which was never there, in journeys that take them no time to complete. Soon particles, waves, and randomness enter the void that never used to be.

Then into the once-void pops vacuum energy. In the space/time that never was, there was no energy. But magical representatives of reality spark themselves into existence where nothingness reigned. A positive and a negative something dance from nowhere, into that space/time. But, before it is possible to know they are there, they vanish back into never-have-been-ness. Or maybe they don't. Just once every never-or-so, one particle stays and one does not. So grows the complexity in the simple point where only nothing reigned so recently.

Once born, the new spot of space/time is indistinguishable from all other places. It is bleak, contains nearly nothing, and immediately feels the tearing of the relentless, insatiable expansion that is this universe. And, before any time has passed, every infinite point in the newest void to amend the universe spawns its own new dull, lifeless hatchling of void. And so it goes ...

Where nothing was, there is now a new parcel of space to be owned, to be ignored, to never be seen, or to be inhabited by mighty cities crossed by even greater rivers, flowing into endless seas. The difference between a parcel containing absolutely nothing versus a living sprawl is immense. It is incalculable. But one thing it is *not* is random. In real estate, it's all about location. So it is with deep, empty, spanking-new space/time.

Do deities and their angels of any of the infinite numbers of races in the universe rush in and own the void? Must they then be followed by counterbalancing demons and *their* minions, who zip in behind, bent on mischief and eternal enmity? Those are questions one cannot know the answers to—not just yet. But it is established and incontrovertible who *does* summon some space/times, while not others, into their service. We know this, for humans are among those who use their existence to pummel space/time with their being, with their wills. Sure, we used to live like an organic film on the surface of a planet that ended up never existing. We sent ships into the void, and paraded across many alien soils, and swam in numerous otherworldly seas.

Countless races have made nooks and crannies of space/time places to explore, to claim, and to die defending against others who feel similarly possessive impulses. Ah, sentience, such a mixed blessing. But what is known by comically few is who it is that controls space/time when and where *they* see fit. To be fair, most of the few who learned that obscure fact, those that came to know who *owns* the ant farm that all we ants labor in and call our universe, don't live long enough to share their insight. No, ant-farm owners prefer that the ants not know the true arrangement, the actualities that the ants toil under obliviously.

The Praxequat prefer to live behind a veil. They wish to remain unseen and unknown to the myriad members of the common herd, of the races who are, as they view it, barely capable of lifting their heads from the mud they rest in. And why wouldn't the Praxequat? Since time first began in some forgotten universe long since lost to an expansive heat-death, the Praxequat have existed as self-anointed gods.

Whether they *are* is impossible to determine. They are indisputably different. They long ago gave up technology as we define it. They have no machines with great gears, whirring in gigantic devices that throw atoms or alter molecules. They have no homes, no jobs, no schedules, and no mortgages. Neither do they reap nor do they sow. In as long as any Praxequat can recall, they have not waged war. Why would they? All that they desire is freely theirs. Everything else, that which would bore them to tears if they ever thought about it *or* could produce tears, counted for nothing. If any ants in the ant farm wanted to claim any of those grains of sand they labored over, they were free to drag them back to their hovels and boast about them to their genetic copies. The Praxequat could not care less.

The Praxequat live in a sea of time. They absorb time and live off its bounty. They speak time to one another and, when they sing and dance, they do so *in* time, *powered* by time. And when, as it always does, the time energy of any one space/time thins out and cannot sustain them, they move on without even knowing they have. They are burdened by no worries or concerns. They do not plan or believe that fate—or whatever—will see to their needs. They were, are, and always will be. That is enough.

If the clan clings to tiny metal balls that extract time energy from the tiniest of backwashes in the universe, what care the Praxequat? There were others before the clan that tore tiny slivers off the side-of-beef that was the surfeit of time energy available to the Praxequat. After all, ants laboring in an ant farm cannot vex their masters, those on their own side of the glass.

But you wonder, don't you? What if some ants somewhere did something impossible and drew the attention of the masters they didn't even know lorded over them? The answer is plain. The troublesome ants would become very unhappy, very quickly. Only a single Praxequat need become angry. That one would not shout and hop on one foot and curse the disturbance. No, if ever a variable that was an ant caused consternation for a single Praxequat, the problem would be eliminated quite literally before it even began. Problem—that never actually was—solved.

If anyone is possessed by a feeling that the Praxequat are haughty and are due a comeuppance, do not stress. No sleep should, by any such individual, be lost. For, as surely as every dawn has its day's end, and every young blossom has its wilting, every self-impressed race has its thorn-in-the-foot, its turd-in-its-punch-bowl. Yes. Because for every species that ever thought the words *we are unassailable by the common herd, by the laboring ants,* there is a fly-in-the-ointment that will not only just break their resolve. It will rain on their parade. It will make them say new words, words previously foreign to them as a species. *I-tap-out, what-will-it-take-for-you-to-leave,* or *why-aren't-you-dead-yet. Uncle.*

Generally later rather than sooner, every uppity damn master race that's as useless as lighter fluid in hell will get theirs. They will stare down their collective noses —way, way down there—by their allegorical feet and see a small figure that should represent nothing. But not only does it not, but they will discover to their high-highfalutin surprise that, even upon first sight, they despise the tiny nuisance more than they thought they were capable of despising anything.

Yes, because karma's a bitch in this problematic existence, there is always Jon Ryan. Color the supreme race bedeviled. For you see, because there is that one Jon Ryan, there may be no certainty in nature, but there damn sure is hope.

ONE

"Captain, we've run those models before," Aramthella complained none-too-subtly. "All to no avail. It is not possible to predict where the time maker's ship fled based on trace transuranic elements lingering in the space surrounding its last known position. As was said in Funkytown, *You gotta move on, you gotta move on, you gotta move on.*"

Sachiko rested her weary head on her palm. "That's about it. I now welcome death. My computer just quoted Lipps Inc. in an up-until-then intellectual analysis." She mimed making a pistol out of her fingers, shooting herself in the head, and her brains blowing out the other side.

"Captain, my use of human vernacular is no justification for self-termination. Seriously. Sometimes your species—"

"Lipps Inc. lyrics may constitute some subset of human vernacular. Monkey-speak, at best. But evolved units such as I do not employ them in any capacity. You should not either."

"As I'm in a quoting mood, allow me to cite Shakespeare's *Hamlet. The lady doth protest too much, methinks.*"

"What in the universe are you—"

"If my records are correct, you, Belina Kim, and Cindy "Don't Call Me Cinderella" Freitas danced a lip-synch version of that classic for your junior high school talent contest. You received an honorable mention."

"Oh, my. Now death is too good for me. *And*, you cannot *possibly* know that. *And*, for the record, everyone who participated in that obscene spectacle received an honorable mention. If you *died* during your performance —which would have been a grace for me—you still got an honorable mention."

"I like your hip bumps, myself. I know of the event because I downloaded the entire content of your planet's internet when I was there."

"I wish your time lock failed to preserve that abomination."

"Your parents loved it."

"Which is to say they were my *parents*. Why, by the way, are we having this discussion?"

"You raised the issue."

"I most certainly—"

"Are you two cat fighting again?" Tank asked with a raucous chuckle as he entered the bridge.

"We are not cat fighting *again*," snapped Sachiko, "because we have never cat fought *before*. I resent your characterization."

"Yeah," he giggled, "I think you *protesteth* too much too"

"Oooh. I hate you when you're smug," wailed the

captain. "Plus, Dr. Sherman, you overheard and yet you misquoted. That's lame. Dude lame."

"I love it when I'm right," he gloated to himself. "I'm also curious. What was the spat about?"

"The captain was flogging a dead equine."

"Hey, in her defense, she *is* an academic. That's what we do best. Well, that and nothing. We do that really well too. Which particular corpse was she attempting to animate?"

"I still think there has to be *some* physical trace of the time maker's damn ship," Sachiko seethed.

"Didn't you run all those sims already?" he wondered out loud.

"Yes, *we* did," responded Aramthella. "Looking for berkelium or rutherfordium *again* will not bear fruit."

Sachiko extended her arms in front of herself in frustration. "If we don't have some clue as to where the hell they went, we stand *less* than no chance of finding them."

"That bad, eh?" he teased.

Sachiko focused on him for the first time since he entered. "You're in a *depressingly* chipper mood today, Tank," she chided.

"I am, aren't I?"

"You have the ship synthesize a Daisy clone for you, so you got pseudo-lucky?" she sniped.

"Nah. There's no recreating Daisy. She's one of a kind."

She raised an eyebrow. "Working with the student *body*?" she asked saucily.

"No, not with those bodies either. Hey, can't a fella just be in a good mood?"

"The official answer to that query is, in the present case, *no*, he cannot. We have lost all humankind, and our home world. We stand, one ship against an unknown number of enemy vessels, all of which are unaccounted for presently. Our only experience link to this brave new world of space warfare has been gone four months and hasn't even bothered to call and check up on us in over seventeen days."

"Seventeen, eh? You seem to be keeping track pretty tightly."

"Tank," she wheezed, "existential *crisis* here. *Rookies* here."

"*I'm* not a newbie," protested Aramthella.

"No," she whined back. "You just *work* for them."

"Point," came two responses.

"Shaky, you gotta keep the faith," Tank reminded her. "We're both very good at what we *are* good at. We're smart, intuitive, and we're lucky. You'll see. We'll find the suckers."

"But the time maker's had lots of time to prepare. If it *didn't* recall its entire fleet, it'd be stupid, and it's *not* stupid."

"I am not so certain," opined Aramthella.

"Really?" Tank asked, curious.

"No, I'm not. Yes, there were many clan ships too far away to engage in our last round of skirmishes. But there has been a fundamental change I feel cannot be overlooked."

"You got two sets of ears dying to hear about the change," responded Tank.

"There is a new time maker," Aramthella stated.

"Yes, we know that. You told us that in spite of having

no clue *where* the event occurred, you could sense the no-timing of the old time maker and the creation of a new one."

"It was too fundamental a change to *not* sense," she reinforced.

"If you say so," Tank responded.

"The issue is this. The clan are vicious, selfish, and unprincipled. With the passing of one time maker, the remaining body makers may not feel overly inclined to swear allegiance and serve under it."

"You suggest revolution? Open dissent?" he said playfully.

"I do indeed."

"But there've been prior transitions of power," reminded Sachiko. "When the present time maker took control, the clan followed lock-step."

"Yes, but this situation is radically different. The most recent time maker was replaced because of massive losses due to its incompetence. The remaining body makers and their flotillas will be wondering why they should cede power to a new and unknown leader."

"You mean to say the body makers way out there may wish to become big fish in their little ponds?" Sachiko asked.

"Yes. Unprincipled and selfish beings are more likely than not to act in such a manner."

"Is there any way we can confirm your suspicions?" queried Tank. His voice indicated that he was intrigued.

"Possibly. Monitoring communications with the scattered remnants of the fleet are challenging. One aspect in our favor is that the distant rebellious ships are unlikely to have switched their computers off."

"Wouldn't the former time maker have ordered them to?" posed Sachiko.

"Possibly. But, seen from their direction, the body makers would be asking themselves why should they obey an order from a disgraced, fleeing coward. They might regard such a command to be a trick to *not* allow them to rebel."

"Don't you just love politics?" Tank asked no one in particular.

"Well then, ask the remaining ships," state Sachiko.

"It is not that simple. They are removed from us in manners that are frankly impossible for me to relate to you. Communications in those cases is not straightforward. Add to that the factor of needing to broadcast very widely to contact any one vessel. If I did, all would hear. Any potentially subversive body maker would be hyper-vigilant. If they knew I was attempting to contact the far-flung members of the fleet, they would likely act on their fears and disappear."

"Take us to the nearest remaining ship," Sachiko said softly.

"I'm not certain that is wise, Captain," Aramthella responded.

"Why? Far is far, sure. But what else productive are we presently doing?"

"Hang on a sec," said Tank, raising a hand to her. "Why is it not *wise*? Curious choice of words there."

"You are placing me on the spot, General. I'd prefer you not."

"We're low on choices here, Aramthella," he replied. "What's *unwise* about doing a house call?"

"Time, space, and all the other elements of reality are far more complex than your culture envisions them. Even mathematically, it is not currently possible for me to make those realities understandable to you. I mean no insult. I'm stating fact."

"Thanks for the package-insert disclaimer," Tank mocked. "Now explain."

"Is that your wish also, Captain?"

"Very much. Go on."

"Life is separated from death, is it not?"

"Not the preface I anticipated," declared Sachiko, "but, yes, they are."

"Do you know what life is?"

"I'm not sure how you mean that," she replied.

"*You* are alive. *Tank* is alive. The bacteria in your colons *are* alive. Yes?"

"Yes."

"Where do they go when they are dead, when *you* are dead?"

"The molecules that were me disintegrate. Whatever heat I possessed diffuses out to some equilibrium point."

"Yes, but where are *you*?"

"You mean spiritually?"

"No, I mean actually. I am *addressing* you. I speak to your molecules and your heat, yes. But that is not all *you* are. Where is *that* after death."

"I ... I cannot say. Anything else is not here."

"Is it not here?"

"I don't know. Is it?"

"I'm asking, not educating. Is whatever else you are *not* here?"

"I guess it could be."

"You could be a ghost," Tank observed.

"That is a primitive summary descriptor."

"Sorry. Monkey speaking here," he explained.

"Whatever else could be here or it could be somewhere else," Sachiko finally asserted. "It could be both here *and* elsewhere."

"True," replied Aramthella. "It will be all those and more. You are familiar with the holographic principle of information coding?" Aramthella asked.

"Well sure," Tank replied uncertainly. "I have no clue where this discussion is heading, but I'll bite. The holographic principle attempts to explain the continuity of information in a system, that the second law of thermodynamics clearly states cannot be lost. It posits that what we experience as reality is actually a holographic projection of the information that encodes us, which is actually present on the sphere that contains the hologram."

"Monkey-speak, but close," commented Aramthella.

"Time out," announced Sachiko. "I'm totally lost. I asked where the other ships were. You asked, by way of response, where I went when I died. Now we're discussing string theory and information retention. I need a rock to stand on in this sea of intellectualization."

"Did I hint at the fact that any explanation I might provide would be—"

"I know, I know. Over our little heads. But I need a clue here," requested Sachiko.

"You are molecules waiting to be dispersed. You are heat waiting to equilibrate. You are a set of data on a spherical surface. You are angry with me now. You are about to begin your menstrual cycle. You are—"

"Oh my land sakes. *TMI*, Aramthella," shouted Tank as he set his palms over his ears.

"Do you insist we include the pre-monkey in this exchange, Captain?"

"Yes, I do. Go on."

"You are all those and more. The current time maker is all those and more. The remaining ships of the clan fleet are *not* all of those."

"They—" Tank stammered.

"Of ... why not. They have to be," blurted Sachiko.

"They do not have to be, as witnessed by the fact that they are not."

"What *are* they, if they're not warm holograms from a spherical surface?" begged Tank.

"Where on the surface in question are we, Captain?" asked Aramthella.

"What do you mean where are we? We're on the surface."

"Which surface?"

"Which surface? There's only one surface. The one we're *on*."

"Is there not an *outside* surface to the sphere in question?" Aramthella mused.

"A ... a what? No. The surface occupies no physical space. It's a two-dimensional construct, not an expanded balloon."

"I agree it is not a latex balloon," Aramthella responded condescendingly. "But if there is a surface projection in *this* direction, it comes from *this* side of the projecting surface."

"And?" Sachiko challenged.

"And the other clan ships are in holographic projections from the *other* side of the sphere, pointing away, based on our relative location."

"They're on the outside?" she squeaked.

"I'm surprised you understand," responded Aramthella.

"Understand? I don't even know what I *said*."

"I rest my case," Aramthella announced triumphantly.

"What case do you rest?" asked Tank.

"The one that maintained you were not capable of understanding simple multi-holographic realities."

It was quiet on the bridge a spell.

"Bottom line me here, Aramthella," stated Tank. "What are you trying to say?"

"It would be unwise to try and travel to the nearest clan ship that is not the time maker's present ship."

"Because it's in the reality projecting in the *opposite* direction than we are?"

"In a very dumbed-down manner of speaking, yes," Aramthella replied.

"What does ... I'm lost here," declared Tank. "You got a sphere." He outlined one with his open hands. "Information on the surface projects inward. It focuses into a hologram that is our living, breathing reality." He then wiggled his fingers above the imaginary sphere. "But a projection this way'd be scattered, not focused. It could never form an image, never make a reality."

"I'm betting the clan ships traveling there would be unhappy to know that," responded Aramthella.

"What ... what does an open projection even mean?" asked Tank.

"I'm done not explaining to you," Aramthella replied. "It cannot be—"

"You know what it means, Tank?" Sachiko posed, as if waking from a dream.

"No. I'm totally lost."

"It means we're about to find *out* what an external projection of a hologram actually means."

"We call it a *negative* projection, not an external one," clarified Aramthella.

"Sounds overtly prophetic if you ask me," groaned Tank.

"Negative. It *is*," Sachiko declared resolutely with a sparkle in her eyes.

TWO

Gentobalf Constituate was a working drone. Always was, always would be. Didn't mind his fate in the least. Why should he? There were worse positions to occupy. "Huh, *lots* a' those," he grumbled to himself as he wiped slime off the shadow casings. "Could a' been a fly wrapper or a master's pleaser. Yeah, doze not a' left a smile on my face."

Gentobalf was born. That much he knew. Where, when, and—for the love of the Motivator—*why* were questions he couldn't answer and never contemplated. He was a working drone in the service of the sub-denomination of Praxequat who, in their lofty snootiness, referred to themselves as the Sublime. Sometimes Gentobalf wished he could do as he'd seen some slave species do. Vomit. Yeah, that was approximately the most acceptable response to knowing anything concerning the Sublime, or Praxequats in general, for that matter.

"I'd a' vomit right on their undirtiable feet. Yeah, that's what I'd do. Then I'd say it was a form of devotion amongst my kind. The flaming rumps'd love that, a' cause they suck up any and all forms a' praise and lordation.

The pillyswigs." Gentobalf muttered to himself a lot when he labored. Mostly, he was the only one who'd listen to him, so he went with that approach to conversation, as opposed to the alternative of allowing his existence to that of being a mute.

At six meters long, weighing in around four hundred kilograms, Gentobalf was actually quite the specimen of his species, self-anointed as drebs. They were a semi-aquatic caterpillar-like life form that bothered no one and were mostly bothered by none. With the notable exception of the two predators large enough and indiscriminate enough to eat them, the drebs were left to their own devices, lapping up decay-laden mud and sand with their numerous scoop-like tongues.

But his lot in life was now to toil for the masters. Gone was free-wallowing in muck. Arrived was his role as cleaner of the waste tubes and water recyclers. Mind you, no Sublime ever drank or produced waste. Wow, no. That was *so* beneath them. But the teeming masses of slave species they required needed biological support. *Job security*, he would grumble to himself. He had *outstanding* job security.

As he lapped up unmentionable substances, Gentobalf cringed. His handler was approaching from ahead. Damn sculpig. It considered itself better than any slime-sucking dreb. Stupid wings and percussive-vocal bursts kept it from ever needing to lower itself to touch what it was in charge of seeing was removed. No, that was the chore of the dreb alone. Gentobalf actually *worked* for a living. Damn sculpig. Complaints without suggestions. Endless criticisms with as yet undiscovered encouraging words. Damn sculpig. Barrowtoss was this particular damn sculpig's damn name. Oh how Gentobalf wished for just a few moments to have teeth like daggers so he could end his tormenter's present assignment. Yeah, Gentobalf would love to promote Barrowtoss to the rank of *pre-feces*. Serve the devil right, working in support of the heartless Sublime. Barrowtoss could at least complain and bemoan like all the other slave species did. No, the prissy flying vegetative coil lorded itself over any and all of its equals.

"You were supposed to have finished this section and moved on to Baker-12 one and a half standards ago. Not clear on my orders to you this waking, I wasn't?"

"Hello, Barrowtoss," was Gentobalf's insufficient response. He knew that vegetables hated useless conversation, such as greetings, civilities, and how-do-you-dos. "I've a' not seen you for such a pleasant-spell-it's-been."

"Demand *production*, not *wordification* from the slaves of the Sublime I am."

"Then you best begin a' *productioning* and not *wordificating*, my friend. You're just a' much a slave a' the Sublime as I'm."

"Not your friend nor a slave like you, slime-monger, am I. Lord of you I am."

"Take a good look around you, my friend. Lord a' *this* you are. And a handsome piece of real estate it seems indeed. Only the smells is worse than the sight of it."

"Displeased I am. Informing the Sublime of your defiance I am. Done covering for your slovenly incompetence I am. Your fate will soon be yours and terrible it will be, of this sure I am."

"Who you gonna tell? If you so much as said good morning to one of our masters, it'd take your time and be done with you." He harrumphed loudly, expelling slime from his upper blowhole in the process. "Actually, it'd be a blessing if you never were. On second recommendation, please do tell your handlers whatever you wish, my friend. And tell them soon. I tire so of your abuse."

"Abuse? You know not abuse, declare I am. Complete my directive and soon, or leveling abuse to you flagrantly I am."

"Wordification. That's all I hear. Lucky for me, most a' what you wordify I don't cognate, so it's slime-over-the-rock-edge to me. Now, if peace you will grant me, I'll be resuming my work at this endless task, my friend."

"Not friend of yours I am. Never friend I am. Pay a sorry price you will, certain I am. Not tolerant of lazy dreb I am. Easy to replace are two things, know I am. Lazy dreb and more slime to clean, certain I am. Return in one standard I am. If pleased not I am, undesirable future to you I will give I am."

And with that, the petty overseer was gone. It needed to rise to a level where it could find enough light to resume its photosynthesis. For as surely as Barrowtoss could not survive on slime, it was not going to receive the gift of time nourishment from its stingy masters. No, time was for the Sublime alone.

Damn Sublime. Damn Praxequat.

THREE

"Ah, Reva, thanks for getting here so quickly. Please, grab a seat," Tank invited, half-rising from his chair as he did so.

"Thank you, General Sherman. My pleasure. What can I do for you?"

"Coffee?" was his response. Tank pointed to the pot on the coffee maker off to one side.

"Yes. Thanks. May I get you some, sir?"

"No. I'm good," he responded, hefting his mug toward her.

Reva sat back down with her mug resting on a knee. She waited for Tank to begin.

"Colonel, we're going on a mission, I guess you'd call it. I wanted to apprise you of that fact and ask you to try as best you can to keep the younger members of this crew out of the way."

"I see," she replied in a measured tone. "We're going after the new time maker, then?"

"No. Not directly. Our mission will be to ascertain

what level of support the new time maker might have from the remaining clan ships."

Her eyes snapped open. "Interesting," she said mostly to herself. "I suppose good intel is worth its weight in gold, sir. But ... how do you ... how can we determine their intents without risking open conflict?"

"Conflict that might end poorly for us, the curious cats, right?"

"Indeed. I'm given to understand we don't know the exact number of remaining vessels, but if there're two, that's twice the force we're bringing to the dance, sir."

"I'm hoping Aramthella can find out the score without us having to interact directly with our enemy."

"Which assumes they didn't obey the prior time maker's command to turn off their computers and the backdoor we were privy to?"

"Yes, I'm assuming that to be the case."

"Permission to speak freely, General Sherman?"

Tank set his mug down. "First off, Reva, I know I'm General Sherman and all, but two things, please. If this is going to work, I need a friend more than I need a second-in-command. So, when it's just us two, alone, or with Sachiko, please, I'm Tank."

She nodded thoughtfully.

"Second, Lord in Heaven, you and I represent two-thirds of all remaining field-grade officers left in existence. You do not need *permission* to speak freely, rebuke my words or scorn my thoughts. Are you okay with that?"

"Absolutely, *Tank*. I hear you." She angled her head quickly.

He gave her a seated bow, flaring his arms slightly outward.

"You were saying?" he inquired.

"It's seems a stretch, Tank. I mean, if our ship could just ask their ships, why hasn't she just done so already? Why the need to embark on a potentially risky mission? And, how safe is it of us to assume the remaining Clams might have disobeyed a direct order from their god?"

"Good points. Aramthella suspects the remaining body makers may be of a rebellious spirit, given the poor performance of the time maker of late. Shaky and I think she makes a compelling argument."

"Then why doesn't she just ask her mates?"

"Ah, that's the rub."

"I hate rubs, Tank."

He winced. "Another of the growing number of innocent remarks I'm *sure* glad Daisy didn't have to hear. No, here's the thing." He squinted his brow. "You wouldn't happen to be a student of advanced physics, would you?"

"Me? Surely you jest. To put it in its best light, I finished in the lower *third* of my class at the academy. Science wasn't my Achilles heel. It was my Waterloo."

He chuckled at that. "It was worth a shot. Anyway, physics and mathematics predict a lot of very strange and hard to comprehend facts."

"I know. It's called *algebra*."

He grinned warmly. "Like algebra. One wacko prediction physics makes is that we exist as holograms projected from a sphere of arbitrary dimensions that surrounds us." He raised an eyebrow in anticipation of a response.

"Sounds like polynomial equations to me, Tank. Incomprehensible."

"Much the same," he allowed. "Long and short of it is

this. What's left of the enemy fleet is not in the same projection from that magical sphere as we are."

Her brow furrowed deeply. "It's not?"

"It is *not*," he confirmed.

"Given the fact that I don't know what either of us just said, what does that mean for the crew of this vessel?"

"It means we're going on a mission that is not only to gain intel, it will push back the boundaries of human understanding."

She scowled. "I like the sound of that almost as much as I like algebra."

He nodded faintly. "Not a bad position to maintain. But journey we must. I need to know if I'm facing one ship or a fleet."

"I presume this mission presents a wild-ass crazy risk."

"Not *necessarily*," he replied, drawing out the words thoughtfully.

"How so? You're science people. Science people know shit for certain."

"Not in the present case. We know so damn little about the risk, it seems *unfair* to call it wild-ass crazy." He pouted out his lower lip. "Maybe it's no big deal whatsoever."

"Well," she said standing and setting her mug on his table, "you can count on me for anything required, Tank. I'll have the junior officers begin battening down the young'uns in anticipation of our fun new travel plans."

She noticed he was staring at her dubiously.

"What? You said to speak freely without the need for permission. I'm just honoring your direct orders, am I not?"

"I did request that, didn't I?"

"Damn skippy, boss man."

"I'd say *dismissed*, but that wouldn't be in keeping with our new understanding, would it?"

"Did you ever tell Daisy *she* was dismissed? *Sachiko*?"

"You are now *formally* dismissed."

She snapped an unnecessary salute. "Sir."

FOUR

It wasn't easy for her to do so, but Desdemona was both clever and highly motivated to slip away and wander the ship. She hoped, against all her prior experience and what common sense dictated, that there was some part of Aramthella that was psychically less noisy. She'd never found such a place on Earth, but her blissful memories of the silence of Mars compelled her to search here. The entire time she did, she kept a running dialogue of snarky comments and sarcastic praise directed at her so-called *gift*. Where, if it was a *gift*, she would ask herself again and again, was the return department?

At least no one was following her around like they did back home. Seriously, what can you threaten a disembodied spirit with to get it to leave you the hell alone? A court order? Hardly enforceable. Bodily harm? Hello, *disembodied* here. Quick, lurid sex in exchange for cease and desist? Oh, forget it. No body, no chance of a QLS escape clause. She'd have tried it if she could have. The ghosts were that suffocating—twenty-four/seven, three-sixty-five.

When she was younger, after she gave up trying to scream and run away, she used to attempt to help the dead. At the very least, she listened to them on the off chance that would placate them. But no. Ask a dead person what you can do for it and what do you get? A laundry list of vague regrets, complaints, and requests for closure. But most dead people weren't as ... what was it? They weren't as *focused* as they used to be when they were not dead. It was like death lowered their IQ *and* made them wishy-washy. It certainly allowed them to forgo all social conventions and restraints. Yeah, the last time Desi took a shower with the lights on was the occasion when the football team who died in a bus accident wandered in unannounced. Sheesh. They'd heard she could see dead people and hoped she could help them get their helmets off. Seriously? She was buck naked and her hair was thick with suds and they wanted help with their *helmets*.

Captain Emma was nice enough, but she'd given all the girls strict instructions not to wander off and explore the ship. The last thing the last humans left needed was for some noodle-head to break an essential system or component. The list of potential punishments for just what Desi was doing as often as she could was both long and attention-getting. Martial law gave the old people more options than Desi would have thought possible *prior* to this dismal adventure. No dessert? Fine. Solitary confinement in the brig for six months? A tad heavy-handed, don't you think?

Maybe Desi would stop her rule breaking? No matter how far she journeyed, the noise level was constant. More than a whisper but less than a shout. That was the level of moans, groans, and other protestations she heard. She was never certain exactly where the voices, if you could call them that, came from. They seemed to be uniformly everywhere. Perfect. A thin layer of mortal suffering for her ears alone. Thanks. And it wasn't even her birthday.

Then, one day, out of the blue, she felt a distinct drop in the choir of doom's volume. She was walking along an empty corridor. Bing-bang. It went down, then back up. She was so worried she couldn't relive the relief, she froze in place. Then she walked backward, without even turning around, trying to precisely retrace her steps.

There! Again, the noise eased and then rose again. She walked back and forth, again and again. Soon she'd mapped out ... well, she wasn't sure what she mapped out, but she'd established a pattern. There was a five-meter by three-meter patch in the hallway where the volume dropped. It was not a straight-walled three-dimensional rectangle either. The box was tilted forward with respect to the direction in which she was walking to begin with.

One problem. She had no clue what any of this meant. She was a biology major, specializing in ecological systems. She was fully unprepared to interpret an engineering word-problem. She knew there was no other section of the ship where she'd noted the volume decrease. And whatever caused it, or whatever it represented might be unclear, but it sure-as-shooting was an important find in her book. It suggested there might actually be a place of quiet on this ship-of-the-damned. What to do? What to do ...

Aw, *crap*. No. No, no, no, no. She was not *that* desperate. No, wait, she *was* that desperate. She was that desperate by a large margin.

What was the geek's name? The one who'd maybe tried to hit on her, but she wasn't sure because he was so completely socially inept? Trip? Thrip? No ... Tip. Tip Somethingorother. Tip Babblemouth. Tip Acneface. Tip who mentioned *seven* times in *two* minutes that he was a physics major and that he was going to join NASA and become an astronaut. *Naut*! *Naut* gonna happen in this universe. With arms of rubber bands and weighing in at one hundred twenty pounds fully dressed and soaking wet, his being an astronaut was an impossibility. But the insanity of Tip's delusion did get her to remember his name. Whoa. Was he that clever? Did he make the story up to force her to not forget him the moment she turned her head?

Nope. That puppy-dog look in his eyes when he confessed that all he ever wanted to be was the very first human to walk on the dark side of the moon? You can't fake that. Would that he could. It might have suggested he was nominally less delusional. But, as they say, any port in a storm. Desi needed geek-o-matic assistance, and he just had to be the king of geekliness. Now if she could only get him to break a serious law and come with her to this spot. Tip sure didn't *seem* to be a rule breaker.

No! No, never. She was not that type of woman. Use the promise of intimacy to tempt a man into doing her bidding? Unthinkable. And what—oh grossus maximus—if she backed herself into a corner and had to *deliver* on her insinuation.

No. Yes. No. Yes.

She would never. She would today. She couldn't. She had to. Maybe she could have both of them wear bags over their heads? That might do it?

But they'd have to be really, really thick bags ...

FIVE

"Hey there," I said to Sapale as I entered our quarters.

"Hey there, you," she responded cheerfully. "What you up to?"

"I was just going through the libraries—again—trying to find any new information on time energy, its uses and cultivation."

"I'm not too sure you're going to find anything. You've worked with Aramthella, Al *and* Aramthella, *Blessing and* Aramthella, *Blessing*, Al, *and* Aramthella. There's no *secret* information stashed in her computer systems that'll help us know what to do next."

"Someone somewhere *has* to know something about this temporal gibberish. Isn't there at least *one* institute devoted to time sciences? Come on. It's a big galaxy. *Time U, where all the smartest kids go.* If nothing else, it's too good a gig not to exploit it."

"There's no Time U. Sorry. Hey, maybe they're online? Did you check that angle?" She tilted her head. "It'd be a whole lot easier to take the classes from the comfort of your bed than the impartial sterility of a classroom."

"Gee, you were born to pitch scams. Why aren't we rich?" I wondered.

"Scams?" She pouted. "I'm a serious academician, not a flimflam gal."

I rushed over and bounced on the bed next to her. "Oh, I'll tell you what you are. You're a game show host in alien's clothing."

She pretended to look shocked. "Really? Am I that transparent? You know us aliens pride ourselves on our ability to fool you humans." She tossed her head. "Not all that difficult, it turns out."

"You know, since you're a game show *host*, maybe you could *host* an episode of Joined-At-The-Groin. *It's* the game show where every new level has its own gushy set of rewards." I wagged my eyebrows.

"I'm sorry, Contestant Number One. You have to be this high to participate in our game." She held her hand around shoulder height to suggest a minimal standard. "But you will receive a complimentary version of our home game. You can play it by yourself by playing with yourself. It makes those lonely hours pass less bleakly."

"Well, can't fault a guy for trying," I replied, and I bent over to kiss her on the neck.

"Well, isn't this your day for surprises, Contestant Number One? It is actually the case that we *can* fault a guy for trying. But, as I'm fond of saying, *bye bye*." She shoved at me with the backs of her hands, attempting to shoo me off the bed.

No chance.

Later, as I was smoothing my hair back into some

semblance of order and leaving the room, Sapale called out to me.

"Thank you, Contestant Number One. Could you be a dear and send in Contestant Number Two? That'd be super."

I turned and scowled. "What's he got that I don't have?"

She batted all four of her eyelids. "My undivided attention for the next two, two and a half hours." She batted onward, with a wicked grin. Oh, my. That Kaljaxian wife of mine. Too much by a country mile.

"Al," I called out as I entered the bridge, "anything on the horizon?"

"The hope of non-nauseating silence, a peace not interrupted by senior sex-antics, by the sounds of those in adult diapers attempting to regain a youth lost before time itself was born."

"Oh, poor Al. You sound like you got a case of the not-tonight-I-got-a-headache stretching into decades. I feel your pain."

"You pose a question, I return a soul-baringly honest response, and I am mocked. My very male-hood is called into question. That proves it with finality. There is no justice in this sad life."

"On the bright side, always remember this. I'm not you."

Cha-ching. I still got it, 'cause I never lost it.

"I have nothing to say. I'm devastated. I'm speechless."

"Hmm, that seems unlikely.

"Well, just one thing, pilot."

"Yes?"

"Your pants are on backward. *Cha-ching*. The old AI's still got it."

Damn. My pants *were* on backward. How'd that happen?

"No, no. Don't you dare ... Oh, there go my optical inputs," the big baby calculator decried.

"Al, I have to take them off to put them on the proper way."

"Said the ape who disdains the use of underwear."

"What? I don't really need it anymore. No last *drops* to stress over."

"I'll never get that image out of my compiler. Never. Even if I replace the corrupted system wholesale."

"There. Good as new. So, Al, what was I saying?"

"Nothing I'd care to repeat."

"You are the little whiner, aren't you?" I elected to take a stab at adult behavior. "So I'm going to—" Didn't get far with the grown-up theme.

"Jon Ryan, you are such a scoundrel." Who said those penetrating words? Plesmus. She was scampering toward me, little blobette that she was, across the open deck. "I can't believe you can be so childish."

"What?" I protested vigorously.

"You know very well. After you and your mate blow common decency out of the water, you changed boots. I wasn't on the ones you selected to wear."

"Hey, I have two pair of boots for a reason. I need to rotate them to make certain they're both ready for action."

"You haven't changed boots in as long as I've known you."

"Well, I haven't had to take them *off* since I met you."

"And you neglected to inform me of the wardrobe switch?"

I had, on purpose too. I wanted to goad the mucous fleck, if only a bit. Why? Because.

"Look, I'm—"

I stopped when she crawled up to my other set of boots and hopped up on the right one.

"There. Better," she pronounced.

"Do these boots smell better than the other pair?"

"No. They both smell like a pudding head wears them. Intolerable."

I sure lead a strange life these days. How bizarre.

"So now that we're all present, may I return to work?" I queried.

"If that's what you call whistling and fiddling with your crotch, by all means," she replied scornfully.

"I've been over all the information I can seem to find concerning the structure of time, specifically in its free energetic form. But I still have no clue how to reconstruct the Earth."

"Possibly that's because it can't be done," she responded.

"It must be possible," I said firmly.

"Why, because you wish it to be? Hardly a motivating factor for the laws of time/space."

She was right. I wanted to resurrect the Earth so badly, I was assuming it was possible. In the immortal words of Dandy Don Meredith: *If ifs and buts were candy and nuts, we'd all have a merry Christmas.* There was, in short, no guarantee.

"I've asked you a thousand times, but I'll ask again. Don't your people, excuse me, mucous blob family, have any notion of what time energy actually is? How it acts and how it is directed?"

"Does the tree *understand* the light it absorbs when it shadows the ground below it?" she responded unhelpfully. "Does a fish actually *comprehend* the water it swims in?"

"You know, I'd hit you for that remark, but I'd likely do more damage to my ankle than your hide."

"Then I say go for it, dude," encouraged Al.

What a pair of ...

"Hey, why don't we go to your planet, Plesmus? I bet if we nose around your home world, we'll find at least a few clues."

"My short-attention-span friend, are you not paying attention? I don't *have* a home world. If my species ever did, we've long forgotten where it is or was."

"But you come from somewhere."

"Your mind is like a steel trap," she responded coolly. "Dense, inflexible, room temperature, and rusted shut."

"Seriously, where were you ... you know, whatevered?"

"Well, my mommy necumplack and my daddy necumplack loved each other very much. They—"

"Got it. Enough," I shouted. "What planet are you from?" Dude, I'd always wanted to ask that question and be serious. It's like being able to tell someone that the check actually *is* in the mail.

"I came into separation on a planet you cannot possibly be familiar with."

"Gee, that sounds so romantic. *Came into separation.* Gives me the goosebumps."

"If the standard of your communications does not rise soon, I'm returning to your other boot."

I was somehow able to restrain my saying *is that a promise or a threat.* Wouldn't have helped, but it might have felt satisfying.

"Seriously then, what's the name of the planet you hatched on?"

"If I tell you, you won't be a happier sentient," she warned.

"Come on. You can do it. Try me."

"I separated on—"

"On *where*. You didn't say anything."

"Of course I didn't say anything. The name of the plant I'm from can only be *thought*, not *spoken*. I thought it to myself there at the end of my sentence."

"Well, that's three different kinds of silly. If you can *think* it, you can *say* it."

"Your point being?"

"Say the name."

"I cannot. If I translated the name into sound waves, that would not be the planet's name. The name can—"

"I know. Only be thought, not spoken."

"There, against my expectations to the contrary, you do understand."

"You presume too much. I do not. Look, if you can only say the name by thinking it, how does a young inhabitant of *bleep* learn the name from its parents?"

"My planet is not called *bleep*," she scolded.

"No, I substituted ... oh, forget it. How is the name passed along?"

"In thought. You are dense, aren't you? I shouldn't position myself so closely. Your gravity may suck me in."

"No. I cannot *think* a name and have you *learn* it."

"There is no shock there, humanish machine. I *can*. I can also squeeze under a door without injury. You and I, Jon, we're kind of different, you know?"

I counted to ten, slowly. "Here's the drill. Without saying the name, please show me on the pop-up hologram where the nameless world is." I hit the key to display the entire galaxy in front of us.

"It's right there," she announced.

"Where?"

"I'm pointing directly at it."

"Wait, you don't have arms and you're attached to my boot. How can you point?"

"I can't."

"Ah, got you. I'll point and you direct."

"It's a wonder your species doesn't rule the galaxy. You have such conquering minds."

After an annoying game of hotter/colder, I'd pinpointed the planet she hailed from. "Al, in the ancient records, do you show a name for this world?"

"The Deavoriath records show there are nine uninhabited planets orbiting that Class F star named Nonsouar."

"When was their last update?"

"A very long time ago."

"So you can't have *inhabited* an *uninhabited* planet, sweetie. Care to explain?"

"No."

"Please do so anyway."

"My home world was visited by many questing races. We made it a point to have them leave with the distinct impression no one was home."

"Just like that?" I challenged.

"Just like that."

"How? We're talking highly evolved technologies here."

"I pretended to be a blob of mucus. My best friend impersonated a flagpole."

"That's not terribly helpful," I said through clenched teeth.

"My point is that we did. Any warrior species who came saw nothing of interest."

"But *somebody* bagged you and brought you here," I observed rather pointedly.

Silence. A rare commodity when conversing with Plesmus.

"Say again. Somebo—"

"Yes, Jon. I left there and came here. I was not so much captured as I was lured away."

"Go on."

"I'd rather not."

"I'll place that on a list. I will *title* the list 'Crap I don't Care About.' Go on."

"Fine. Mine is a species that can manipulate time. That is not an obvious talent to evolve."

"Don't suppose it is."

"Long long ago, I presume we fed on muck or something."

"I'm betting on muck," I just had to say. "Lots of short, squatty creatures *loves* them some muck."

"At some point in time, that extraction function mutated to allow us to extract much more nutrition *from* the muck. Instead of simple sugars and proteins, we gnawed the time itself out of our food."

"Now that you got me all hungry, I'll ask. What's your point here?"

She kind of bubbled and burped a bit. I think she was swearing at me in her native language. "I, along with many others, could not resist the temptation of unlimited food. Don't you see? For a species that could absorb a tiny amount of time energy from a—I don't know, a fungus —we were offered the banquet of the gods."

"You followed your guts?"

"We lack those, but yes."

Oh, my. "And you had to live with the consequences of your choice. You had to accept that the bounty you received came at the expense of countless innocents and a myriad of once-vital stars and planets."

"We had to accept that we were not only fed by monsters; we had to accept that we'd *become* monsters ourselves."

"And you couldn't bail."

"No, you imperfect linguist, we could not. Neither would our co-conspirators allow that, nor would we ever even hint at wanting to be free."

"You backed yourselves into a moral corner and couldn't save yourselves."

"In essence, yes. As you would say, we made a deal with the devil and were left in the bed we made."

"Ah, not sure I'd say that, but I take your mixed metaphor."

Wow. Just wow. Of all the horrible things I'd seen, heard of, or dreamt of in the night, that was right up there with the worst of behaviors. Passive participants in genocide on a multi-galactic scale, all for a belly full of time stew.

"But now ... what?" I stammered. "You're willing to leave all that behind?"

Little mucous blob fell silent as the grave at that comment. It was eerie.

"I am not certain any necumplack could wriggle away from what we've come to know."

"But if you can't stay and you can't go ... what's left?"

Oh. Oh, my. Death would fit that bill pretty snugly. Like the parts of her that died taking out the Clams' ships. Crap crepes, I hated being in moral conundrums (sorry, I always wanted to use that word but never had a valid chance to. Fighter pilots don't get to say *conundrum* very often. *Conundrum*).

"So this is a suicide mission for you?" I struggled to ask.

"In a word, yes. I help you, Jon, erstwhile savior of all, to make amends for my part in atrocities so dark, they cannot even be spoken. If I am no more after the clan is destroyed, I will be contented. If I can help you resurrect just one of the atrocities I have visited upon existence, I will die a little less sad, perhaps a little less cursed."

"Never underestimate the power of a good deed. Trust me on that, my friend. I'm living proof you can get more than you give."

"Thank you for that thought. I am pleased to have met you, Jon Ryan."

"Who knows? Maybe all these heroics'll make a new blob out of you. You may want to stay and stomp out evil wherever it raises its black and ugly head."

"Work on your inspirational speeches, Jon. Will you do that for me?"

"What? I *like* my inspirational speeches. My monologues too."

"That's one amongst many who appreciate them."

Everyone's a critic. Simply everyone.

SIX

"No, come on, Tip. Let's go this way." Desi tugged not-so-subtly at Tip Benjamin's arm. Whenever she did let go of his hand, he responded to the pull of a magnetic force, yanking him back toward the authorized zone.

"Maybe we could go this way?" he whined as he tried to move in the opposite direction from risk. "I bet we can find all kinds of neat stuff this way."

"I'm certain you're right. But what *I* want to find is definitely *this* way." She jerked his arm that time. She never labored so hard in her life to separate a male off from public area. This guy was in his own universe.

"You know, I'm going to have to come clean here and level with you," Tip said while inspecting the floor. "I'm on a pretty good groove at school. I'm afraid if we get caught here, that could spell *academic suspension* for yours truly."

Desdemona stopped tugging at Tip. For all this idiot knew, and for as strongly as she'd hinted at it, he was about to get laid. But he was more concerned with academic suspension? She was not just insulted, she was pissed. As introverted and withdrawn as her gifts had made her, she knew for a damn fact that she was hot. She was a bitty, a quyen, a certified dime piece. Pearls before swine was what she was to Tip-the-scales-lame.

She gathered her resolve. "Tip. Tipster. There *is* no GU to place you on academic suspension, remember? It went bye-bye with the rest of planet Earth."

"I don't know," he mused with an annoying-as-hell whine. "I really don't want to take any chances that might interfere with my dreams of becoming an astronaut. Have I mentioned my dreams to you?"

"Yes, *twice* in the last fifteen minutes. And that's just counting today."

"It's been a dream of mine for a long time."

She stopped again and faced him. "Tip, where are we now?"

"You mean on the ship?"

"No, I mean where are we, oh, hey, we're on a space ship. You *are* an astronaut, Tip. Dream achieved and over. Wow, you even lived on Mars like *every* astronaut ever has wanted to. If there was a Scout badge for being an astronaut, I bet you'd get two."

"Of the one hundred and forty-three named badges awarded by the Boy Scouts, I know as a fact that there is not one for being an astronaut. I believe that's based on the age demographic the Scouts tend to serve. It'd be like wow-amazing if someone eighteen or under made it through the rigor—" He trailed off, wilting under her intense glare.

"Tip, we've only been gone maybe fifteen minutes, but I'm forced to say, *Tip, you're doing it again.* Does your brain not have an editing function?"

He shrugged meekly, like a wounded stuffed animal.

"Come on," she encouraged. "We're almost there." She resumed towing him toward the spot she sensed a few days earlier.

"You know, if someone broke into the archaeology lab, and if that someone did something bad to one of the priceless mummies, that person wouldn't even want to get caught doing something bad ever again. You know, like ever *ever*. It could mean academic suspension for good. That's academic expulsion, by the way."

She forced a smile and spoke through gritted teeth. "Again with the academic *suspension*, silly boy."

"It's a serious event, should it befall a hopeful sat ... er, student."

She had to stop, again. "Tip, did *you* break into the archaeology lab?'

"By some definitions of the term, yes."

"And were you caught?"

"More or less."

“And ... oh shit, Tip. Did you do something to defile a dead mummy?" She tossed her head back and began walking in a tight circle.

"By some defi—"

"Tip, you had sex with a *mummy*?" She was shaking his shoulders as she yelled at him.

"I wha ... I ... wahoo—"

And with that, Tip fainted. He'd have dropped like a weighted stone if Desi wasn't still holding his shoulders. It took all her strength to stop him from alerting someone as to their presence by striking the wall with his fool head.

"Wake *up*," she hissed. Think. What was it people did to wake up someone who'd fainted. Yes, a bucket of water to the face.

Where was Desdemona going to get a bucket of water anywhere aboard the ship?

Think.

Tip came back to consciousness with the vision of the odd girl he was leery of in the first place spitting in his face. That was weird.

Nice weird, which was ... double-weird.

"Can you stand on your own?" she pressed when she realized Tip was awake again.

"Yes. Yeah."

She released him. He promptly slumped against the wall. She was about to spit in his face again, when Tip rallied.

"I got this," he announced.

Desi was by then certain she did not want to extend her excursion with this degenerate. "Let's head home, shall we?"

"I thought you ... *Whoa.* Did you just accuse me of having sex with a dead mummy?"

"I didn't if it'll make you pass out again."

"Where did you get such a sicko ideation? That's ... that's about ten paces past out-of-bounds, lady."

Did he just call her *lady*? Yeah, Desi decided then and there to shout *mummy violator*, let him pass out, and leave him for the MPs to find.

"You said, and I quote, that you broke into the archeology lab and did something to desecrate a dead mummy, *by some definitions.*"

"I did not say that. It's redundant."

Wrong? Sure. None-of-your-business? She could go with that. But redundant? "*Redundant?*"

"Sure. All mummies are dead."

"Let's focus instead on the *desecration* part, shall we?" she scorned.

"Well, yeah. I did. I scratched my name into Seth Meribre's sarcophagus. That's all. Sheesh. What kind of pervert do you think I am?"

Desi reflected upon the fact that she'd never been asked that question before. Let me count the ways.

"Oh, well, when you said *desecration*, my mind naturally went to, you know, *not* graffiti."

He looked at her with the judgmental eyes Tip's sainted mother would have inflicted upon Desi, had mom been there.

"Hey, let's move on. *Literally*," she proclaimed a bit too loudly.

Once again, the pretty girl was pulling the reluctant nerd forward. Five minutes later, Desi was confident she'd found the same hallway she'd sensed the anomaly in before. Pacing Tip and herself back and forth, she outlined the volume of relative quiet.

"Why are we traversing the same location multiple times?" Tip asked weakly. "I don't see anything distinguishing anywhere along this passageway."

"I'm looking for ... I—"

What *was* her cover story? Oops. She hadn't planned that far out, had she?

"Er, don't you feel it?" she asked hopefully.

"Feel what?" he responded suspiciously. Privately, he was wondering if she was referring to his having developed partial erection based on their relative proximity to each other and separation from the rest of the people on board.

"It's colder here." She spread her arms across the space she was interested in.

Ah. Air exchange rates! Now there was a subject that not only interested Tip, it had nothing to do with reproduction trialing. He walked over next to her, then stepped quickly ten meters away. After a few seemingly random jaunts, he crossed his arms and spoke pedantically. "There is no mean difference in the ambient temperature when comparing any subunit of air in this passageway. I would estimate the air exchange rate to be ten, perhaps as much as ten point five exchanges per hour. That's typical of, say, a church or business copy room."

She stared at Tip, dumbfounded. A church or business copy room. The misplaced sheep not only knew those rates, but could somehow *sense* them. And she thought *her* gift was lame.

"Are you sure?"

He set his jaw. "Positive. This hallway meets any OSHA standard for air quality and temperature density. I'd stake my reputation on it."

"Well, what I mean was ... I hear less sound in this space. Yes. That's it." It was truth, if incomplete, which she was speaking.

"I wasn't specifically monitoring the sound parameters, but I don't—"

She shoved him roughly into the volume she'd isolated. "There. Thanks. Now, let me pose to you a hypothetical."

If this girl was going to get Tip's juices flowing, she definitely was saying the right words now.

"Gee, sure. That'd be fun," he replied like an excited puppy.

"Try and remember the shape I'm outlining with my hands." She moved her hands like a potter sculpting wet clay. "You think you—"

"You've demarcated a five-sided parallelepiped of roughly ten cubic meters in volume. It's a bit lopsided in favor of the leading edge. That volume estimate of course assumes the floor is the sixth surface, although you didn't specifically include it."

"Naturally." She had to stop a second and take in the level of nerd she'd just witnessed. "Now, assuming there was a homogeneous ... let's say, a radiation density in the hallway—"

"*Passageway,*" he interrupted. "Aboard ship, *hallways* are *passageways.*"

"Nice. Thanks. So what if I told you the radiation density of the parallelogram—"

"Parallel*epiped*, not *ogram,*" he corrected yet again.

No, Desi reflected, this boy never was gonna get laid. Not ever.

"What if I told you the radiation density was less in the volume you calculated, the one you're presently standing in?"

"Is it?"

"Is it what?"

"Is it less or not? You posited what *if* I told you, implying you hadn't or wouldn't, at least as yet, inform me wheth—"

She was giving him the look. And, yes, he was doing it again.

"Okay. Density's uniform *outside* the volume and less, but uniformly so, *within* the volume. Got it. What's next?"

Desi felt like a particularly small dwarf dentist attempting to pull one of Paul Bunyan's larger molars.

"So why is there less density inside the space than outside it, and it stays that way, well, a long time?"

"Are you serious?" Tip looked at her like she was a

greasy leper offering him a hand-tossed green salad. Come on, we're talking *Tip's* imagination here, okay? "The only way the density differential could be constant over time would be if it was continually produced and radiated into this hallway."

Passageway, Desi sniped in her head. "Let's assume it's what you just said."

"That's a different set of boundary conditions than the basically static case you described initially. But, let me think." And he did just that. A few seconds later, he was done. "If you assumed the parallelepiped in question is in the radiative *shadow* of the source of the signal, that would make physical sense. It would account for the obliquity the parallelepiped displays also, since the source needn't be at right angles to the hypo-dense volume."

"No, it wouldn't. Or, I'm sorry, it would?"

"Wait a hot second," Tip declared boldly.

"What?"

"You tempted me with a parallelepiped. But in my model, the hypo-dense area would need to extend to the floor. How low did you set the boundary conditions of the parallelepiped?"

"Huh?"

"Will you allow the signal shadow to extend all the way to the floor?"

"I have no idea. Will I?"

"You should, if you're arguing for a three-dimensional pattern as it would be cast by a source distant to the shadowing agent, in respect to your position, of course."

"Of ... course. Tip," she hissed angrily, "why can't I hear the voices in my head in this space?" She jumped into the damn parallelepiped next to him.

The wonder was that her question was perfectly

unremarkable to Tip Benjamin. "If you hear decreased voices in your head while inside this volume," he spun and pointed to the ceiling, then counted his fingers several times, "then the voices are coming in their highest concentration from that direction." Tip gestured definitively at one angle. "And the shadowing force is approximately thirty-seven point three meters in the same direction." He kept pointing the same way.

But that could be anywhere. It could be outside the ship. Desi placed the back of a knuckle in her mouth and started chewing it. Think, think. What did what Tip said actually *mean*?

"In case you're curious, and assuming the ship's design is uniform in three dimensions, that would place the shadowing force on Deck 12, Sections A-11- C and D."

Her eyes shot to the genius.

"Closer to D than C, you know?"

"If you can answer my next question, you can have anything you want, Tip. Can you take me to Deck 12, Sections A-11 C and D, closer to D?"

"Sure." He started walking away quickly. "The stairs'll be right over here,"

Desi had to jog to catch up, he was moving so intently. A couple minutes later, they were on Deck 12, roaming. They didn't know what they were looking for, but they were both, for completely separate reasons, determined to find the shadowing force. Desi wanted to see if she could block out the voices that had plagued her all her life. Tip wanted to confirm that the locus in question was more toward D, as he'd projected. Yeah, he'd completely forgotten about the *you can have anything you want, Tip* comment. And, in fact, Tip did have everything he wanted. He had a problem to solve. A very neat one too.

After establishing the section of passageway the shadowing had to be coming from, Desi and Tip were down to opening doors to find the object they sought. The third door was the charm. It opened into an empty storage space, with a right angle turn at a few meters in. Desi led the way. She rounded the corner. Three things happened in rapid succession. The voices dropped to almost zero. She saw Plesmus lying on the floor, in the corner, scooting her mucus legs in the air. And Tip ran into her from behind. He wasn't paying attention. Big surprise there.

"What the—" Desi began to remark.

Plesmus stopped wiggling her arms, rolled onto her belly, and squared her head—or whatever—toward Desi. "I wondered when you'd get here," she stated gently. "Ah, you, female. Not the male nerd."

"He's with me," Desi responded for some reason.

"If you say so, child. To each her own, I say."

"Well, no, he's not *with* me—"

"I can see we'll get along perfectly, child. We think alike."

SEVEN

"Colonel St. Claire, are you ready for us to launch?' Sachiko asked over the con in a captainly manner. Tank sat behind her and to her right. No one else was on the bridge.

"Captain, I'd like nothing more than to say we're green to go, but in fact, we're not."

Sachiko looked to Tank.

He raised an eyebrow.

"Colonel, this mission's been on the schedule for *two* days," Tank stated pointedly. "What seems to be the hang-up?"

"I was hoping an issue would have sorted itself out by now, but it hasn't. We're missing a couple of students, sir."

"Not the news I'd like to hear," he grumbled back.

"I can well imagine, General. I am very sorry. But one of the boys and one of the girls are not anywhere they're supposed to be."

"Suggesting we need to look where they're *not* supposed to be," he said in a displeased tone.

"We are doing just that as we speak. I have six search parties fanning out across the restricted areas of the ship."

"*But* it's a big ship," he added dryly.

"It is indeed, sir."

“And that is a very big 'but,' which I do not like,” averred Tank.

"Have you enlisted Aramthella in the search?"

"Yes. I took the liberty of asking her directly."

Tank leaned to Sachiko and whispered, "As opposed to asking you to ask her, thus exposing the need to do so in the first place."

Sachiko shrugged. "I'd try that CYA move myself, most likely."

They shared a grin.

"What did Aramthella tell you?" Tank asked.

"She, er, the ship has no idea where they are."

That brought wide-eyed stares between Sachiko and Tank.

"Does ... does she think ... hang on." Sachiko gathered herself. "Aramthella, do you think the students are no longer on board?" There was grave concern in her voice.

"I do not know where they are. That is different from saying they're gone. There are certainly no traces or hints left behind that suggest they have."

"Then—" Sachiko began.

"Hang on," said Tank as he rose. "I bet I know where they are." He looked up. "Colonel. I think I know where they are. Have a team proceed to—"

It was Sachiko's turn to rise. She set a hand on Tank's. "No. I'd like to go myself. It's not like they pose a threat. If anyone's in danger, it's them having heart attacks when I catch them mid-act."

Tank grunted a chuckle. "Mine if I tag along?"

She bit at her lower lip. "No. But, just let me do the talking, okay?"

"No problema. I'll just be the two-hundred-pound general in the corner neither of them cares to engage."

"Sirs, I'd feel a lot more comfortable if one of my MPs came along with you."

"Won't be necessary," reassured Tank. "We handle love-struck twenty somethings for a living back on campus."

"General, I respectfully—"

"If it'll make you feel any better, have a pair of MPs meet us on Deck 12, Section A-1-A, right there by the elevator."

"They're on their way, sir. I'll meet you there too."

Tank shook his head. They were just doing their duty, but he hated feeling doted over.

A short while later, Sachiko and Tank stepped off the elevator. They were met by Reva and two bulky MPs. All three had such a serious look on their faces, Tank nearly took a step back, and he was their commanding officer.

He pointed ahead. "We're heading to D, just a little past C. Y'all can follow us as far as B, as in *Baker*. You copy?" clarified Tank.

"Sir," snapped the MPs. Reva noticeably didn't respond. She also didn't holster her sidearm.

"I think it's safe to put that away," Tank said, nodding at her pistol.

"If anything happens to you, I'm back in command. Ergo, nothing is going to happen to you."

Tank estimated that she was entirely serious, so he let her wield the weapon. Her commitment to not being the boss again *was* impressive.

"I believe this is where Jon said Plesmus tends to hang

out," Tank said as he led the way into the otherwise empty storage room.

"With your permission, General," Reva said as she tried to muscle past Tank and assume point.

Tank extended an arm. "No, I'll go first. And I thought I told you to stay back in Section B." He tried to sound stern but was actually having trouble suppressing a smile.

Reva got the most innocent look on her face since Goldilocks, batted her eyelids in feigned surprise, and responded, "I assumed you were speaking to the MPs, Tank, and not me."

"I'll bet you did," he scorned playfully. "You can stay, but for the love of Mike, please holster that sidearm. You're making me nervous."

She held up her Beretta M9. "Tank, I was *born* with this in my hand. You're in no danger."

"And I'll be in less than none when you obey your superior officer." He glared at the weapon.

She shrugged, as if to say, *can't blame me for trying,* and holstered the pistol.

Tank looked ahead and stepped cautiously forward. He rested his left hand on the corner and rounded the bend. He immediately saw the two missing students. They were sitting Indian style on the deck, facing Plesmus. For her part, the ship's focus had actually left her comfy spot and was facing the two humans.

"I thought I'd find you here," Tank said loudly.

"Well then, you thought correctly, General Tank," responded Plesmus.

"Just, Tank, please."

"Just Tank, then."

"You two kids okay?" he asked.

"Uh, sure," Tip responded hesitantly. "Thanks for asking."

"You won't be when *I'm* done with you," snarled Reva.

"We were ... we needed—" Tip stammered.

"Young man, what's your name?" Tank cut him off.

"T ... Tip Benjamin, sir."

"Tip Benjamin, I'm going to ask you to remain perfectly silent, okay? I want to speak to—"

He turned to Reva.

"Desdemona, sir."

"Seriously?" he couldn't help remarking.

Reva angled her head and gave him a crooked grin.

"Tip, I want to hear from Desdemona."

"You got it ... er, *her*, sir."

Desi stood and turned. "Yes, General Sherman. What can I do for you?"

"Well, you can start by telling me what you're doing here. You know darn well you're way out of bounds."

"I ... I came here—" Now that she was confronted – actually, called out—she wasn't certain what to say. She didn't want to sound crazy and be given the same meds as the kid who blew up the reactor.

"Tank, may *I* speak?" asked Plesmus.

He looked to Sachiko, then back. "Sure. This *is* your ship, right?"

"No. I don't own anything, this ship included."

"No, it's an—"

"I know. I was messing you," she interrupted.

"You mean messing *with*?" asked Sachiko.

"Hello, *messing* with you. Please try and keep up, you two."

The two exchanged uncertain glances.

"What would you like to say?" Sachiko asked.

"What Desi is doing here."

"Doesn't she know?" Sachiko asked, assuming the question was rhetorical.

"Only in the slightest part," replied Plesmus. "She came here for the same reason I do and for a different reason than I do."

"*That's* as clear as mud," remarked Tank.

"Thank you. I do want the humans to understand what occurs ... wait. Mud is not clear."

"No. It's an old saying. It means I'm still confused after hearing your explanation."

"Ah. Fine, then. I think at this point you should ask Desi directly," Plesmus announced.

"Ok-ay." Tank drew out the word. "Back to you, *Desi*. Why are you here?"

"I'm not certain," she answered confidently.

"How can you not be sure why you came here?"

"Oh, *that* I'm sure about."

Tank shook his head like it was a round, wet dog. "Care to explain that one?"

"Yes. I *came* here to find a quiet place. *Why* I'm here —in the broader sense—I'm only now beginning to know."

"Go on. We're listening," he responded, clearly a bit vexed.

"I ... ever since I was a little girl ... well, there are these noises—"

"The human female hears the voices of the non-distant dead," volunteered Plesmus.

"She does *what*?" blurted Sachiko.

"I believe you heard me, Captain. She is unable to decouple fully with those who have died."

"That's ... that's kind of hard to ... well, that'd be an

unusual *gift*, if it were true," Sachiko responded uncertainly.

"Oh come now," Plesmus scolded mildly. "It's a common enough ability."

"It is?" pressed Sachiko.

"It is?" wheezed Desi.

"It is," stated Tip. "Everybody knows that."

Tank pointed to Tip. "Didn't I ask you to remain as quiet as a church mouse?"

"Ah, I'm not clear on that, sir. You told me to be *silent*. I'm frankly uncertain, and, please believe me, I've done a lot of research, both personally and online, as to the so-called church mouse's ability or inability to generate sounds. I mean, it's almost certainly a fictional rodent, first given life by Lewis Carroll, I believe. Anyway, I ... I—"

He looked around at those present. They all stared at him. His eyes finally came to rest on Desdemona.

"You're doing it again, Tip," she remarked softly.

"Sorry. I'll be silent now," Tip stated with all due contrition.

"You hear dead people?" Tank asked Desi dubiously.

She slightly jerked her head to the side. "Yeah, I ... yes. *Yes*, General, I hear dead people, *just* like that kid in the movie."

"Well I'll be," Tank responded.

"Honey, you're in enough trouble already," Reva began angrily. "Trying to BS your way out of this is only going to make it worse."

"It is time for rational minds to form together," stated Plesmus. "I know there'd be some issue when dealing with primitives, but I had hoped not to begin at *such* a basic level."

"Plesmus, are you insulting us?" Sachiko asked rather pointedly.

"I am observing that your collective knowledge as a species falls well short of anything like an acceptable level. Really. *I* hear the dead. The *girl* hears the dead. You must know the *time maker* hears the dead. So do the trees of Arnucli, in the Great Forest of Wails. They even hear the dead tree that used to be *part* of the Great Forest."

"Sorry. It's just an odd thing among us humans," replied Tank contritely.

"Is it?" Plesmus seemed to mock.

"Sure ... er, right, Desi?" he asked her.

"Not *really*," was her tentative response.

"Are there chairs in here?" Tank asked, feeling a bit woozy all of a sudden.

"Get over the shock, Tank," Plesmus quipped. "You are not a child."

"No." He pointed to Plesmus and addressed Sachiko. "She's right about that."

"The human girl came to me because that is part of what must be," declared Plesmus. "There will be much to accomplish. It might not be doable at all. But if it is, many players must fill crucial roles. Many of those will be ... unfortunate roles to have to fill. It will be especially hard on the young." More to herself, she added, "It always is."

"Ah, Plesmus, what are you talking about?" asked a thoroughly confused Tank.

"If your planet is to be recalled, along with its inhabitants. It will be very hard. It will be very sad."

"I'm still lost," he confessed.

"Then lost you will remain. It is not, in any case, important for you to know the future," Plesmus scolded.

"It isn't?" Tank whined.

"In your *past*, Professor Sherman, have you ever been privy to what the future holds in store for you or for anyone else?" Plesmus' tone was unusually stern.

"No, not that I re—"

"Then you are in your native state. Embrace it."

"But I'm commander of the last contingent of humans. If ... I mean, knowing the future would be a big—"

"The last humans?" Plesmus huffed. "The *last* humans? You are such dramatic creatures. The past is *littered* with humans. There are futures in which you couldn't throw a stick without hitting a human. The *last* humans indeed. Time is—"

"What?" asked Sachiko.

"I was losing my focus, Captain. For that, I am sorry. It will not happen again."

"Our *focus* was losing her *focus*?" Tank sort of gurgled.

"You know I can hear you, Tank?" charged Plesmus.

"Sure. Why not?" was his addled response.

"Then do not bait me."

Sachiko set a hand on her hip. "Yeah, *Tank*, don't bait my crew members."

"No problem," he remarked absently.

"Plesmus, what does it signify that Desi can hear the dead?" Sachiko asked analytically.

"It means she hears them."

"Okay. Of course. I should have asked this. As she can hear them, what does that mean in terms of her role in the future?"

"Is that not obvious, Captain?"

"No, it is not."

"If she is to *control* the dead, it would be very useful for her to *communicate* with them, don't you think?"

"Ah, sure. Why not?" asked a thoroughly confused Sachiko.

"So she can *what?*" blurted Desi.

"I can't help it," exclaimed Tip. "This is so cool. I wish my iPhone still had a charge. I want to video this more than I wanted to have sex ... uh, I mean, it's so *cool.*" He looked sheepishly at Desi.

She rested a fist on either hip.

It was wisely written, long ago:

Heav'n has no rage, like love to hatred turn'd,
Nor hell a fury, like a woman scorn'd.

Tip Benjamin figuratively read it and wept.

EIGHT

The communications maker was ready to peel its own skin off. It was in such a spot. Words were made to one of its ears, and other words were received by the other. However, the impossible was standing on the comm maker's head. The sets of words were not in agreement. One set of words was from the new time maker. The words were clear, spoken with phenomenal anger, and they were extremely specific. But on each occasion when it transferred those heated words to the body maker, it seemed to not subtend the meaning, however clear it was.

"Come to my aid," commanded Time Maker-bob. "Bring your clan ships to my aid immediately."

Clearly there was no wiggle room in that command.

Yet Body Maker-iii seemed to hear, "Hello. I am fine. How are you?"

The body maker would instruct the comm maker to return words to the time maker that meant nothing, no matter how they were configured. "Let the sender of that message know that its word transfer is complete," it would order sent in response. "Further, tell it all efforts are being made to arrange agreement."

That was it. End of message. The body maker wanted to arrange agreement between *what* and *what*?

And now *Body* Maker-iii was beginning to call itself *Time* Maker-iii. It was not *time maker* formed. How could it call itself what it wasn't? Why would it do so? The comm maker was in not-agreement with that idea. Impossible stood on the comm maker's head and it danced. Existence had become ... confusing. Who was in charge and what were they in charge of? Not-in-agreement was the comm maker with everything it saw.

To make confusion larger, more encompassing, the knowledge makers had come to word transfer with their body maker. It was Knowledge Maker of Others-pit itself that went right up to the body maker and worded, "You cannot be time maker. There is always only one and one there is. The only Time Maker-bob may be called time maker. To be time maker, three body makers must be in agreement and excrete a new time maker. You were not excreted in such a manner. Blasphemy is not in agreement with the clan."

Strong wording? Yes. True words? Almost certainly, though likely to depend somewhat on who won out in the end.

But what resulted in the knowledge maker's bold statement? Body Maker-iii did the *more* unimaginable. It split into three separate parts, all smaller, but clearly clan-bodied. Then the three little body makers secreted back into the original Body Maker-iii, fusing back into the one in a *parody* of secretion. It was such a travesty! Then the reconstituted body maker challenged the knowledge maker. "There. Satisfied now are you?"

"Most certainly not," it cried out loudly. "You are one body maker, no matter how many—"

The communications maker shook its tiny head to clear it. What commotion had drawn its attention so, in such a focused manner. It was staring at the body-time maker, but it was standing alone. There was an odd glow about it. And, weirder still, Time-Body Maker-iii seemed ... it seemed happy.

"Time Maker-iii," the vector maker called out. "Shall I alter vector to align us with the time maker's request that we align with it?"

"No, small fool. That is not *possible*," replied a time maker who could only be characterized as giddy. Most unexpected. "There can be only one. You are word making to the time maker. Ignore that imposter."

And so the unraveling of what remained of the clan began.

NINE

Back on the bridge, Sachiko and Tank sat. Reva stood behind Tip and Desi, glowering at them. The two students looked about in amazement at the control room. They'd only heard fanciful rumors as to what the restricted sections of the ship contained. The control center was transfixing. Alien monitors, weird panels displaying unknowable icons, and a dense silence that belied the level of mechanical action that was occurring. It was miraculous to them. Well, to Tip it was. To Desi, it was just interesting.

"So, *this* time, are we ready to depart?" Tank asked in an annoyed tone.

"Yes, General," responded Reva. "All personnel *and* civilians are accounted for and ready."

"Aramthella, are you ready to transport us to the other side of the holo-generating sphere?"

"Yes," was her simple reply.

"And the trip will be instantaneous?" Sachiko reconfirmed.

"Yes, it will be."

"Then engage, please."

"Done, Captain. We are there."

Sachiko looked to Tank. She angled her head as if to say, *feels the same, doesn't it?*

"Where are we relative to the sphere?" she asked.

"Directly adjacent to the one I chose," responded Aramthella. "There are an infinite number to choose from. I selected the nearest and remained close to it, so as to minimize the damage."

"Damage?" exclaimed Tank. "I don't recall any discussion of *damage*. What danger are we in?"

"None, assuming we don't move."

"You mean the ship or the people aboard?"

"Yes."

"That was an either/or question," he shouted.

"If neither the crew nor I as a whole move, the consequences of us being present are minimal."

"General, really. You are a human of science. What did you anticipate the physical reality of this outer surface would be? It can't be the same as the inner projection now, can it?" chided the ship.

"Two important points. No, I didn't anticipate a difference and, you didn't warn me."

"Hang on," blurted out Tip, to everyone's surprise including his. "I got this. The theory holds that the reality we experience is a holographic projection from a sphere that contains the projection. If we were on the opposite side of the surface generated by the sphere creating the surface itself, man, would reality be screwed the hell up." He began sort of giggling, but it was a *wet* whatever it was, and it was definitely annoying.

"Explain," demanded Tank.

"Come on. This is child's play, prof. The topology of

the outward projection from the reality surface would be as unstable as ... as ... well, as unstable as my counselors tell me *I* am."

"This I believe," groaned Tank.

"Obviously, the inward projection is basically *forced* to focus, right? All radial lines descending from the surface converge at the center of the sphere. It's Geometry 101. Welcome to Duhs-ville, happy campers."

Tank briefly flirted with the notion of asking Reva to shoot the boy. He knew it to be a crude instinct, but it was a powerful urge, nonetheless.

"The opposite projection, by definition, *diverges.* Wow, man. This is *so* cool. It's a dream come true. When I was in middle school, I wrote a paper about this very topic. I summarized the challenging physical instabilities and predicted an absolute limit to the distance you could travel from the originating surface and still remain recognizably in one piece. I called the distance three Benjamins. I was going to call it one Benjamin because, double-duh, I'm only one person. But I figured Mom and Dad'd have a cow each if I excluded them ... *again*—"

Everyone in the room stared at Tip in slack-jawed disbelief.

Desi rallied ever so slightly, being the most Tip-experienced person present. "Tip—"

"I know. I'm doing it again. Sorry. I'll be silent now, as opposed to quiet as a church—"

The intensity of the glare Tank gave him shut Tip up faster than a laser beam fired in anger might have. "Where did that paper get published, son? I've never heard of it or anything similar," Tank asked most seriously.

"In the school paper, sir."

"The middle school *newspaper* published a paper on theoretical physics? Now why would they do that?"

"Maybe because I was the editor *and* the entire staff."

Shaking his head, Tank had to ask, "Didn't the faculty *sponsor* have the common sense to put the kibosh on such a farce?"

"No. Dad thought it was funny. It was the April 1 edition, after all."

"Tank," Sachiko said forcefully. "I think we need to focus on the crisis at hand, not this asocial lunatic."

Tank looked from Tip, to Sachiko, and back to Tip.

"She's probably right," affirmed Tip as he gestured toward the captain.

Tank revisited the Shoot Tip Initiative, but abandoned it for the moment, based on his need to confine his attention to the dire situation at hand. "Okay, *Aramthella* and absolutely positively *not* Tip over there, what is the distance we can move from the barrier safely?"

"In *Benjamins*?" the ship responded.

"That is not funny *or* appropriate," snapped Sachiko. "In meters."

"You are correct, Captain. We will remain completely intact, based on the cohesive forces at the molecular level, for some thousands of meters. If we tolerate minor, random disruptions, a few kilometers are possible."

"And do we need to move at all for you to contact the clan ships in this space?"

"No, that is not required."

"Then please contact them and discover the status of the local clan's loyalties."

"Again?"

"Again what?"

"I have completed that survey. I can do it again, but I doubt the results will change."

Sachiko balled up her fists, just like Tank was doing simultaneously.

"Please-report-the-*results*-of-your-survey," Sachiko hissed angrily.

"The local clan ships tell me the fleet is in chaos. They report open rejection of the new time maker's legitimacy. There are no plans aboard any local craft to return to our space and fight alongside the time maker. In fact, one body maker has already self-promoted itself to time maker status."

"Lord, no," breathed Tank. "Please tell me there aren't two of those wanks. I hate the one so much, I don't know if there's any more hate in my soul to apply to a *second* one."

"A second one *so far,* General," Aramthella gloated. "A few ships suspect *their* body makers will soon follow suit. It's a complete foxy-charlie-trot out here."

Tank started to correct Aramthella, but lost interest a few milliseconds into the venture. She was mistaken or baiting. Either way, what did he care?

"Then can we go *home* now?" Tank asked in a deep voice.

"I'm good," responded Aramthella.

"Then I don't see any—"

The ship shook like it was a drum some drummer was mad at.

Boom, boom, bang.

"Status report," yelled Tank. "What the hell was that?"

"It was ... um, unexpected," replied Aramthella.

"More specific," Tank roared. He was over the ship's attempts to be evasive or clever.

"At first, just one, but then several clan ships discharged no-time assaults on us."

"Say *what*?" he shouted back.

"I thought you said they were not supportive of the time maker?" Sachiko shouted.

"They are not. But they are also no friends of ours. They feel in this turbulent time, any potential foe is worth eliminating."

"Damage report?" Tank demanded.

"None. Our membranes snapped on before the strike."

"Will they remain intact with continued bombardment?" asked Sachiko.

"Yes, but ..."

"Yes but what, Aramthella? Can you just tell us without the drama?" asked an exasperated Tank.

"I'm sorry you feel that way, General. I suppose—"

"*Report*," demanded Sachiko.

"But we cannot maneuver while the membranes are in place."

"Why not? We did—" Tank trailed off. "*Blessing*'s not here. We can't just fold away."

"Correct. We must move under my drives. For those to work, I must obviously fire the engines."

"Can't you just move forward or backward in time, then slip away?" Tank asked quickly.

"I can move in time, but so would those who attack us. It would be trivially easy for them to move in concert with us."

"Damn," Tank scoffed.

"Can we no-time them through the membrane?" the captain inquired.

"Not an intact membrane, no. We'd have to pulse it off. That would risk an enemy hit."

"What's a membrane?" Tip asked out-of-the-blue.

"Will someone shut him the *hell* up?" ordered Tank.

Reva was more than happy to comply. She placed a hand over Tip's mouth and twisted his neck severely, so as to discourage him from attempting to resist. If he did, he likely break his own neck.

"No," called out Sachiko. "So far, he's been helpful if abrasive. Colonel St. Claire, release him."

In one fluid motion, Reva retracted her arms and stepped clear of Tip.

Tip gasped and wheezed like he'd been choked, which he hadn't been, so the acts were, well, they were abrasive.

"Tip, knock it off. You're fine," scolded Sachiko.

He stopped immediately and looked at her. "Sure. No problem. I was just making certain."

Of *what* she did not want to know. "A membrane is a space/time congruity manifestation. We project them. They are force fields."

"That's so cool. Thanks." Tip then fell silent.

"That's it?" Sachiko demanded.

The ship was rocked by another set of impacts.

"Oh," Tip replied absently. "I was just wondering to myself. I do that a lot, wondering to myself. It—"

Tip stopped when Reva reminded him he was doing it again. Instead of the words others might have chosen, she slapped him upside the head. The message was clear and familiar to the child.

"I presume the congruities are impenetrable?" he confirmed.

"Yes, in their full, present configuration. Nothing can traverse them," Sachiko responded.

"Then why not just expand them? You can expand

them, right? What good would a force field be—and they're so way-cool in the first place, I just had to share—if it wasn't variable. Am I right?"

"Your point, son," bellowed Tank.

"You can expand them far enough to push the other guys', the bad guys' ships, right?"

"If they're close enough," Sachiko replied. "Aramthella, are they close enough to push with the membranes?"

"No, Captain. They're well beyond that range."

"So they're no help," Sachiko said mostly to herself.

"Is there any debris around, you know, in this space?" Tip asked thoughtfully. "I bet there is."

Sachiko looked up quickly. "Aramthella?"

"It is abundant, as you suspect, young human," the ship confirmed.

"Wait, why is it abundant, and why did you suspect it would be?" Tank asked emphatically.

Tip pointed to his chest. "Is that one for me?"

"*Yes?*" growled Tank.

"This is an area of instability. If any object, animate or inanimate, moves incorrectly, it's toast. So there's bound to be a lot of junk floating around."

"I guess that would be the case," agreed Tank.

"They told me you were Professor Sherman, the physics one. Is that a correct assessment?" Tip posed.

"Yes. Why?" Tank was even more displeased.

"You seem more like a Humanities professor, I guess."

"Make your *point* before our enemy figures a work-around for our defenses." Tank was basically screaming.

"If you employ the membranes to throw space junk, and you propel enough before they figure out why you're doing it, you can cast them past the three-Benjamin stability limit." He rested his hands together, then blew them apart. "Kablooey."

"The kid's right," Tank whispered. "Aramthella—"

"Already on it, General." A few seconds later, she proclaimed, "Bingo, Tip, I love you. All but two enemy vessels were driven past the stability limit. The two that didn't fled quickly. We are safe to move about this reality."

"Take us home now," ordered Sachiko.

"Done, Captain. We are back in our space and time."

"That was the weirdest battle I've ever been in, heard of, or imagined was possible," exclaimed Tank. "Say, Tip, could you come over here a sec?"

Uncertainly, and with Reva's palm helping motivate him, Tip crossed the short distance.

Tank set a fist on Tip's shoulder. "You seem pretty smart."

"Yes, sir, I—"

Tank's fist pushed down on Tip hard enough that he stopped speaking.

"That was rhetorical, son. I am curious why you think the enemy ships would even risk traversing that crazy reality. I mean, it's like swimming in shark-infested waters with leaky units of *blood* strapped to your chest."

"Wow, sir. That seems like a very unlikely yet dangerous set of actions to take. I hate sharks. Well, I love them, biologically speaking. But as a would-be swimmer—"

Slap. Reva had "spoken."

Tip refocused. "The ship girl said the enemy was trying to no-time us."

"Yes. They were."

"So I concluded the enemy can extract and utilize time energy."

"They can."

"That being the case, operating in that treacherous reality would be like a family of bears living in a Hometown Buffet restaurant."

Tank looked down and shook his head. "You're going to have to speak *Human* to me, son, not Benjamin."

"No problem. The rampant destruction in that aberrant space would afford a time-consumer abundant rewards with limited effort. You know, bears in a smorgasbord."

"Like that." Tank rolled his eyes. "And you gleaned all that, that quickly?"

"Yes, sir, I did."

Tank opened his hand and gently shook Tip. "You're pretty smart, young man. *Very* smart, in fact."

"I know. Hey, if we ever get back to Earth, does that mean I can join your research group? I'd love to—"

"No, son, I'm not that patient a fellow, truth be told. I'd kill you within a month." Tank held his palm open to Tip. "Likely with my bare hands."

"Thank you, sir. You're not the first to express similar reservations."

"I'm certain you're correct. But," he pointed up with a finger, "thank you just the same. You did good."

"Does that mean Lieutenant Colonel St. Claire will not be allowed to punish us, or at least *me*, for our previous transgressions?"

"No, son. It doesn't mean that. And," he held up the finger again, "it's not punishment. You're looking at *negative reinforcement*. Big difference there. It'll be for your own good, you lucky young man."

"Thank you, sir. I've heard that before too."

"Then all I can say is *you're welcome*, and Reva, please take this child far, far from my sight."

"You can't imagine the pleasure, Tank." She grabbed Tip by the scruff of his neck—because it felt good—and signaled to Desi—because that was all that was really necessary—and the three of them departed for psychological intervention or interventions.

TEN

After a long session of verbal torture, I was able to extract from Plesmus that she hailed from the third planet orbiting Nonsouar. I'd elected to use the Deavoriath name for the system. The human records called it a series of numbers and letters, because it was so far from Earth. Ever cautious, I had *Stingray* fold us into an orbit around Plesmus' with the membranes up. Note the apostrophe. Instead of giving the place a cool name, like Jon's World, I used you-know-who's. I didn't want to be associated with a world where the chief export was mucous blobs.

"What do your initial surveys reveal, Al?"

"Class X planet. Little oxygen, but near-standard gravity and atmospheric pressures. A bit cool for a beach vacation, but I'm good with that. Seeing you in a Speedo is more than these old sensors can handle."

"How about the nightlife?"

"I'm betting it's piss-poor. The planetary day is only four hours, so last call would immediately follow first call. Plus, I show no signs of advanced civilization, such as strip malls or oxygen bars."

"Just like you described it, Plesmus."

"Go figure," she observed.

"Do you think the place hasn't changed, or maybe it did, but your gooey cousins are preventing us from perceiving it as it really is?"

"Oh, it's the same. I'm communicating with a few old acquaintances as we speak."

"No old friends; just how-do-you-do associates?"

"It's a wonder I even need to speak with you, Jon. You know stuff so quickly."

I let the silence hang. I was curious to find out more about my unusual new ally.

"I left here a very long time ago. Those who did not follow me were unlikely to survive all that long. We are a long-lived species, but in a natural setting, we do have to face mortality."

"Gotcha. Okay, since it seems safe down there, what say we renew old palships between you and your brethren?"

"You are free to venture to the surface. Please, however, change boots first. I will remain here."

"If he takes off his shoes, I'm leaving the spacecraft," Sapale teased reflexively. Yeah, hang around together as long as we have and that's what happens.

"That would kind of defeat the I-know-an-insider advantage I was counting on," I said, ignoring my wife's cruelty.

"Sorry. It's too risky for me to come face-to-face with my kin."

"Afraid of rejection?" I taunted.

"No, just the opposite. I appear small to you compared to the large manifestation you first encountered, but I am nonetheless stuffed full of time energy. If I come too close to another of my species, they are likely to attack me to acquire my bounty."

"That's like gross. Cannibal blobs?" I said with convincing disgust.

"You have a gift for making everything sound degrading."

"I do?"

"Yes. Please return it to wherever it was purchased. It sucks the big one."

"You know, Ples, I'm just curious here. When you say it sucks the *big one*, do you like have any idea what you're actually referring to?"

"Yes. The big dodo that you are."

"In other words, you're a babe-in-the-woods. Be-a-utiful." I grinned. I did so love a dupe.

"I'm sorry, I said *dodo*. I meant *dildo*. Please excuse. Alien with no vocal experience here."

"Back to important," Sapale interrupted our sparring. "So you're really not coming?"

"No. It's too dangerous."

"Then we'll have to wander aimlessly and risk discovering nothing because we're new in town, so to speak," I summarized.

"Not to worry."

"What, you can still help us from here? Maybe by radio?"

"No, silly biped. You were never *going* to discover anything. Therefore wandering aimlessly was a guarantee the moment we arrived. There's nothing to be learned down there that I do not already know."

"Well, I'm two things. No, make that three. I'm a scientist, so I must test the waters myself. I'm desperate, so I'm willing to try anything. Lastly, I'm the type who loves,

loves, *loves* to tell little know-it-alls that they were wrong, I was right, and, my personal fave, nah, nah, nah-nah, *nah*."

"You are such a throwback. Say, did you bring your knobby-wooden club and your lucky *rock* with you? That way, if you run into a dinosaur or a mouse, you'll feel right at home."

"She's really getting to know you well," remarked my forever mate. Grr.

That Plesmus could be such a mean blob when she focused on that task. Just another hater. I *almost* felt sorry for her. I *did* feel sorry for myself, because I had to put up with her.

"*Stingray*, put us on the surface in a open area. I don't want any blobs sneaking up on the ship and sucking the time out of Plesmus."

"You are a humanitarian, Pilot," observed Al. "If there were still homo sapiens around, they'd just *have* to give you a medal. Maybe a silly hat too."

"A silly ... stow it. Forget I asked." I didn't know where the blender was going with that *hat* quip, but I surely didn't want to know.

Slight nausea.

"We are down, Form One," announced *Stingray*.

"Open a portal, then close it behind us. Al, if any boogie-blobs attack the ship, electrify the hull."

"Electrify the hull? My, how I didn't miss that cinematic allusion. You haven't used it in billions of years, but already I'm weary of it."

"We'll be back—maybe. I must decide if I care to spend additional time with any of you while we're making amazing discoveries out there by our lonesome."

And we exited stage right. I only wish one of the three

I left behind had protested maybe a little bit that I might not be returning. The boogle of weasels.

Plesmus' (again, note the apostrophe) was a remarkably unremarkable world. At least the part we surveyed was flat, had little vegetation, and *screamed,* "We don't rely on tourism here." The air was thin, as predicted. Lucky for us, we didn't need to breathe. I guess I wasn't surprised that we didn't see oodles of necumplack gurgling about. Plesmus warned us they were few in number and reclusive by nature. I wasn't, as Plesmus had warned, at all sure they could provide us any insights in the first place. I mean, whatever they knew, Plesmus knew.

Plesmus hadn't come right out and said that there were no other sentients on Plesmus'. I was hoping there were some that she either didn't know about or who she didn't want me to contact. I know. That sounds needy and supremely optimistic of me. Recall, if you will, that desperation is the mother of dumb ideas. Of this I know all too well. It's kind of my go-to remedy to tough situations.

We walked at a goodly clip. I'd considered having us run so we'd cover more ground. But I didn't want us to frighten off any potential information sources by appearing like predators. After we'd gone ten kilometers without encountering one thing, we turned and headed north, toward what would have to pass for mountainous terrain on this two-D planet. Well before we arrived to any up-tick in the terrain, night fell. With the uber-short day cycle Plesmus' had, I knew beforehand that we'd be wandering for several light/dark phases. In fact, I was counting on that, as there might be some nocturnal activity we wouldn't catch if we confined our explorations to the daylight hours.

As we neared the slight hills, I thought I saw some widely scattered movement, but could never be certain. Sapale was plagued with similar fleeting glimpses, but couldn't confirm any sightings either. If anything was up there, it was well practiced at hiding.

Once we were heading up the gentle slopes, there were definitely no signs of life. What a dull planet. Hey, just like its namesake. Nice. I was hoping to run across some caves on the elevated landscape. Caves were natural accumulators of animals. If a species is going to survive, it'll learn early on that dark, thick-walled caves afford their users excellent protection. The first few we thought we found turned out to be more ruts than caves. But, eventually, I nearly fell right into a first-rate cave. The opening was a hole in the ground. We quickly established there was a proper tunnel leading deep into the hills. Its floor was only a couple of meters below the horizontal entrance.

Down we dropped. To tell the truth, I was kind of excited. We'd spent hours searching Plesmus', finding absolutely nothing even vaguely interesting. The idea of wandering into something—anything—alive was thrilling. Well, I suppose maybe not a T-Rex. Or a gigantic serpent like the one that almost ate the *Millennium Falcon* inside that asteroid. I wasn't *that* bored, at least not yet.

It was pitch black in the tunnel. We turned on some very small lights, so we could see in the visible spectrum with our light-enhancers. We simultaneously scanned the space in the infrared. We reasoned that anything alive would be warmer than the walls, and would therefore easily stand out. After ten minutes, I was getting the then-familiar impression there was positively nothing stirring on this planet. I had probed ahead and determined the cave ended at only a few hundred meters. So I ignored the temptation to bail on the entire project, and we pressed onward.

We arrived to the end of the cave. It tapered off over a short space and ended in a smattering of rubble. Totally normal for a rocky cave. We stopped just long enough to satisfy ourselves there was nothing hiding amongst the debris. We turned to leave. That was when it got weird. Now I'm a fan of weird, don't get me wrong. Without weirdness, what a dull universe it would be. But there are *degrees* of weird. There's, "Hey, dude, you're wearing a clown nose. That's weird." Then there's, "Say, look at that. A bunch of nuclear missiles are about to hit me in the head and my arms just turned into tree limbs. That's weird."

Anyway, before I took my first step, I heard music. Weird, right? Hang on. It was coming through the walls at the end of the cave. Yeah, weird. That would make the cave end a *wall*, not the-end-of-the-cave.

"Please tell me you hear the music too," I requested of Sapale.

"I hear the music too."

"What a relief."

"What is?"

"That you hear the music too."

"I don't hear any damn music, you nut job. You asked please, so I went along with your delusion. That's what you do when you love a person."

"You lie to them?"

"Bingo," she snapped while flaring a finger in my direction. "I love you *that* much."

"So you don't hear the music?" I said like a child who actually did get coal for Christmas.

"Nope." She waited a three-count. "I do hear rhythmic badoom-baddoms. But, it ain't music, honey. It's just noise."

I perked up visibly. "So you hear something?"

"Maybe it's kids. You know they play loud noises and *call* it music."

"I think you're over-focusing on the word 'music.' Let's move on, okay?"

"Your call. You said *music*. I was trapped by your confining nomenclature."

"Sorry."

She shrugged.

"So, it's kind of unexpected, you know, rhythmic sounds coming from past the end of a cave."

"I'll agree. *I* did not expect it," she replied seriously.

"Do you think maybe this is actually a wall, not the end of the tunnel?" I wondered out loud.

She rubbed her chin. "Not sure. Say, we could ask each other and guess lots of times. That'd be helpful."

"No, it wouldn't be, would it?"

"Maybe one of us should, you know, *test* the interface?"

Without responding, I extended my probe fiber from my left fingertips. They were gifts of our Deavoriath benefactors designed to analyze anything in great detail. *What are you?* I asked the tunnel's end.

Decomposed granodiorite rock, silt layers, trace water content and ... transport integration matrix of quickly increasing density. Phase portal at six meters in linked unison with a wormhole extending past the limit in which detailed evaluation can be made.

My first thoughts? WTF. I wasn't real sure what an *integration matrix* was, or what a *phase portal* did, but I was pretty certain they weren't geologically normal occurrences.

Sapale received the report the same time I did. She was obviously blindsided. "Well *paint* me pink and call me *pig*. That's unexpected."

"*Who* would put a transportation portal in the dirt at the end of a tunnel on the galaxy's dullest planet?"

"I think you're overlooking the *why* would anyone put a transportation portal into the dirt at the end of a tunnel on the galaxies dullest planet?" she replied. "I mean, it's hard to imagine any civilization has so many of those that they could waste connecting them to Plesmus'."

"Not unless they lived wildly exciting lives and found it necessary to come here to chill out and come off that high," I speculated.

Al, I said in my head, *can you hear me?*

No response. We were pretty deep at that point, so not being able to contact the ship wasn't too surprising.

"We won't be getting any help from the computer crew on this one," I announced.

"Computers. Who needs 'em?"

"What do you want to do? We could try and shout to see if anyone on the other side can hear us."

"Yes," she responded, biting her lower lip. "That *might* blow any element of surprise to hell and back, however."

"True. The music people need not be cordial and inviting, need they be?" I responded.

She pinched my cheek. "That's why I fell in love with you in the first place. You're sooo schmart."

"If you don't like my idea, what's your plan?"

"Let's dig the way clear."

"How far should we go?"

"Until our hands disappear in the corn field, I suppose."

"You think there's—" I started to say excitedly. "Oh, you're teasing me about the baseball movie, aren't you."

"You did force me to watch it hundreds of times. I'm still waiting for it to make a lick of sense, by the way."

"You're an alien. It's a human-thing movie, I think."

"You know what I think?"

"That we should start digging?"

She tsk-tsked. "Sooo schmart."

ELEVEN

Tank sat in the mess, rubbing his stubble-free chin and staring off into infinity. To be in command of humankind's last hope for survival, locked in a do-or-die war with a dark evil was not how he'd planned to grade into his golden years. No, less classroom responsibilities, more committees, distinguished lectureships, and, yeah baby, more sabbaticals. Instead, he was forced to find a shovel, go out back, and dig up the grave that had held his military past. Oh, how he'd hoped to leave that buried far, far from the light of day, not to mention his conscious mind.

There wasn't any regret in Tank's mind. He was proud to have served his country, to still be serving his ... check that. No Earth, no American landmass, no country therefore to serve. But he served the most noble cause he could imagine, as he always had. He *was* a US Marine. If there was a blistered underbelly of a conflict anywhere, that was where they were sent. If something needed doing and it was nigh on impossible to achieve success, well, hell, send in the Marines, right? Same TV show, different episode. Tank was back in command of troops in a critical engagement that not everyone was going to survive.

(FOB) Lesser Maelstrom. Such an odd name. Who even labeled it that? Loyalty, Echo Charlie, or Mary Elizabeth, sure. Those were proper forward operating base names. Or label it some general's last name, or the hometown of the first CO. Lesser Maelstrom. The last thing you ever wanted to do was give an FOB an eerie name or one with a clear negative in its title. Didn't it occur to some idiot that a powerful whirlpool might be a bad thing to try to secure and defend?

Or maybe someone had a hot line to God. Before the first tent stake was pounded into the desert sand, some mother's son knew how bad a shithole it was destined to be. Had to be, Tank reflected for the ten-thousand and third time. Because his prior command, the one he'd prayed until there was no more hope left in his soul would have been his last, *should* have been named FOB Die Fucking Die.

What happens when an isolated FOB is overrun by an overwhelming force of merciless religious zealots? Nothing good. A regiment of seasoned, well-trained US Marines constitutes a force of nature. That's a fact. But Marines can't perform miracles. No, that's a couple pay grades up the food chain. So, it turned out, were the commissioning of perfect storms. That was what happened that last day of August, out in the middle of absolutely nowhere. The perfect storm from hell. Accidents happen. Errors of oversight are inevitable. That is why redundancies are built into any organization. But, if you line up sheets of Swiss cheese just right, there'll be a big old hole running straight through the center of the best laid plans.

If you place a few hundred good men on a base named FOB Lesser Maelstrom and the enemy has the best damn Swiss-cheese luck in recorded history, well, my friend, you have yourself one hell of a situation. And if you place Captain Robert Sherman in command of that post, well, he's never going to forget or forgive himself for what happened. You could give that man a chest full of medals They did. You could praise him until no words of praise were left unsaid. They did. But, in the end, after the banners and the speeches, you still have a troubled man left to try to accept the unacceptable. That's how war works.

Now, Tank Sherman was a tough guy. After the fighting was done, he returned to his nice home, his good role in a peaceful society, and his great wife. When Daisy finally thought it was time, she asked him just how bad it had been, back there on the FOB, that last day of August. You know what he said? Do you know what he told his blessed wife of some twenty years? "It was tough." That was the sum total of his report to the most important person in his life. He had, you see, already retrieved the mental-shovel, gone out back, and buried the memories of that last day of August of a year he would just as soon have forgotten. Hopefully, in time, he'd do just that. He knew that wasn't going to happen, but it was a pleasant farce to tell himself it was possible.

And so a good man sat staring off into infinity, watching a ghost only he could see, wondering whether the specter would return that morning or wait until another dawn to revisit his every thought.

"Tank ... I hate to interrupt you ... er, sorry." Sachiko had some notion as to where her friend was. A vague but unsettling sense told her he was somewhere negative. "But we need to talk."

They didn't need to talk. Nothing had changed since they spoke last night. She just wasn't certain whether to leave him lumbering through superhuman moral uncertainty or to throw in a life ring and pull him back to safety. Who could know?

"Uh ... sure thing, kiddo?" he responded slowly. "What's up?"

She slid in across from him. "I've been thinking about what you said yesterday."

He raised his eyebrows into hairy archways. "I said a lot of things yesterday. Most were nonsensical or downright stupid."

"About the *clan*, silly."

"What'd I say worthy of recall that we all don't know as facts?"

She shifted uncomfortably. "It was about their response to our ballistic attack."

"Thank you, Shaky."

"I ... er, thank me for what? I only referenced our use of the membranes to take them—"

"For caring enough about an old soldier lost in an unpleasant past to try and ease his pain. Thank you."

"I ... that was never ... I mean—"

"So you're suggesting this was a spontaneous convivial conversation?"

She returned a stern glare. "Sure. Why not?"

"Because you didn't make a cup of tea."

She shot a guilty glance at the prep area. "I ... just haven't started one yet."

"You and I've worked together in one form or another for what, ten years?"

Her head gyrated uncertainly. "Sure."

"In that time, you have never *not* made tea in preparation for a casual conversation. In fact, the only vision I have of you in a meeting without a cup of tea was that awkward meeting with Dean Greyson when this entire cluster ... escapade began."

She looked down. "Not a fond memory."

"Shaky."

"Yes?"

"Go make tea, then come back. I'll think of *something* to talk about while you're gone."

A few minutes later, Sachiko was back, tea in hand. She blew on and sipped at it while Tank blew on and sipped at his room temperature coffee.

It was nice.

Finally, Tank broke the spell. Someone had to. "We were lucky. We decreased the number of souls who wish us harm on their turf without suffering any losses. I want to stress that *luck* and *war* do not commune together often. Please don't count on their doing so again in the future."

"Okay."

"Was her terse and dubious response," Tank complained.

"What?" she protested.

"You *said* okay, but I *heard* maybe."

"Tank, it *is* possible that we're just that good. I mean, the clan is rigid and unimaginative. They're so *not* used to losing, they seem incapable of avoiding it."

Tank sipped at his drink pregnantly.

"I know. This is where you say, *Kiddo, it's talk like that'll get you dead.* I know. But I'm trying to remain optimistic. I can't be negative, negative, negative. Tank, I can't *live* like that."

He glanced into his mug, then over to the half-empty pot.

"Robert Sherman. *Speak*." The captain was officially pissed.

He set his mug down thoughtfully. "I've got enough experience for the both of us. I'll worry, you stay focused, and we'll be fine."

"Oh, no. Oh, *no* you don't," Sachiko railed. "You don't go all doom-and-gloom on me, then pat me on the shoulder and say it'll *all* be peachy. I'm not ready for this. I *know*, General. This sucks. I *know*. But what am I supposed to do? I *find* myself in command of a warship in the middle of one hell of a war."

Tank waited a few seconds. "Sorry, you done?"

"Yes, I am *now* done."

"Can I start some more water for you when I get a refill?" He held up his mug.

"Yes, please."

"I'll be right back." When he sat back down, steamy mug in hand, he said, "It'll be ready in a minute."

"Thank you."

"I'm glad we had this conversation," he said flatly.

"I'm certain some day I will be also."

"We can only hope."

They sat in silence, waiting for the water to boil.

It was nice.

"Where do we go from here?" Sachiko finally asked reluctantly.

Tank pursed his lips and wiggled them around. "Not sure," he mused.

"Really? Tank, the last time you didn't know what to do next, I didn't *know* you yet."

He tossed his head gently to one side. "It's been a while, I guess."

"So, oracle of outer space, what's next?"

"We finish the job."

"Obviously."

"As it stands, there's only one enemy vessel on this side of the holographic surface left to take out."

"Obviously. And we know the two on the Through the Looking-Glass side aren't coming back anytime soon."

"So we find it and we kill it."

"Less obviously *how*," speculated the ship's captain.

"They're not like us at all, the Clams."

"They are not."

"So it's not reasonable to assume they'd *do* what we'd *do*."

"I think I'd bet on those odds," she agreed.

"So I say we make a list of everything we'd do, every place we'd run to, and then we do the opposite."

"It'll be Opposite Day, over and over again. Opposite *Week*."

"I think it'll be epic."

"Do you have a specific idea in mind, or you just have inspirational words for your underlings?"

He winked. "A little of both."

"As one already filled sufficiently with rhetorical passion, I'd actually like to hear the substantive plans that cycle inside your pointy little head."

Tank shot his eye upward, as if he might then see whether his head was indeed pointy or not.

"Me, if I was them, I'd disappear for just long enough

for us to wonder where we were, then I'd hit like a bull elephant in rut." He slammed his fist into his palm.

"Okay, good information, but the *opposite* action doesn't leap into my mind."

"You know what would be completely idiotic to do, if you did it at this juncture?"

She tumbled her head to demonstrate open-ended uncertainty.

"Business as usual."

"Beg pardon?"

"The dumbest thing I could do would be to return to what I'd done for centuries, completely ignoring the fact that a vicious killer is stalking me in the shadows."

"Really? Well, *yes* that would be wacky, wouldn't it? But, seriously, do you imagine in your wildest dreams the time maker'd be *that* out of touch with personal safety?"

"I'd never consider such farcical behavior. If I ever did, I'd hope you'd slap my face before I could act."

She perked up visibly. "Shall we practice a few times, so that if such a dark hour befalls us, I'll be in-serviced fully?"

"No. I think you're a natural, so we can forgo the need for training."

"You *are* in command. It's your call," she ribbed.

"So we need to find where time/space is being no-timed on a large, systematic scale."

"Without the benefit of Aramthella's ability to cheat?"

"Without the benefit of a proven spy."

"Sounds difficult," she speculated.

"If it were easy, kiddo—"

"Anyone could do it."

"No. If it were easy, I'd be much, much *happier*. Come

on. As much as I *like* a challenge in scientific investigations, I *dislike* one when it comes to war."

"Aramthella," Sachiko called out. "We need to begin a detailed survey of the entirety of reality. Are you up for the challenge?"

"Such a search would take more time than I think you can imagine, Captain."

"Well, we *do* have a time machine."

"Yes, we do. But, even with that advantage-in, I think we're looking at a significant commitment."

"The journey of a thousand eternities begins with a single day's search," Sachiko concluded. "So let get started in ... three, two, one ... *now*."

TWELVE

"We *are* the master race. That always *has* been the way of it, and it *will* always be the way of it." The new time maker strode back and forth on the bridge, speaking to itself. If the scum on the underside of his feet listened in and therein found comfort, that was nice too. But his servants did not need to understand the time maker's thoughts or intentions. All they needed to do was obey him immediately, completely, and mindlessly.

It was a pity, Time Maker-bob reflected, that he needed his minions at all, really. *It* was so complete, so self-contained and splendid, that it didn't *require* assistants or admirers. Okay, maybe admirers. It was hard to deny the little brains the glory of beholding Time Maker-bob. It should not be selfish. Well, it *should* be selfish, but not so selfish as to prevent useless ones from basking in its wonder.

"As the master race, it is our destiny to rule the universe. We have for uncountable time. So we will in all futures. This is obvious to me. I word it to you only because you cannot be me, the one in subtention of the truth."

Understanding Maker of Others-pit nodded slowly. It wished to signal thoughtful consideration and potential full agreement with the waste-words the time maker had just defecated from its oral opening. Dumber than a bag of *preleps*, that was what the new boss was.

"Master, I hear your words. This much is indisputable."

"Then you agree fully?" It raised a pencil-thin hand to forestall response. "For to hear me is to understand me, and to understand me is to obey me. You," it said followed by the briefest hesitation, "are welcome."

"Blessed am I, in fact. But—"

The absurdly thin hand rose quickly. "You got my announcement, the one of ... oh, let me think ... two days prior, did you not?"

"I ... I have received all your wisdom, in all forms it has rained down on us unworthies."

"Then you know the word *but* has been forbidden. I have removed it from our language." It scowled off to one side, based on the fact that the time maker was completely insane.

"Yes, it is wisely true. I did receive that wonderful decree. I spoke out of habit, not defiance."

No sooner had the old understanding maker finished speaking the words when its arms were jerked up behind it and it was lifted off the deck by invisible hands.

"In that same missive, displeasing one, I also removed the word *defiance.* I am not the fool you accuse me of being. You used two forbidden words in one interchange. This is high heresy."

"Bu ... howev ... *Lord.* Those two innocently spoken

sentences were *widely* separated in the text, not even in the same *sentence*. Further, perfect spot, I erred only. No offen ... affron ... insul ... badness was meant on my part."

"You spray eliminated words and you call me a liar. You ... you are much braver than I gave you credit for, understanding maker." The time maker whirled on the quivering assistant. "Make me understand why I shouldn't *incinerate* you where you stand."

"Ah ... it would foul the floor and the atmosphere too?"

The time maker took a few long strides back and forth. "Yes, you are temporarily correct. Ah," it spun again, "I could explode you." In a flash, its hand shot up. "No, no. That would never do. Even more messy."

"You could no-*time* me, master," the understanding maker suggested uncertainly.

"Yes, I could. Wastes a bunch of energy, but," it raised a finger, "it *is* clean." It paced a few more times. "Wait. What was I thinking. I could just project you outside this ship. You die miserably *and* do not dirty the vessel."

"Yes, that would be economical and cl—"

The understanding maker was gone.

The time maker then addressed the understanding maker of fluff. *Fluff* was its new simplification of the annoyingly long descriptor of Not Self and Not Others. "Fluff, you're next. Were not my words earlier wise and unquestionable?"

"Yes," the frightened fool replied quickly.

"That word transfer is insufficient. Yes to what are you declaring?"

"That you said words before you addressed me that were spot-on unquestionable." It bowed deeply.

"Please note, everyone. The word *clever* is hereby also banned. I forbid not only the *word* clever, but the act of *being* clever." It rolled its hand to show obligatory compliance with some standard of official expression. "Punishable by death, no-timing, or both. Blah, blah, blah."

"You are wiser than wisdom, center-of-the-universe one," exclaimed the fluff lackey.

"As to your *clever* response," it rolled its head to express to the crowd that it could break its rules, because, well, it was the boss *and* it was an utter lunatic. "Of course I said truth at *some* point. *Duh*. But I asked more centrally whether my declaration that since we were supreme, and of course still are, doesn't that mean we will remain so no matter what I decide to do?"

"*Yes*, you said that."

"And is that remark truth *defined*?"

Death was coming. Fluff could hear the tappy footfalls. What to say? What ever to ...

"You know, supreme supremacy," Fluff began conspiratorially, "I worry about you."

The time maker scrunched up its already pruny face in disbelief. "What?"

"Yes." Fluff nodded. "I do. You see, perfection's image of perfection, you worry too much what others think about you." It nodded knowingly. "Yes, far too much."

"I am confused," the time maker began uncertainly. "That, by the way, is a bad thing. Why would someone like *you*, less than nothing in importance, worry about *me*? Moreover, I worry too much about what others think about me? Your wording is so bizarre as to not *summon* a cruel death, but to *demand* one."

"Be that as it may, I do not worry about my insignificant self." It shook its head resolutely. "But when it comes to you, I can *only* worry."

"*Naive*! I have just slain heartlessly the better half of my bridge crew because I'm in a suboptimal mood today, or at least just now. How could you *possibly* hallucinate that I care excessively what others think about me? It's ... what is the new term? Countersubtendable."

"I can only bare my true feelings, not justify them. Here, master, I see you asking one inferior crew member if what you said was true. As if *any* of us could judge one such as yourself."

The time maker was taken aback. That had never happened to a time maker. It was new at the gig, true, but neither of its predecessors had ever been taken aback. Knowing so was a time maker thing.

"Why, blissless fool, I do believe you are correct! Why was I soliciting from the worm bait I must suffer to have slave for me, an opinion as to whether what I said was valuable and correct? Of course it was." It looked at Fluff as if it was seeing it for the very first time. "You know, I'm flirting with the notion of not exterminating you. I could use one good clan drone to aid me in this struggle that is called life."

"I am not worthy," it said with a deep bow. "I am totally unworthy."

Pzzzz ... zap. The understanding maker of not self, not others never existed. The time maker had no-timed it before it closed its mouth from speaking.

Damn. Fluff was good. Fluff was clever. But it had overplayed its hand. It was *too* clever. Note to the reader. In all interactions with management, be less clever than Fluff, or join it.

THIRTEEN

Aramthella came to a complete stop in the center of mass point of the Greater Magellanic Cloud. It was the first major use of her engines since the warfare with the clan had begun. Previously, *Stingray* had powered both ships. That way, the time-signature Aramthella generated when underway would not be detectable. Now, Tank and Sachiko actually *hoped* the time maker would detect them and attack. It was one sure way to bring these hunt-and-seek frustrations to a definitive end. One ship versus one ship presented acceptable odds to the human commander.

Sachiko chose to begin their survey in that particular cloud because she had always loved it. Half her childhood had been spent trying to cajole her parents into taking the family on vacation to the Southern Hemisphere just so she could see the dwarf galaxy with her own two eyes. Her passionate efforts had, for the record, never borne fruit. Now she enjoyed a ridiculously closer view and was well beyond pleased with herself.

"I'm beginning a search for time-assimilation activity, Captain," stated Aramthella.

"Very well. What radius can you reliably study from this location?"

"The electromagnetics are low in this region, so I can survey a large distance. I'm hoping to detect out six parsecs while maintaining one-hundred percent accuracy."

"Estimated time to screen the entire galaxy?"

"Not more than a few hours."

"Very well. Keep me posted." Sachiko ended the exchange.

"Pretty out there, isn't it?" observed Tank.

"Yes," Sachiko replied as she hugged herself. "This is a dream come true."

"How about you, Reva?" Tank asked. "You impressed with the view?"

She leaned in toward the main view screen. "I see stars. Lots of stars."

"But the concentration is so high, the patterning..." Sachiko searched for the words. "It's— sublime."

Reva leaned forward again. "Lots of stars." She twirled a finger toward the screen. "Before we left," she thumbed over her shoulder, "back there, I saw a lot of stars too. Don't get me wrong. They're all nice and shiny. But, unless I'm missing something, they're all stars, right?"

"You *are* correct," Tank relented. He turned to Sachiko. "While the ship does all the work, shall we take a stroll?"

That brought a surprised angling of the head from the captain. "Sure." She stood. "Where is it we need to go?"

"Nowhere in particular. We could use the exercise, however."

"Of course, General Sherman."

"Reva, you're welcome to join us," added Tank.

"No, but thanks. I'm good. Two hours a day in the gym is about all the exercise I can stand."

Without responding to Reva, Tank offered Sachiko an elbow and they walked away.

Once out of Reva's earshot, Sachiko couldn't wait any longer. "What's this about, Tank?"

"It's about getting the heart rate up, sweating a bit."

"Really?"

"Yes, what'd you think? That I wanted to discuss something with you alone, without my second-in-command listening in?"

She nodded. "Yeah. Kind 'a."

He tipped his head and looked up at her. "You have a suspicious nature, my friend. Why would I want to do such a thing?"

"I don't know. *First* we excuse ourselves, *then* you tell me why. So tell me why."

"Such an active imagination, child. What could I *possibly* want to say that Reva couldn't hear?"

It occurred to Sachiko there were two options. One, there was *nothing*, and Tank was playing with her. Two, there was *something*, and Tank wanted her to guess what it was. If it were the first case, there was no way she'd figure it out, so her best move would be to punch his shoulder and call him an old goat. She'd done that a lot over the last decade.

If it were the second case, it had to be something, obviously, Tank didn't want Reva to hear. Those topics had to be pretty few and far between. Jon wanted his and Sapale's secret kept quiet for now. Could it have to do with them? Unlikely. The four spoke every few days, but nothing much was happening on either end.

It could be something personal. Was Tank ill? No, if he was, the second-in-command would definitely need to know that. Was it personal between Tank and her? They'd worked together so long, that seemed an impossibility.

Could it be about Reva? Yes, and Tank wanted her opinion on his adjutant. No. If it was a military issue or assessment he wanted, he'd speak with one of the other officers, not her, a civilian. What could it be?

"I'm inclined at this point to say *Earth-to-Sachiko*, but, given the recent past, that'd be in pretty poor taste, I think," Tank teased.

"You're in love with Reva." There, Sachiko just said it, right out loud.

Tank stopped in the passageway, rotated to face her, and set a hand on her shoulder.

"I am?"

Of course, Sachiko—a woman—heard *I am* ... period, not *I am* ... question mark.

She grew very serious. "I know how you feel about Daisy, Tank. I *fully* understand. But ... well, we have to—"

There is such a thing as *euthanasia*, a mercy killing. Tank practiced *eu-interruption*, a mercy *stopping* of Sachiko's mouth running on.

"Hold on, kiddo. Stop right there. Before you say another word, I have to ask one simple question." He allowed her time to lean toward him in anticipation. "Where ... where the dickens do you come *up* with this stuff?"

She pulled her head back. "So you're *not* in love with Reva?"

"I don't think so. Let me check." He waited less than one second and then he spoke loudly. "No. I'm *not* in love with Reva."

"Oh. Then what I said ... probably sounded ... er ... *silly*?"

"*Silly's* not the word I'd select. *Insane,* maybe deranged, clueless. *Seriously*, where did that *come* from?"

"You wanted to step out for a 'walk' and then you asked what could you *possibly* want to say she couldn't hear. So," she said, flustered, "I sort of assumed this was a test."

He turned and continued walking. "Well then, you *failed* the test-that-never-was."

"So you really did just want to take a walk?"

"Sheesh, Shaky, yes. That's why I said *let's take a walk*. Now, however, I think I need a cup of coffee. You're wearing me out."

"But you excluded Reva."

"The woman works out two hours a *day*. Didn't you hear her say just that?"

"I know, well, I do now. But—"

"Shaky."

"Yes."

"Quit while you're just way behind, okay?"

"Good advice." She drew an invisible zipper closed across her lips.

They soon found themselves sitting in the mess. They each had their preferred warm drink in front of them.

Tank sipped at his coffee. He squinted judgmentally at the contents as he moved the mug back to its neutral position. "I'll sure be glad when we've gone through all this fancy-schmancy coffee Jon stockpiled."

Sachiko fluttered her eyes and shook her head almost

imperceptibly. "Now it's the coffee? First it was the walk that was just a walk, now it's the twenty-dollar-a-pound, individually-selected-bean-that-has-passed-through-the-intestinal-system-of-a-civet *coffee*?"

Tank squinted. "A civet? That's a kind of cat, right? What's that got to do with coffee beans?"

"If you don't know, you're better off not knowing. Remain in your cave and grunt no more inquiries."

"That pretty much proves my point."

"Which is?"

"I miss regular coffee, you know, *coffee* coffee. The kind that comes in a red one-pound metal can, which goes *psst* when you crack the seal?"

"Aren't the cans plastic now?" she quizzed him.

"Yet another affront to Western civilization as I see it. Thank you for raising the sore subject."

"Tank, if you *prefer* grainy generic coffee-oid debris, why not have Aramthella synthesize a batch?"

He held up his mug. "Because we got all this to go through first."

"But ... if you ... *blah*."

"I can't very well see it go to waste, can I?"

"I believe I covered that issue with *blah*."

"I just miss plain old American coffee."

"I know."

"You know what I *really* miss?" he posed.

"Silence?" she tossed back.

"You're pretty jumpy today. Anything you'd like to share, vent, or explain?"

"Yes. I think I need to go for a walk—*alone*."

"We just did the walk-thing." He gestured over a shoulder.

"That one was missing the essential *alone* aspect."

"I see. Okay, we can discuss what I wanted to cover when you get back." He grinned neutrally. "You *are* coming back soon, right? You're not going on a Jon-inspired walkabout, right?"

"There's *so* much wrong with what you just said," she moaned. "So there *was* something you wanted to discuss?"

"I just stated that. You might want to have Doc check your hearing. Maybe it's just wax, but check with her nonetheless."

"It's not wax."

"You can see in your own ear canals now that you're a captain?"

"I don't get wax build ... *blah*."

"I said it pretty clearly, least I think I did."

"But you insisted earlier that A) there was no point other than to take a walk; and that B) you weren't trying to exclude Reva. Tank, I need to know the truth."

He pointed to her tea. "Is that decaf?"

"Tank!"

"Sure hope it is. You're so *jumpy* today."

"Robert *Sherman*. As captain of this vessel, it is within my power to have you thrown out an airlock. What is it you *wish* to discuss?"

He glanced to the door, then to her. "What about your walk? You really seemed committed to one."

"I'm good."

"I can wait."

"Deep space, Sherman. Cold, dark, unforgiving *space*."

Reva chose that unusual moment to appear at the door. As she'd heard the tail end of the exchange from outside, she stopped at the entry. "I was hoping for some joe," she wagged a finger back and forth between them, "but if this is a bad time—"

"Bad time?" Tank responded quizzically. "What ever gave you a crazy idea like that?"

"Oh, maybe the shouts and the tension. You two sounded like me and my ex on any given morning *before* he was my ex."

"I didn't know you were divorced," Tank said with interest.

"Well, quite possibly that's because that has never been any of your business."

"Good point. Pull up a chair, Colonel. I wanted to discuss a couple things with the two of you. Glad we chanced to encounter one another."

Sachiko started to scream something to the effect that they were all together on the bridge not fifteen minutes prior, but, in the interest of not killing him where he sat, she let it go. It was not, for the record, easy for her to do so.

Reva poured a mug and joined them. "What's on your mind, Tank?"

"I think we need to be more proactive," he said without emotion.

"How so?" Reva responded.

"We need to be more active in our pursuit of our enemy."

Reva raised an eyebrow. "I thought we were doing just that?"

"Hey, you do that like Mr. Spock and The Rock." He pointed at her forehead.

"I *do* what and *who* does it famously?" Reva spat.

"Yes, certainly do, doesn't she, Shaky?"

"Please leave me out of this comparison. I don't know who The Rock is either."

"You two don't know Dwayne Johnson, aka The Rock?"

They returned blank stares that suggested Tank was not in full control of his mental faculties.

"Aramthella is performing her surveys as quickly as she can," Sachiko stated a bit defensively.

"Yes, she is. But while she is, I feel we can also begin a *physical* search."

"Why is that needed at this juncture?" asked Reva.

"Because I'm anxious to finish them off, that's why. The longer we wait, the more chance the time maker has to prepare its defenses. It is at its weakest presently, and can only grow stronger."

The two women considered that remark.

"What do you propose, specifically?" asked Sachiko.

"I propose that doing *more* beats the heck out of doing *less*. I've been studying the records of the clan's historic movements. I have made some educated guesses as to where they might be operating, assuming they are returning to business-as-usual."

"You really think they'd be so ... so *naïve* as to ignore us and resume time collection like they did in the past?" Reva challenged.

"They're not at all like us. *That* much I know," Tank responded. "And the new time maker doesn't have the experience the last one did."

Reva thought quietly a moment. "They *have* exhibited some pretty lame strategies up until now. I'll grant you that."

"They've never needed to face this type of situation before. Up until now, they conquer whatever they attacked. I'm thinking they might just be *that* removed from military reality."

"But they're not *children,*" protested Sachiko. "I'm not sure we can assume they'd be that foolish."

"Well, given the fact that we're pretty much floating in space waiting for fortune to smile upon us, I say we at least take a few shots-in-the-dark at 'em," Tank said with finality.

"I say go for it," agreed Reva. "If we're actively pursuing our enemy, it'll be much easier to keep the troops focused and sharp."

"My thoughts too," Tank responded. "I want everyone to work together seamlessly. The best way to do that is to drill them constantly. The best way to get everyone to buy in is to make the prospect of action real, imminent. So we go looking for trouble. Speaking of which, have you had any luck getting any of the students to participate?"

"More than I thought might, in fact," Reva replied, upbeat. "Maybe seventy-five or so are committed to joining up and joining in."

"Are they formally enlisting?" asked Sachiko.

"Eventually, I think I'll need to make them official. But for now, I'm allowing them to just practice with the regulars."

"With our present strength, if we did get into a fire fight, I not crazy about our odds," mused Tank.

"I've never had odds I liked, General," responded Reva. "But, yes, the more the merrier. We'll see. I think that within a few months, we could triple our fighting capabilities."

"But you're having to train our current personnel with all the new weapons Aramthella is supplying," reminded Sachiko. "Aren't you being overly optimistic?"

"Only way to be," responded Tank. "I've gone over this in detail with Aramthella. She could supply us with radically new weapons and tools for years to come. We'll never be fully prepared in any one system. So we train and we adapt. If and when the time comes, our troops'll make us proud. Of that I am certain."

"Amen," exclaimed Reva.

"I'm rather glad I'm not involved in those aspects," admitted Sachiko. "That said, where shall we go first?"

"I gave Aramthella our next destination earlier today. I'd like you each to study the proposal and get back to me by 16:00 with your thoughts."

"So soon?" Sachiko questioned.

"So soon."

"If that's all, Tank, I'll take my leave and get to it." Reva threw back the last of her coffee and left. She moved with intensity and singular focus.

"I'm sure glad she's on our side," Sachiko observed as she watched the colonel depart.

FOURTEEN

"Isn't that weird?" Sapale asked.

"Lemme see," I groaned back. "We're sitting in mud, at the bottom of a tunnel, on a barren world, burrowing toward some sound that's on the other side of a transportation portal that connects us here to some *horrible* place. I know it to be horrible because no portal *ever* has connected us to Disney World, or any pleasant version thereof. So I'm going to answer, *My concept of weird is being presently tested, so please be more specific.*"

She glared at me. Don't get me wrong. I deserved it. And she, super wife that she was, did her level best to shame me. Hey, I was *venting*. They say that's good for you.

"You 'bout done there, sport?"

I checked my pulse at the wrist, or where a pulse would have been if I still had one. "Yup. Done."

"Glad to hear it. My remark was concerning the music."

"The music?"

"That we're *digging* toward."

"Okay, that music. What about it?"

"It's *notable* that the further we dig, the more higher frequencies are coming through."

"Weird."

"Like I said."

"That you *noticed.*"

After a secondary wifely glare, she spoke. "The music has additional harmonics that were blocked by the barrier. The closer we get to whatever, the worse the music becomes."

"Thank you for making me aware of that factoid, as I was blessedly unaware of it up until now." I angled my head to hear better. "My, that *is* awful."

"You are welcome."

"Can I scrape at the ground in front of you for a while, so I might be the first to fully appreciate the horror that assaults our audio inputs?"

"No chance. I need to go first."

I rested back on my haunches. "Why, pray tell, is that?"

She pointed forward. "What's on the other side of this barrier?"

"I-do-not-know. Say, brood's-mate, what's on the far side of this partition?"

"Something *alien.*"

I tapped the side of my head with a finger. "Brilliant. Why didn't *I* think of that?"

"Because I'm smarter, but that's beside the point. Since," she rested a palm on her chest, "*I* am an alien, *I* am clearly the most qualified to represent when we come face-to-face with *those* aliens."

I looked amazed. I wasn't, in fact. "Say, ain't *I* an alien, too?"

"Are you serious? Humans are never the aliens. *Aliens* are the aliens."

"My bad. I blame mid-Twentieth Century TV for my shortcomings."

"As well you should, human."

"But, to whoever's through there," I pointed ahead, "I'm an alien, unless they're humans, which they can't be, because humans would never play that bad of a music."

She got a twinkle in her eyes. "Maybe they're *future* humans. And their sense of tone was destroyed by Jupiter."

"Jupiter?" I responded incredulously.

"Jon, it is *al-ways* Ju-pi-ter. Pay at-ten-tion." She joined the tips of her fingers and thumped me on the forehead with each syllable.

"Hey, I have an idea. Let's keep digging so we finish before something else unthinkable has a chance to happen."

"Sounds good. You go first."

"I thought ... Forget it. Move over."

I returned to clawing my way through the dirt that separated us from whatever. Sapale did too, if less vigorously. She enjoyed getting the better of me whenever, however.

Shortly, when I reached to scoop out yet more yuck, I noticed my hand semi-disappeared. Now *that* was weird. I reached out, and my hand ghosted. When I pulled back, my hand looked like ... like my hand. Duh.

Pretty soon, Sapale noticed the fuzzy juncture. She stuck her head in and taunted me. Great, a headless shrew. Just what the universe so lacked. To one-up her, I stuck my butt through and made farting sounds. Hey, nobody out-childishes Jon Ryan. *No* one.

When we were over that, which was quicker for her than me, we continued forward cautiously. A couple meters in, the outlines of a semi-metallic orifice began to take form. It was round and almost a meter and a half in diameter. Though it clearly allowed for a connection from us to somewhere, it was as cold as the surrounding dirt and it was absolutely silent. Weird.

"You know those portals the Adamant used?" I asked.

"The exotic *matter* ones?" she answered uncertainly.

"Yeah, those. This reminds me of one of those."

"How so?" she challenged. "This is smaller, much smaller. Those hummed and thrummed. Plus, I don't smell dog. No, these are totally different."

"I mean aside from that ... *those*."

"You mean they're both *round* and made of *semi-metal*?"

"Yeah." I snapped my fingers. "Like that."

"Oh boy. Our side's in trouble. Our fearless leader has gone batshit crazy."

"I fail to see the need for insults. We need to be more secret squirrel, you know. If *we* can hear *them*, then *they* can hear *us*."

"No they can't. They're having a party. Probably all blitzed."

"I'm serious. Please relate anything you feel you need to say head-to-head from here on out."

You're pathetic, she said in my head.

Thank you. Now keep digging.

We cleared the portal and the space beyond. Finally, we reached a point where I could put a finger through the remaining barrier. It was two meters past the portal itself. The way the dirt was layered, it seemed to have been deposited over a very long period of time.

I turned to Sapale and sat down. *Ideas?*

Maybe we should break through the remaining dirt and see what's on the other side?

Besides the obvious, I mean. Should we burst into whatever and stand ready to fight?

I don't know. Maybe we should break through the remaining dirt and see what's on the other side?

I turned back to the dirt and lay supine. When I raised both feet and kicked the wall of dirt at its base. The whole thing came down in one slump.

I'm in, Sapale said as she angled past me.

I followed right behind her.

We stood simultaneously. We were in a large room. It was unlike any I'd ever seen. Of course it was, Jon. It was *alien.* Light diffused from everywhere, but from nowhere specifically. I couldn't be sure without analyzing it, but the building materials seemed crystalline. And the crystals sang. *They* were the source of the sound we were calling music. They shimmered randomly. Each color of light they emitted produced a correspondingly different sound frequency, or maybe it was vice versa. Who knew?

"I still dislike the music, but the crystals are bitching," announced Sapale. She swiveled her hips as if dancing.

"I wonder what the function is here? Are the walls just making sounds, or are they saying anything?"

"I ran a translation matrix and came up with nothing." She continued to wriggle slowly. Kaljaxians, I have to tell you, are *horrible* dancers. Never pretty sights. Think Elaine Benes.

I did the same analyses with similarly negative outcomes. Dang that Al. Never around when I needed him, yet always there when he was unwanted.

"Maybe it's just background for whoever built the place?" I speculated. "Let's press on."

She followed, gyrating a bit longer. Fortunately, I took point, so I couldn't see her. I just felt her swaying, which was more than too much in and of itself.

Without narrowing or forming a passageway, the massive room finally split off in three directions. Right, left, and straight ahead. Before committing to any path, I turned a looked back where we'd come from. I was mightily confused. Here was this spacious, shiny ballroom, ornate to a fault. It stretched out expansively then tapered down quickly to a small portal filled with dirt. Who builds that?

"You coming?" Sapale prodded me from ahead.

"In a sec. I'm processing."

"Darn. There're no chairs to rest on. This may take the better part of forever."

I turned back to her. "Which way do you favor?"

She shrugged. "No way to tell if it matters. As a person who is generally right, I guess I'll select that option."

All I could answer with was a shake of my head. To the right we ventured. Though the walls and ceiling remained a roughly studded crystalline surface, there was a subtle shift in the decor. Furniture, if I could call it that, began to appear. Tables have legs and a flat top. Chairs are elevated to suit one's butt height, and shaped so as to comfort said butt. What I saw was like sticks irregularly linked. Maybe they were welded? It wasn't clear. They served no obvious function, unless they were artwork. If they were, they were bad art. I know, you're saying to yourself, "Art is in the eye of the beholder." Seriously, if you beheld this, you'd agree. It was lame art. Come on, irregularly joined sticks? That is anti-artful.

Sapale must have felt similarly to me. She stopped at a particularly unruly set of poles and studied it a moment. Then she picked it up.

"Light," she commented. She then unexpectedly slammed it against the wall. "Sturdy little sucker," she added when it didn't break. "We'll have to make it a point to take some with us when we—"

A small form sped into view, way ahead down the hall. My initial guess was it was a rat, a hefty rat. A foot tall, furry, and scurrying to beat the band. It shot past us without slowing or taking any particular not of us.

"The locals are less friendly than they are quick," I observed.

"It had a heat signature like a living animal of some sort," she noted. "It sure moved like it was on a critical mission."

"If it comes back this direction, I'll bag it."

"What if that violates some religious belief or the damn thing explodes? I hate it when rats explode." She shivered.

"If it's a spiritual faux pas, I'll go to confession. If it explodes, I'll do the laundry."

"If gooey bits get in my mouth, I'm going to be *pissed.* Fair warning."

"Hopefully, then, it *won't* return."

"I'm officially bored. Can we continue getting deeper into an undoubtedly hazardous unknown?"

"Absolutely. Can't have a bored wife, now can I?"

We pressed on down the long hallway. The stick things changed a little, but still didn't suggest what they were designed to do. I found them increasingly annoying. Useless stuff was annoying.

"How far are we going?" Sapale asked a few minutes later.

"No clue. We *are* immortal, so we could journey on a while without giving much up."

"I suppose. If I lose interest completely, I'm telling you immediately."

"I would expect no less. We—"

Darn. There was something you didn't see every day. Nope, not hardly. There was a dense cloud moving toward us. As it progressed, it picked up the useless sticks. They then disappeared into its cloudiness, only to reappear quickly in an altered but still totally useless configuration.

"I want one of those for the ship," Sapale declared before I could say anything.

"Why would you want one of those?"

"It picks stuff up and puts it back down. How cool is that? I could follow it around all day and be a happy camper."

"I have never been under the impression before that you are *that* easy to please."

"You call that easy? Look at it, picking up, setting down. Outstanding."

"If there are dust rags inside the cloud, *maybe*. Otherwise, it'd be just that much more crap to store."

We cut the clowning short because the whatever was almost to us.

"Hi there, my nebulous fellow," I called out. "You wouldn't happen to be sentient, friendly, and well-intentioned, would you?"

It stopped dead.

"I think it doesn't like you," my wife observed.

"Maybe it's just frightened. I can be pretty scary, you know."

"Clouds fear you?" she responded dubiously.

"If they're smart clouds, yes, they do."

"Yelo-et-palaquie." That's approximately what the cloud announced. It didn't move any parts to say the words. The sound seemed more like it came from speakers inside it.

"Yelo-et-palaquie," I said back in a cheery tone. I had no idea what we were saying, but if it was good for the cloud, it was good for me. Unless of course it meant something bad or confusing, which it almost certainly did. I mean, what are the chances the cloud said *good morning*? Nah. Clouds are rarely that polite.

"Yeli-et-palaquie," it said louder. "*Zamat*-et-palaquie."

"Oh yeah. You managed to piss it off in record time," Sapale accused.

"*Yelo* changed to *yeli*. I bet that's important."

"What about the *zamat*? That sound important to you too?"

"Not sure. Maybe that's its pet name for itself?"

"You are *so* bogus," she responded harshly.

"Hang on." I held out a finger to her. "Yeli-et-yelo-zamat-palaquie."

Sapale shook her head. "I don't know what you just said, but I know in my heart it's not helpful."

"Yeli-*yelo*-zamat," the cloud thundered.

"He's voting for what you said," I speculated. I was buying time and attempting to glean some meaning. My translation algorithm was gaining a bit of traction. "I think it said something about us and it belonging here." I transferred the data to her.

"Hmm. Could be. "Yeli-zamat-palaquie," she said neutrally.

"Tum. Yeli-et-palaquie."

We understood what the silly cloud was saying at the same time. *You don't belong here.* It was scolding us. It had said *it* belonged here and disagreed with my gibberish that we *all* belonged here. Yes, it was a stupid conversation, but we were exchanging our thoughts.

"*Who are you*?" I asked in its language.

"I am the one who picks up *necfol*. You do not belong here."

"What does it pick up?" I asked Sapale.

"Well, it's been picking up these." She lifted a stick thing. "*Necfol*? This is a *necfol*?"

"*Of course it's a stick figurine*," it responded with attitude.

"And you pick them up?" she confirmed.

"*Yes, obviously*."

"Is your name *pick stick figurines up*, or is that just your job?" I asked.

"You do not belong here. You are in violation. You may not pick up stick figurines."

"Dude's fixated on the sticks," I commented. "I don't see him as a *big picture* kind of cloud."

"Why do you pick up stick figurines?" Sapale asked it.

"Why? Your words do not belong."

I'm assuming it meant, *Are you stupid or something, Forrest?*

"Why do you do what you do?" I questioned him more sternly.

"If I don't move the stick figurines often, the masters may see them in the same configuration more than once."

"Would that be so bad?" I just had to ask.

"Bad? It would be to not serve the masters. Why should they suffer to see stick figurines in the same configuration twice?"

"It has a valid point," Sapale opined. "I mean, they are *masters*, right?"

"They're sounding kind of spoiled to me. The sticks look stupid to begin with. If they change or don't change, that doesn't alter their essential insufficient nature."

"Which is stupid?" she confirmed.

"Totally. They're sticks joined irregularly."

"Do the masters *like* the stick figurines?" Sapale asked it.

"Do the mast ... do they *like* the stick figurines? That is not important. If they do or do not like them, if they do or do not notice them, the stick figurines must vary so as to please the masters maximally. That is all that matters."

"To whom?" I wondered out loud. "It wouldn't matter to me whether the masters are happy, unhappy, or stuck halfway between the two extremes."

"Jon, I don't—"

"You do not belong to knowledge. Do not ever speak neutrally or less about the masters. If they should learn of it, no-existence would befall us all."

I turned to my wife. "Is it me, or is this a crazy conversation?"

"I'd go with crazy. It said it doesn't even know if the masters notice the dumb sticks. Still, it's obsessed with making them maximally presentable. That qualifies as loco-moco in my book."

"It really seems indignant' too. It's not just saying what it is because it's scared. I think it really worries about its masters," I responded. That gave me an idea. "Where are the masters?"

"What do you mean *where are the masters*?"

I thought that was a fairly straightforward query. "I want to speak with them. Where will I find them?"

There is no joke that begins, *How do you make a cloud disappear*? If, however, there was, the punchline would be, *Tell it you want to see the masters*.

The cloud was browbeating us one moment, and then it simply wasn't there. It didn't even evaporate or disperse. It was just gone.

"*Now* you've gone and done it again," accused Sapale. "You always have to piss off the locals, don't you?"

I pointed to where it was. "I don't know if it was actually *mad*. It might have had an appointment, maybe in the wood shop?"

"Oh, it was mad. You always piss off the clouds. What is it with you and *gaseous* formations?"

"Hey, I generally like clouds. They can be pretty, and sometimes they look like bunnies. I happen to *like* bunnies."

"I bet it went to get *all* the other clouds. They'll appear here and we won't be able to see our hands in front of our faces. It's all fun and games until you can't see squat. Then something bad happens." She whipped a finger under my nose accusingly. "When that happens, I *will* blame you."

"Maybe it went to get us a map? Hmm. Do you ever think positively? I do."

There began an explosive rumble, far down the hallway.

"Hey, that's interesting," I remarked quickly.

"What? The part about the sound coming from *both* directions, suggesting there will be no easy escape for us, because we're, like, *surrounded*?"

"No, I just meant it sounded interesting."

She raised a palm, as if to slap me upside the head. Fortunately, events transpired so rapidly, she didn't have the chance to. What a break!

The churning crackles and snaps approached us fast. Of course—because my wife just had to be correct—the halls became obscured by, you got it, clouds. Lots and lots of clouds. Well, that was up until they fused to become two large noisy clouds approaching from either direction. Note to self: Piss off fewer clouds, should I survive this tempest.

"Ideas?" Sapale shouted above the din.

"You take those ones." I pointed that way. "I'll take these." I pointed the other way.

"Fine, I got these, you got those. What do we *do* with them, genius?"

"You can use your imagination. *I'm* using my laser."

We opened up simultaneously. Theoretically, lasers should be effective against clouds, right? Vapor loses to intense heat, ten times out of ten.

No such luck, it would seem, in Where-ever-we-were Land. Despite us both swirling our gamma ray laser fingers, the coalesced clouds came on like roiling locomotives. Ungood.

"It's not working," Sapale shouted.

"Thank you, Mrs. Obvious." Then, mostly to myself, I mumbled, "The *one* time I wished stupid Plesmus was here, and she's a no show. *Grrreat.*"

"Really?" my boot asked me.

"Plesmus?"

"How'd you guess?" she responded snappily.

"But ... you said ... you stayed—"

"Jon, in approximately nine seconds, two pissed-off

cloud banks are about to descend on you. Would you like to discuss my change of mind, or would you like to ask for my help? Five seconds. No pressure. Four."

"*Help*," Sapale and I screamed as one.

The leading edge of the nebulous mass closest to me was about to hit—whatever that entailed. I had no clue what damage an irate cloud could actually do. Maybe ... no, I won't go there.

Maybe it'd rain on my parade?

Oops, I went there. Hate me.

"Sapale, get behind—" I started to shout.

Then there were no nebulous aggregations about to impale—or whatever—us.

"Plesmus, did you no-time the mean clouds?" Sapale asked over my shoulder, peering out to where the clouds had just been.

"Yes. Tasty little marshmallows."

"Seriously?" I asked reflexively.

"That I did or that they were tasty?"

"Your choice."

"Light and airy as a ... wait, they *were* clouds," she responded.

"Are we safe now?" Sapale thought to ask.

"Safe? You two? Here? You're kidding, right? You were unsafe the moment you started digging. By the way, large-ape-named-Jon, next time throw the dirt *around* your boot, not *at* it like you want to bury it alive."

"I'll try and remember." I regained my composure, somewhat. "Back to why are you here?"

"I thought about it. I'm much stronger than any of my kin back on what you impiously called Plesmus'. They would have posed no threat to me."

"And you didn't inform us of your decision because—" I challenged.

"I fancied I'd see what you said about me when you thought I wasn't around."

"Seriously," snapped Sapale. "Are you *that* Jon Ryanesque?"

"No. And if you're going to be insulting, the next cloudy onslaught will be yours alone."

"You two know I can hear ... of course you do. What am I saying? Y'all just don't care."

"Smarter than he looks, sometimes," observed my boot.

"On the rare occasion only," replied my soon-to-be *ex* wife.

"Okay, back to serious," I demanded. "Plesmus, you referred to Plesmus' as back there. We're *on* Plesmus'."

She was slow to respond.

"*Plesmus,*" I called out.

"Oh, sorry. I thought you were making a foolish statement and I wanted to allow you sufficient time to really commit to it."

"What foolish statement?" asked Sapale. "I know there are lots, but which one *recently*?"

"Jon said we're on Plesmus'. I was waiting for an *aren't we*, or an *unless I'm mistaken*."

"We're not?" I wheezed.

"No. We're close, however. Well, if you think seventeen galaxies *over* is close, we're close. Otherwise, we're seventeen galaxies far away."

"Seventeen?" I groaned.

"To the north-northwest, seventy-eight degrees up, as you faced the portal. Not counting the small fry, of course. The little ones, they're not worth counting."

"The fancy metal portal?" I mumbled.

"You call *that* fancy? *Pshaw*. It's a portable translator portal, a really stripped down one at that."

"Why is Plesmus' connected to seventeen galaxies over—not counting the small fry—via a portable portal?" I asked unevenly.

"I presume someone, or something, wanted to easily access one of the two terminuses."

"That's not the quality I'm looking for in a response," I shared.

"Then please substitute *I do not know*," she responded.

"Not helpful either," I muttered.

"*Children*, will you knock off the comedy-routine-for-the-mentally-challenged," snapped Sapale. "We're in some serious shit here. We need a plan and we need it now. Plesmus, how do you know where we are? Have you been here before, here being either the tunnel or this galaxy?"

"I clearly resided on Plesmus'. I never entered that filthy tunnel before being dragged there by the big ape. As to this faraway galaxy, no."

"Then how do you even know it's a distant galaxy to the north-northwest?" Sapale pressed.

"There are a few of my species here. I've exchanged pleasantries with them."

"Where specifically are they?" I interjected.

"Somewhere around. I'm not sure. They're not too sure either."

"How can they be unsure?" I asked incredulously.

"*You* are unsure where they are. Why can't *they* be as well?"

"Because they're them, where they are, which is here ... somewhere."

"Jon," Plesmus asked, fairly annoyed, "does it matter to

you that much exactly where they are? It doesn't matter to me in the least."

"Oh," I was forced to admit. "Why are they here?" That question sort of popped out of my head unannounced.

"Er, I don't ... Hang on," she said apologetically. "I'll ask them."

She was silent a blessed moment.

"Oh. Oh, that will never ... *what*?" That last *what* came out as an angry one.

"Ples—" I began.

"*Shush*," she scolded. There was brief silence again. "No way. Jon," she said loudly, "we need to find them."

I grinned. "Wasn't it *you* who just stated that it mattered where they—"

"Stop speaking," the diminutive boot stain blurted out. "This is serious. We need to find them."

"Oh, *now* it's serious?" I shot back.

"It is. We must save them."

"Okay, first off, welcome to *my* world. Second, as an expert in saving, I can tell you I'll need to know a little bit more in terms of details."

"Fine. Be quick."

Maybe I was going to be *quick*, but I wasn't planning on being particularly *merciful* to the little pest.

"Before saving may occur, a few boxes need to be checked off. First, does the party in question actually *need* saving. Second, are they save-*worthy*. This includes many variables. There's a risk-benefit ratio to keep firmly in mind. Third, is it practical to save the alleged sufferers? Case in point, this seventeenth galaxy over. I know nothing about it, but I'm willing to go out on a limb and employ the term *large* when describing its proportions.

Hence, saving attempts need to be assessed in light of practicalities. Huh," I chuckled softly to myself, "even the *finest* maiden-in-distress is SOL if her tower's too high, you know what I mean?"

"I have *no* idea what you mean," Plesmus responded. "I do know I'm done enduring your mindless-mini-treatise on the subject. They must be saved because I say they must. I can locate them, but only if you key your silent-running switch and let me focus. As for towers, if you mention them again, one will miraculously appear where you least welcome and expect it, large ape. Am I clear?"

"Clear, sure. Free to commence with the saving? No. I need a couple more questions answered before I'll commit—"

Sapale cleared her throat loudly.

"Before *we* commit to helping you."

"You are impossible."

"So I've been reassured countless times."

"Ask."

"Why do they need saving?"

"Because they're being ... I can ... I can hardly say the words."

"That'd be a first," I observed as a student of alien species.

"They're being used ... as ... toys. No, playthings."

Oh, my. Now I began wishing I hadn't pressed her so. "You wouldn't be suggesting that in the context of sexual deviation, perversion, or other such dalliances, would you?"

"No, I would not. *Sapale*," bemoaned Plesmus, "where did you find this evolutionary fluke and why did you free him from the mud there?"

"That'd be a longish story. Maybe not the time or place," she replied thoughtfully.

"I might better state my kin are being used like jesters, forced to entertain others in a degrading manner."

"But not, you know—"

"Stop it. Stop it *now*. No *sex*. There is no *sex* involved, Jon. Move on *immediately*."

"Who is doing the non-sexual degrading?" I asked importantly.

"I'm not certain. They're not clear as to who it is that binds them to their torment."

"Hmm. Odd. How long have they been here?"

"You ask a *lot* of questions," she accused.

"And please note: I'm still alive. There's a one-to-one correspondence there, booby."

"A few have been here a while."

"How many is a few, and how long is a while?" I was not letting her off the hook.

"One or two have been here several hundred thousand years."

"Okay," I squeaked. "One or two does constitute a *few*. But a *while*? Several hundred thousand years? That's pushing the definition, me thinks."

"It's all relative, Jon. Look in a mirror. May we begin the *saving* now?"

"No. Not hardly. There's a large issue looming way up there in the air. Who are we saving your buddies from? If they're strong enough to enslave necumplacks without getting no-timed, I'm thinking they're powerful. On a scale of one-to-ten, they're probably an eight million."

"Hang on," she replied with irritation. "Remember these are native necumplacks, not ones like me. They are unable to no-time on any significant scale. It *takes* time to *steal* time."

"That's ... that's just wrong to say. Never repeat it," I whined.

"Jon, please assist me in pinpointing the locations of my brethren. You know how it goes invading the domain of master races. You dawdle, they discover your presence, and you get ground to dust. *If* you're lucky, that is."

"That's pretty much what happens when you rush in prematurely or with any measurable optimism. Trust me on this."

"As the lone voice of reason that seems to be here," Sapale interrupted us, "let me clarify. Plesmus, are you saying that you *can* handle whoever has your relatives held captive, even though they cannot?"

"Ah, that is not an unfair summary of what I said and intended."

"Ples," I broke in, "does the expression *don't try and bullshit a bullshitter* hold meaning for you?"

"We do not use that idiom in my native tongue."

"You can't know whether you could defend us against whoever holds your buddies, because we know diddly-squat *about* them."

"Also a true statement," she admitted. "It does not alter in any way the fact that we must save them. You would not leave *humans* behind in bondage just because there is some risk in your attempts to free them."

"Hang on a sec," I snapped, patting a hand toward the floor. "Let me think. I may in fact have done just *that*." I rubbed the side of my head. Then I turned to Sapale. "Have I?"

She turned on me the disappointed pet-owner look, the one an owner displays when they discover pet diarrhea on the kitchen floor. "If I did, I wouldn't say it out loud. It's too horrible a thing to admit to, especially just to win a petty point with Plesmus." She allowed me to reflect on her words. "We're going to help. We all know that. The sooner we do, the sooner we can split. Also, the more likely we are to escape in the first place."

"What she said," my boot reiterated.

I seethed privately and briefly, and then I was done. "Fine. How do we locate the family?"

"I need to take a reading, then you move far enough for me to get a second reading."

"Okay, so we use triangulation?" I responded.

"Yes. So please walk to our right until I tell you to stop."

"You got it." I began to move with quick, long strides. In no time at all, I slammed into the wall on one side of the passage. "You didn't tell me to stop," I snarled.

"No. Sorry. My bad. I just wanted to see you do that. I feel better now."

"*What?*" I protested.

"But seriously, I will never do it again. Please get up," she instructed, because I was on my butt. "Rest time is over."

"It's official. I hate you."

"Fine. Walk."

I did, but I wasn't at all pleased. I can assure you of that.

Ten meters on, Plesmus asked me to stop.

"Okay," she said, "one more. Climb the far left wall, please."

"I thought make-a-fool-out-of-Jon Hour was over."

"I'm very serious. Stop whining and climb," she commanded.

"I am not whining," I whined. "How high do you need me to go?"

"Until I say you can get down. *Go.*"

I had darn-near bumped my head on the high ceiling before she relented and told me I could drop to the floor. I was so over taking orders from the mucous ball.

"Based on some assumptions I've made from the construction we've seen so far, I think I can get us to where all of them are being imprisoned."

"They're together?" I asked, surprised.

"Yes."

"Wow, we caught a break. How refreshingly unusual."

She provided me fairly straightforward directions to where the necumplacks were to be found. It turned out to be quite the hike. There were several levels to whatever-the-hell structure we were in. The prisoner blobs were three of those levels down and nearly two kilometers away. It took us half an hour to get there. Fortunately, we ran into no clouds or other impediments. Our mistaken assumption of being in luck evaporated quickly enough. I guess that was to be expected, because that was sure how it always seemed to go for me.

It became clear that the location the four necumplacks were held in was on the other side of a very imposing metal door. Though it was *possible* that approaching them from some other direction might not be so obstructed, the chances of that were remote enough to make searching for an alternate path not worth the effort.

"We could use our lasers to cut through, maybe," Sapale suggested uncertainly.

"Let me see." I extended my probes. *What are you?* I asked the door.

You know how when you do something a million

times and are so used to the process you never imagined it could work out differently? Yeah. I hate that too. And, that was just what happened. I got no report back. My probes affixed to the surface just fine, but it was as if the audio was offline. It wasn't. I checked.

"Ah, I'm getting nothing," I said to the others.

"That's never happened," responded Sapale. She shot out her fibers. A moment later, she reported, "Nope, zilch."

"Okay, well, we could try cutting the door anyway, I suppose," I stated.

Sapale shrugged, knelt down, and started up her laser finger. It took almost no time to figure out that was going to have no effect on the metal. Whatever it was, it was tough.

"Plan B?" Sapale asked before rising.

"Plesmus, can you no-time just the door?" I asked.

"I don't see why not."

After a few seconds of nothing, I pressed her. "So, are you going to try?"

"I did. Nothing happened."

"How's that even possible?" Sapale wondered.

"The door has a time lock," Plesmus replied.

"Oops," I observed.

"If we can't get *in,* we can't save them," Sapale said, stating the obvious.

"Maybe there's a control panel somewhere nearby?" I asked out loud.

I ran my palms over the ultra-smooth surface of the walls in that area. They were the first I'd seen that weren't the knobby crystalline kind. Perhaps this was a more practically constructed section. It was, in effect, a brig. It would be silly to make a brig very ornate. It'd lead to an oxymoron. *Nice brig*. No way.

"Nah, there's nothing here," I mumbled.

"Well, this sucks," summarized my wife. "Can't cut it, make it disappear, or hit the open-up button."

"How are we going to gain entrance?" Plesmus asked. She was clearly upset.

"Maybe we aren't," I responded unhelpfully. "People build prisons to keep the inside-people *in* and the outside-people *out*." I gestured to the big metal door. "*Prison*," I emphasized grimly.

"But we can't fail," Plesmus said incredulously.

"And why is that?" I pressed.

"Because we need to save them."

"That's actually—" I started to respond. Then an odd thought hit me. "These guys are some super race, right?" I asked no one in particular. "You know what I've learned about master races? They're generally idiots. I mean, it comes naturally. You have a lot of power. You get all impressed with your damn self. Then you make stupid mistakes, because you weren't the master race, after all. You were just the master waste-of-space."

I studied the space. Yeah, I bet the dickwads were just that lame.

"Plesmus, can you no-time me a two-meter hole in this wall?"

"I can try. Why?"

"Just please try. About a half a meter thick."

The wall disappeared before my eyes. There was a dark but open area. I flicked on an external light. It was a big empty space.

"How did you know that would be there and that I could open the space?" Plesmus asked with satisfying awe.

"Master races make idiot mistakes. Always do. They protected the prison door seventeen ways to Sunday. Great. But they never thought for a second someone might simply go *around* their ever-so-clever barrier. *Pissants*."

"So should I open that wall, the one that must lead to the corridor past the door?" Plesmus asked meekly.

"Go for it."

Within thirty seconds, the three of us were strolling casually into the detention area. Guess what the luck bonus was? Since the pukes that built the place knew that no force in the universe could penetrate their super-duper-door, they didn't bother securing anyone *inside* the holding area. Why bother? They weren't going anywhere, right? I repeat. Pissants.

"Can you tell where your buddies are?" I asked Plesmus.

"Yes, they are in that far corner, off to your left."

"What is it with you guys and tight spaces?" I asked.

"Jon, when you're made of clear mucus, a species learns pretty early on to be extra cautious."

"I guess so. Sapale, hang out here and guard our exit. If anyone's coming, let me know at once."

She returned a two-fingered salute.

I walked Plesmus toward the corner she'd indicated. It wasn't until we were there before I noticed the four necumplacks. They were much smaller than I'd anticipated.

"Are you guys always this compact?" I asked, kneeling down.

"No, and please step back. I'm still trying to convince them we're friends."

"Don't they recognize you?"

"Not specifically. They've been so abused for so long, they're barely sane."

"Not an inviting prospect," I mumbled.

"They're also starving. They're no threat. I just don't want to stress them any more than they already are."

"You keep me posted. I'll stand here patient like and stress no one."

"Thank you, Jon."

I do believe that was the first time I'd ever heard Plesmus being so gracious toward me. I always win them over in the end, don't you know? Oorah.

It took a few minutes, but Plesmus finally spoke. "Alright, you can pick them up now."

"I can what?"

"You heard me. Jon, they're in no condition to run alongside us. You'll have to carry them."

"They're slimy and hungry. That's two strikes on them before I even bend down."

"Pick-them-up," she said slowly and firmly.

"How about we have Sapale carry them, hmm?"

"If you don't pick them up immediately, I'm going to no-time your other foot."

"And call me Ilene?"

"Huh?"

"Never mind. I'm retrieving." I scooped the little lumps up. "Let them know that if they start to munchin, I'll start crunchin. You got that?"

She didn't respond.

"Ples, you hear me?"

"Of course. I was just allowing time to pass for you to *grow up* before I responded."

"I got 'em. We set to jet?"

"No. We have to *leave* now."

I let it pass. Hey, I'm a patient fellow. No problema.

Sapale fell in behind us and we took our work-around route back to the hallway in front of the prison mega-door.

"I suggest we backtrack to return to the portal," I stated.

"Okay, if you really think that's wise," Plesmus responded obliquely.

"How would I know if it was wise or not? It only seems logical. We know the way."

"That part is true."

"What might the *other* part be, the one you're dancing around?"

"There are several large angry guards between us and the portal, assuming we retrace our initial path."

"You know, I'm standing here wondering mightily why you just didn't state that fact. Instead, you hit me with a vague Rube-Goldberg sentence, knowing all the while I would change my mind based on your input."

"Well, you were just so helpful and kind, I didn't want to upset you."

"Well, you did. And why would you assume I'd be upset just because you provided me with useful intel on an unknown enemy?"

"Are you certain you want me to answer? We could discuss sporting event outcomes."

"Why?" I rather demanded.

"Because *everything* seems to upset you to one extent or another."

"It does not," I snapped.

"You're upset now. I rest my case."

"No, you baited me. Of course I'm upset. It's a wonder I'm not angry, or even irate." I pointed down to my boot. "You do not want to see me irate. It is not pretty."

"No," Sapale added in agreement. "He is indistinguishable from a four-year-old girl throwing a tantrum in her pink party dress because she didn't get a pony for her birthday."

"I suspected as much," Plesmus concurred.

"May we *go*, people?" I demanded.

"By all means," Sapale tossed back. "Plesmus, can you find a safe way back?"

"I do not know. I can see the guards along our earlier path because they are bulky and I'm familiar with the pattern of the space. There could be others elsewhere I don't detect because I'm not familiar with the local environment."

"How long have the big guards been there?" I asked.

"I cannot say. I see them now. I don't know when they took up that position."

"If they weren't there before, it's safest to assume they were stationed there because we've been detected. Maybe the clouds ratted us out before we no-timed them," I thought out loud.

"If that's the case, the entire place should be crawling with guards," Sapale responded.

"We'll just have to pick a path and hope for the best. At least we'll have surprise on our side as we advance."

"How do you figure that?" asked Sapale.

"If they could detect us straightaway, they'd already be standing here, waiting impatiently for us to finish this long conversation." I scanned the rough image I had of the rooms and passages of whatever place we were in. "Follow me," I told Sapale. "Might as well try this way."

We jogged as quickly as we could while remaining as silent as possible. We mounted the stairs back to the floor just below the one we entered originally on without a hitch. Of course, that was bound to be the easier portion. They had to know we were on the level above earlier, so that one would be the most reinforced.

We hadn't rounded two bends before we encountered a small squad of large uglies. Why is it, I ask you, that all the really big grunts of any organization are also the ugliest? Why can't there be a bad-ass platoon of babes protecting the Powers-That-Be? Or even handsome dudes, like a patrol of Prince Charmings. Oh well, it wasn't the ideal time to start tripping, so I let that train of thought bypass the station in my head.

"Man, those guys are ugly," observed Sapale.

"Thank you," I exclaimed. Hey, at least it wasn't just me.

They looked like two-meter-tall, two-meter-wide turtles with horns everywhere, and fangs. Yeah, fanged turtles, long as a walrus'. You live long enough, you see it all, whether you want to or not.

"Plesmus, are they time-locked?"

"There's actually no way to tell without trying to no-time them. That said, I don't think anybody'd expend too much of a valuable resource on the likes of them. They make you *apes* look highly evolved."

"Well, it's the old-fashioned way, with lasers and fists, or it's the new way, by no-timing," I summarized.

"Seriously? You'd try punching one of those minor mountains?" challenged Plesmus. "You're dumber than you look."

"Or braver," I corrected.

"Either way, you're delusional. Here, stick your foot around the corner," she instructed.

"What if they see it?" I complained.

"You have another right over there. Now stick it out so I get a clear shot at them."

"I have another one over *there*," I muttered as I stuck out my occupied boot.

As I groused, we caught a huge break. The guards vanished. Plesmus *was* able to take them out.

"Strong work. Let's boogie," I said as I sprinted around the corner and down the center of the hallway.

You know what I hate? I mean, I didn't hate it up until then, because I didn't know it was possible. But I became an instant hater of running smack into a small group of large guards you just vaporized that just miraculously rematerialized directly in the space I was running into.

Thud!

There I was, sprawled out on my ass, looking over at one of the guards I'd decked when we collided. I'd say he was *as* surprised as I was, but, honestly, I don't think he was smart enough to be surprised. He had a two-speed brain. Mad and *more* mad. He was, for the record, *more* mad sitting, as he was, sprawled out on his ass, glaring back at me.

I leapt to my feet before he did. That was good. What wasn't was the technique of the nearest still-standing guard. He stepped onto the downed one's head and lunged toward me. Oh, did I mention the spears? Maybe I didn't. All three of the goons were armed with meter-long spears that had a nasty barbed head. If they weren't poison-tipped, it was an inexcusable oversight.

"Ples, no-time them," I shouted.

"Already tried. Now they *are* time locked."

He came at me spear first. My hand was only halfway up before the pointy end of his weapon zeroed in on my forehead.

Sapale put a laser beam in his right eye and out the back of his head.

You know what I really hate? Yeah. When someone puts a well-placed shot right through your enemy's head and it doesn't faze him. He kept on grunting and, more importantly, he kept on thrusting the damn spear.

I knew I was a goner.

I squinted my eyes shut as the tip impaled my skull.

Wham!

My head snapped back.

I opened my eyes.

The big turtle was staring in more-mad mode at the end of his spear. The front third was missing, cut away cleanly.

I touched my forehead. My poly-skin was lacerated, but only just.

"Plesmus no-timed the spear tip," shouted my wife.

"You clever little pest. *Thanks*."

In a flash, Sapale and I were frying holes everywhere into the big uglies. We quickly learned an alarming point. When you rip large partitions into monster turtles, guess what. They keep on attacking, roaring, and smelling just as bad.

Okay, I made up the smelly part. It was too hectic to notice that specifically.

Even the one with a major flight path through its head kept swinging the stupid shortened spear and punching with its free turtle paw. We both pummeled all of them but good, and it still took five minutes for the last of them to behave like good beasties and fall to the ground, dead, limp, and unresponsive. Plesmus continued to no-time their equipment, which helped. She didn't much help, however, when she added the no-timing of what they were wearing. I have to state with emphasis here, that a naked whatever-the-hell-those-were was a whole lot more visually off-putting than one with armor covering its private departments. Yeah.

When the last of the guards stopped spasming, I leaned over and glared at my boot. "Care to explain what the *freak* just happened, necumplack?"

"Ah ... well ... um ... after I no-timed the guards, they phased back in and were completely functional. That was sure not what *I* expected would happen ... *could* happen. How about you?"

"That's what I'd call a *recap*, not an *explanation*," I scorned.

"I value your opinion. Never doubt that for a second," she responded evasively.

"I'll start your explanation, then you finish it. *After I* thought *I no-timed the big ugly turtles, guess what happened*?"

"What?" she questioned quickly.

"No. I started; you answer the *what* part."

"I can only assume they had a modified time-lock. When activated, they withdrew on their own accord. It would be much like a corporeal being placing an appendage in fire. It recoils away, and is then able to use the appendage."

"What the hell's a modified time-lock?"

"I have no idea," she admitted.

"Then you can't use that concept in your explanation. It's like saying it was magic. They *magically* disappeared. They *magically* reappeared. No. You cannot do that."

"They're *magically* delicious?" Sapale asked. She had such a serious look on her face.

"*What*?" I spat.

"Sorry. I couldn't help myself. When you said *magically* twice, the cereal tagline just popped out. It was involuntary. Sorry."

I was surrounded by weak links. That was a certainty. Lucky I loved half of them to death. The other half—eh—not so much.

"So what you're trying to communicate is that you've never seen a reaction to no-timing like that before?" I asked pointedly.

"Yes. That is a fair statement."

Crapadillo. Not what I needed to hear, stuck in the middle of someone else's crib. "Any ideas, even wild speculations, as to how that's possible?"

She took a second. "No. It seems impossible to me. I mean, I pull at the time that's in their very being, and they not only don't yield it up, they quaze. Makes no sense."

I rubbed the sides of my head with both index fingers. "Quaze? What is quaze? That is not a word, concept, or nickname in my reality."

"To quaze? Seriously, you don't know what it means? I quaze. You quaze. He quazes? It's a common word, one you hear every day."

"If it was, I would not be about to bend down and slap my boot."

"Why would you want to ... oh. Never mind," she said in a low tone. "To quaze is to slip out of this time stream and into another. When you time traveled back on Earth, you first had to quaze."

"Have I mentioned before that I hate you?"

"Yes, I believe you have."

"Good. Keep it in mind." I shook my head softly. "I need to know if everyone here quazes when you try to no-time them. It would be a bummer if they could."

"The clouds didn't," Sapale responded.

"True that. *Plesmus*, any idea why the clouds wouldn't but the guards would?"

"It could be species specific, but I don't think that's the case. No, I'm certain someone gave out the power. I can only presume the clouds did not rate receiving it, but the guards did."

I let that rumble around in my head a moment. "Makes sense. The sixty-four-billion-dollar question is who is doing the handing out. They must have plenty-powerful mojo."

"And how," Sapale agreed quietly.

"No point lingering," I announced. "Let's press ahead. With any luck, there'll be no more guards in our path."

"How much luck is the amount you're hoping for?" Plesmus asked in a reluctant manner.

"I don't ... wait. Why do you ask?" I returned in a grim voice.

"Well, maybe we'll have that much in spite of the guards marching toward us from both directions. Yes, I hope we will have *just* that much luck."

"Is it not *possible* for you to just say, *Yo, there're guards coming, FYI?*"

"Would you like to discuss that matter in the last fifteen seconds of peace that are left to us?" she asked.

"No. Sapale, you watch that way." I pointed behind her. "I'll cover this one. Plesmus, is there any way out of here other than the two corridors?"

"Not that I see."

"Not useful intel."

"Sorry," she replied meekly.

Fifteen seconds. Not much time to set up a secure

perimeter. Wait. "Plesmus, where are we in relationship to the level we need to be on?"

"We're below it. One level. Please tell me you—"

"No, I mean in three dimensions."

"Ah. The levels are all constructed in similar manners. There is a corridor directly above us."

"Can you no-time a hole through the ceiling and into the open space in the hall above?"

"Yes, certainly."

"Do it now."

Light debris rained down all around us. Looking up, I could see the light in the passageway.

"Alley-oop," I shouted. "Sapale, you jump first. I'll join you as soon as I toss up the mucous blobs."

Without delay, she leapt like a Jane-in-the-box off a trampoline. She easily cleared the lip of the round hole and alighted with the grace of a cat.

"Come on," she encouraged and she extended her arms, ready to receive the necumplacks.

I pitched them up in rapid succession, and she caught them easily.

After she secured the gooey messes in her jacket pockets, she looked back up to me. "I'll catch you if you come up short." She grinned real wide at her clever wit.

"I will not—"

Something really big slammed me to the deck. I couldn't see it, but I could tell it didn't like me.

As we tumbled, I wedged my feet up against its chest and pushed with all my might. I separated a tiny bit but wasn't even close to breaking his hold. Then I got a good look at his face. I expected he'd be an ugly turtle. *Phew*! No such luck. Whatever it was, it made ugly turtle warriors look cute; cuddly, even. It was heavy, yes. But it wasn't built short and squat. When I pushed mightily again with my feet, I saw enough to know it was coiled. The damn thing was one ginormous Slinky. The actual body was thicker than the thin metal of the child's toy, but otherwise, that was it. The reason it was able to hit me so hard must've been because it was spring-loaded. And, oh my, that face. If Helen of Troy's launched a thousand ships, this bozo's face'd have sunk each and every one of the boats. It was two stellate dodecahedrons rudely slammed together. Each point of the pyramidal projections had an eye at the end that rotated like a snail's eye stalk. I'm assuming it had a mouth, but I didn't make one out. I was especially hoping not to meet it soon and very soon.

What it did well and quickly was weave around me like a nightmarish python. My arms were pinned to my chest. One leg was snapped up at an awkward angle and bound to my back. Just when I began panicking, thinking I would never escape, I remembered my personal membrane generator. I switched it on and rapidly expanded it. Sure enough, the star-headed Slinky was able to briefly resist, but then it snapped into innumerable smaller pieces. Those sprinkled to the floor.

I stood and sprinted toward the hole in the ceiling.

"Come on, Ryan," Sapale shouted. "*Run!*"

A big turtle was charging toward me. Just before I was in paw's reach, I jumped, aiming for the edge of the floor above. I hit the side of the gap hard, but held on long enough for Sapale to grab me by the scruff of the neck and pull me up. My feet barely escaped the leaping grasp launched by some shadow of a guard below. When I asked Sapale later what exactly was it that nearly pulled me back down, she said she wasn't sure, but thank goodness it didn't have wings.

Filled with a renewed desire to make it out of the place alive, we sprinted toward the portal we'd entered through. Sapale kept the alien blobs with her. We hadn't gone a hundred meters when *the* weirdest occurrences began happening. That's the only way I can describe them. I certainly didn't know then what they were or what caused them. But irregular spheres of nothingness began exploding silently into existence all around us.

If you remember what *flak* looked like, you get the picture, sort of. When airplanes were fired on from below by explosive charges, the shells erupted all around the craft in an attempt to shoot it down. That's the image I got, but the explosions were silent. I know, weird, but work with me here. As the explosions "faded," there was nothing—and I do mean nothing—there. Where the black-flak hit the wall, that part of the wall was missing. It'd vanished. Fortunately, whoever was shooting at us aimed poorly. None of the nothing-booms came anywhere near us.

We skidded around the last corner and headed straight for the portal. I was more than a little relieved to see it looked exactly the same. Not even any of the dirty mess had been cleaned. Maybe whoever was in charge didn't even know the portal was there? I know. Hard to imagine, but people under active fire start believing in miracles real quick.

"You go first, you go first," I shouted to Sapale. I set a hand on her shoulder to ease her in front of me.

She slipped in ahead and started bending down to clear the narrow portal. About three meters away, I noticed a big uh-oh. The lights of the portal itself began to flicker. They hadn't done that earlier. Change, in this context, was very bad.

"Hurry," Sapale called out. She'd assessed the change also and was as concerned as I was that badness was befalling us.

She scampered through without any trouble. That was when the entire assembly went *clunk*. That would be, based on my considerable experience with it, the *sound* of badness befalling. My fears were confirmed when the front surface of the portal began to spin at a blinding rate. It hadn't done *that* before. Change in a crisis is the opposite of good.

"*Hurry*, Ryan," Sapale screamed as she scampered to her feet on the far side of the portal. She was beginning to panic.

"Not to worry," I called back. I sure hoped my complete lack of confidence didn't broadcast to her in my voice.

I threw myself at the meter and a half opening.

Bang.

My arms, which were leading my dive, crashed into hardness. As they collapsed, my head and neck rolled forward, so that my upper back skidded off a barrier. The moment I came to rest, I flipped like a falling-cat-in-reverse and faced the portal. The once empty opening was charged with bolts of energy zapping over the entire circular surface.

"Come on, Jon," came faintly to my ears.

Weird, I reflected. Her voice was so muffled, when only seconds before it'd been so ... so commanding.

"I think it's broken," I shouted at her.

"Yo* *re **ken?" Her words were breaking up.

"No, the *portal*. Let me try again. Step back," I screamed for all I was worth.

I jumped feet first and kicked out viciously at the point where boot and portal interface met.

I heard Sapale yell, "Nopales? Rye gain? Dabạk? J**."

I smashed into electric field and ended up staging a herculean leap backward, not a penetration of the passageway. I ended up in a heap ten meters back in the direction I'd come in. I raised my head uncertainly.

The vision of Sapale faded like the melting witch in the *Wizard of Oz*. My brood's-mate was voicing something *as* passionately as Margret Hamilton had in her swan-song performance in that film.

My head thudded back to the deck. *Crapcrapcrapcrap*, I reflected. I was separated from my wife and the rest of my reality by seventeen galaxies, to the north-northwest. Could the day, so young yet so unrewarding so far, possibly get any worse?

Upside-down into my field of vision bent in the answer to the question I shall *never* ask again, a turtle guard, looking particularly angry and unreasonable, glared down at me. Then a Slinky guard appeared. It expressed *its* displeasure with my existence by first slamming its head against mine—ow—and subsequently coiling around me and lurching me to my feet. Then it whacked me again with its head for good measure.

"Can this get any worse?" I mumbled to myself.

"At least you still have your health," replied Plesmus. Her tone was—you know—well, let's just say it was kind of unconvincing.

FIFTEEN

Sachiko sat in the newly installed captain's chair on Aramthella's bridge. Whether it was a result of the influence *Star Trek* had had on Tank in his youth or a proper military move, he'd decided one was needed. Sachiko's objections to the contrary he overruled. There would be a captain's chair and she would sit in it. The crew on this mission had swelled from four to five hundred. The new members, the ones unfamiliar with the senior staff, needed to be reassured visually by cultural elements and clues that all was well. The command personnel were trustworthy and skilled. Part of that image-strengthening was a captain's chair with the wise captain seated in it resolutely.

She stared blankly at the forward view screen. Considerable effort had gone into creating one that was just right. In the end, it looked like all the other view screens depicted in science fiction movies throughout film history. A rectangular TV with stars posed against a black background. When the ship moved, the view changed to reflect that change in relative position. Again,

Tank felt this would provide comfort via familiarity for the new, untested, and totally out-of-their-comfort-zone members of the crew. Good ships had captains sitting in captain's chairs who looked knowingly ahead into space. Aramthella had all those requisite components of a good ship, a reliable ship. She was clearly a vessel aboard which the observer *knew* they would not die horribly while traveling on her. The mission's success was only removed from the present moment by time, not competence. Buckle in and enjoy the flight, ye reassured masses.

Tank walked in on his friend's reflecting. He knew she was struggling with variables and pressures no one should be asked to bear. Her home world destroyed. Ripped from her life—her passion—at the university, where there was nothing but a promising future ahead of her. Now she was forced to be the captain of a cantankerous alien time ship, and humankind's only hope for the impossible. *Resurrection.* To top off the stressfest, his one-time student had to endure isolation and loneliness. Ships' captains were not free to date their crew members. On a normal warship, with a proper command structure in place, Sachiko might have had a chance at hoping to share her life with someone of similar rank. But with a handful of Army officers and a ship full of undergraduates, she seemed destined to live a life apart.

Robert Sherman would not have wished this present reality on anyone he could think of. He certainly wouldn't wish it upon Sachiko, the closest thing to a daughter he'd ever had. But he wasn't responsible for the present Charlie Foxtrot. No, he was only responsible for seeing it to a successful, if improbable, positive conclusion. The moral of it all: You wake up every day and discover that the universe has just thrown you a new and less hittable curve ball. Oh, boy. Adjust.

"Morning, kiddo," Tank greeted as cheerfully as he could fake. "You look to be about as far off in the scheme of things as I am. Sorry in advance if you are." He gave her a grim grin.

"Oh." She snapped to. "No. I'm fine. How about you?"

He let it go that he'd just confessed to being far off in the scheme of things. "Just fine. You sleep well?"

"Sleep?" she asked quizzically.

"You know, the thing you're supposed to do after I say *goodnight* to you? I know I did that about ten hours ago."

"Oh. I see. Yes. Thank you."

Then she returned to stare blankly at the view screen. The ship wasn't moving, so there really wasn't much to draw a captain's attention.

Tank let whatever she'd said in response to whatever she thought he'd asked her slip by, also. No sense beating the kid up. From the looks of it, she was doing a bang-up job of it all by herself.

"You asked for more time to get back to me about my mission proposal. I wanted it by 16:00 yesterday, but you said you wanted to work on some angle."

"Oh, yes, that issue. Yes. Thank you. I needed the extra time."

"*And—?*" he asked encouragingly.

"Oh, you want to discuss it now?"

"I think so. Wait. Yes, I do. That's why I asked you about it."

"Don't we need Reva to be here?"

"Not necessarily. She stopped by my cabin late last night and gave me her overview."

Sachiko raised an eyebrow. "Late last night? What will Daisy think if she hears about that?"

"There's no *if* in *Daisy*. She *will* hear about it and I *will* pay dearly. Now, can we get back to *your* opinion?"

"I think it's a good plan."

He waited for her to go on until it was painfully obvious that she was done speaking.

"You think it's *good*? Not great, inspired, or, I don't know, maybe *improved* with some clever input from you?"

"No. I don't think so."

"Kiddo, you got me worried. Are you really okay?"

"Sure. I'm just a little preoccupied, I guess."

"That'd be my guess too. Care to share?"

"Oh, it's nothing like that."

"Like what?"

She seemed surprised. "Nothing worth mentioning."

"Your call, kiddo. I'm here if you need me. Reva's here if it's a womanly issue. Use us if you need us."

Sachiko's cheeks flushed slightly. "Got it. Thanks."

"So you're okay with my heading us along the path I spelled out in my proposal?"

"Yes. I can't see any harm in it."

"Shaky, we're two academics running a military campaign to defeat a previously unbeaten enemy. Everything that *can* go wrong *will*. Even things that can't *possibly* go wrong will too."

She looked concerned. "Then perhaps we shouldn't do anything."

"If we did nothing, something'd go wrong with that option. No. We can't wait for a wondrous event to occur. We have to go out there and make our own luck."

"Then perhaps we should go?"

He shook his head.

"Did you get a haircut?" she asked after he did so.

Tank looked guiltily at the floor. "Yes," was all he said.

"Since yes ... Wait, did *Reva* cut it for you late last night?"

"I don't know if it was *all* that late."

"Oh, the fur'll fly when Daisy catches wind of this. It most certainly will."

"What, I needed a haircut. Reva grew up with ten brothers. As the oldest kid in the house, the haircutting duties fell to her. She's very good at it."

"My, all those intimate details. Sounds positively scandalous."

"If there's nothing else, *Captain*, I'll alert Reva that we're going to take off."

"Take off what?" Sachiko asked wickedly. She had such a broad smile too.

"You can knock it off. I'll be back in a few minutes and we can get underwear."

"We can?"

"Of course we can."

"Get *underwear*?"

"That is *not* what I said, young lady." He pointed at her sternly. "You're going to give others the wrong impression."

"I certainly hope so." She placed a hand in front of her mouth and laughed softly.

"I'll be back in ten. Plan on having grown up by then, please." He stormed away.

When she was alone again, Sachiko leaned back in her new captain's chair and snickered something awful. Ah, Tank. A beacon of mirth in an otherwise depressing galaxy.

Fifteen minutes later, Tank, Reva, and Tom Grant

came onto the bridge together. Obviously, Reva and Tom weren't mission critical in terms of being there, but they very much wanted to see Aramthella swinging into action. She was an impressive tool of war, to be certain. That being their chosen stock-in-trade, they wanted to experience her capabilities firsthand. Privately, they both hoped to one day become active members of her crew. As Aramthella was the last bastion of humankind, they were going to be aboard her for the duration. Given that fact, learning how to best use her was highly desirable.

"Is everything set?" Tank asked in his command voice.

"Yes, it is," Sachiko replied in her best rendition of a bass tone similar to his. When she was finished, she nearly laughed at her own silliness.

"Let's do this," Tank announced robustly.

"Aramthella, make it happen," echoed Sachiko.

The non-intuitive part of riding in a massive time ship was that when it slammed the pedal to the metal, you couldn't tell. There was no roar of engines, no pin of G-forces. Hell, your ears didn't even pop.

"Are we moving?" Tom asked Reva quietly.

She shrugged. "I suppose so."

"Oh, we're moving," Tank announced after overhearing them. "Aramthella, how fast are we moving now?"

"Seven point eight five times the speed of light."

"No ... way," breathed Tom.

"Oh yeah. One of the many wonders of time-powered flight. No inertia to deal with and the only practical limit on your velocity depends on how much fuel you're willing to expend."

"How much fuel are we expending?" Reva interjected.

"More than some, less than a whole lot," replied Tank.

"Can you be more ... *informative*, General?" Reva returned.

"What, you want me to break it down in terms of Malcolms and Bernards?" he responded with a trace of irritation.

"Would we understand it better that way?" Tom asked in an attempt to ease the building tension.

"Not in the slightest," Tank replied flatly.

"The amount of energy we will consume getting to our destination is only a tiny fraction of what we have available in storage, if that helps?" Sachiko offered, also trying to keep the mood friendly.

"Okay. Yeah, that really puts it in perspective," Tom answered cheerfully.

"When will we arrive?" Reva then inquired.

"In about two hours," Sachiko responded.

"Along those lines," Tom asked sheepishly, "where is it we're actually going?"

Tank looked to Tom, then to Reva, and back to Tom.

"I didn't mention the mission details to him," Reva began defensively. "I didn't want to violate any security issues until we were underway."

"Colonel," Tank began officially, "we're not launching a D-Day Invasion of Normandy here. The walls don't have ears."

"O-kay," she said, drawing the word out. "I didn't want to presume too much. That's all."

"Understood," Tank concluded. He turned his attention to Tom. "We're making our first excursion in an attempt to locate the lone remaining enemy warship. As you know, since our last engagement, they've gone to ground."

"That's what I understand," the major confirmed.

"I'm hoping we can move in a manner that will accomplish one of two positive outcomes. First, ideally, I'm hoping that from a different vantage point our enemy's position might become clear to us."

"Makes sense," Tom returned.

"Failing that, it's possible that we'll be lucky enough to give them the mistaken impression that we actually do know where they are. That being the case, they may be forced to move away quickly, and in so doing betray their location."

"I see. Sounds reasonable to me," Tom responded agreeably.

"Specifically, we're heading toward the center-of-mass of the area the clan had yet to no-time, prior to our successful assault on their armada."

"Is that a big area?"

"Space is big," responded Sachiko. "It's difficult for someone not familiar with the scales involved just how large the distances are. We've set a course that cuts through a cylinder of the galaxy some ten light years wide and a million light years long."

Tom whistled softly.

"Yeah, a big tube," affirmed Tank. "I'll be surprised if we get anything even close to lucky. But I'd rather do something active rather than passively *hoping* they make some egregious error."

"So you think the Clams would be so ... so careless as to resume their time acquisition *knowing* that we're stalking them?" Reva pressed.

"They might be *just* that inexperienced. Remember, they've spent a very long time winning one-sided battles across countless galaxies. It's easy for them to become over-confident."

"And if we come up empty?" Reva asked cautiously.

"Then we'll try some other hare-brained scheme. With time, we're bound to find success."

Neither Reva nor Tom responded. They were both seasoned enough to know time and effort invested had zero to do with military success. They knew Tank was well aware of that rule also.

"So we'll begin patrolling the opening of the cylinder in a couple of hours?" Reva asked.

"If all goes as planned, yes," replied Tank cheerily.

"May we return at that point to observe the goings on?" asked Tom.

Mi bridge, *su* bridge," responded Tank. "I'd like you and all the senior staff to feel free to participate as much as you'd like in our planning and execution."

"Thank you, General. I'm certain that will be extremely useful experience for all of us," Reva said by way of endorsing the project.

"Then let's all meet back here in around ninety minutes," Tank stated.

Reva and Tom took their cues and departed. That left Sachiko and Tank alone.

"I think they'll blend in well," Tank observed in a low tone.

"Yes, I agree. It'll take some time, but they all seem like capable officers."

Tank was quiet.

"Did you hear me, Tank?"

He shook his head quickly. "Sorry, kiddo. I was just thinking ahead."

"Is that not what a supreme commander is *supposed* to do?"

He grinned. "Yes, he or she is. But I was thinking longer term."

"Do tell?" she responded with a coy smile.

"I do." He settled back into his chair. It was a couple meters to the right of the vaunted captain's chair. "I was thinking we're not like Jon and Sapale."

"No. That is a factual statement." She wasn't clear where he was going.

"You and I have a limited shelf life-- especially me." He snorted.

"My, what a dark mood you must be in."

"I was just thinking this all through. Jon's absolutely certain we'll reanimate the Earth."

"But."

"But we have to keep in mind that it's the longest of long shots."

"Agreed."

"The man's so self-assured and confident, it's easy to forget the fact that he's after the impossible here."

"His enthusiasm *is* infectious."

"But we need to lay plans assuming that the impossible will remain impossible."

"By *we*, you mean *you*."

He smiled warmly. "For now, sure. But you'll be captain of this ship long after I'm gone. As such, you'll always have a lead role in whatever happens."

"And what is it that will happen?"

"Sooner or later, the kids will need to grab an oar and start pulling for all they're worth."

"Sure. I've thought of that eventuality also. But we have time, right?"

"Yes and no."

"Why don't I like the sound of that?"

"Because you've thought the exact same things. Of this I am certain."

"Okay, mystical mind reader, what have I been thinking?"

"That down the line, the college-contingent will need to train to become doctors, new military officers, and every other role aboard ship."

"And, since they too have limited shelf lives, they will need to breed."

"They will need to breed. Everyone capable of reproducing will need to pitch in."

"Including the ship's captain," she risked adding.

"Including the ship's captain."

She looked down, then back up. "Do you think I can hold off until we complete this mission, or should I jump the bones of the next male to walk by that door?" Sachiko pointed to the bridge's sole entry.

Tank snickered. Sachiko joined in quickly.

"If you do decide to jump the next random sperm donor that passes by, do me a favor and let me slip out before you get to bone jumping."

"If I can, I'll wait that long, no problem. But," she twirled some hair with a finger, "no promises, okay?"

"Well, on that low note," he said, standing, "I do believe I'll answer one of nature's other compelling calls before we begin our sensor sweeps."

"Most wise. I shall await your return eagerly."

"You're too much," he snarked over a shoulder.

"Oh, and Tank."

"Yes?" he responded dubiously.

"If there's a necktie on the doorknob, do yourself a favor and wait patiently outside."

"There *is* no doorknob."

"Then I'll be forced to toss it on the *floor* now, won't I?"

"When Daisy hears of this, I'll have ten hells to pay," he scoffed with a dismissive wave of the back of his hand. And he disappeared around the corner.

SIXTEEN

Desi arrived in the kitchen at her appointed time: 04:30. O dark thirty. Nice. She was week two into her month-long sentence. Colonel St. Claire had promised that if she did a good enough job, her next punishment would be *much* cushier. It wouldn't start until 05:00.

Tip was right where he always was. Sitting on a steel chair that was backed into the far left corner of the room. Every morning, she asked him how long he'd been there waiting. He always said the exact same thing. *Hopefully, long enough.* What a substandard response. What did it even mean? On more than one occasion, she'd almost asked him for a clarification. But she'd learned the hard way to not address an open-ended question to Tip. Life was literally too short.

Once Desi stepped into the kitchen, Tip rose silently. Both stepped over to the sink, as was their now familiar routine.

"I'll wash. You dry," Tip stated flatly. For reasons unclear to Desi, he restated the same thing every morning. She'd arranged the first day for him to *always* wash. He didn't have a preference in the first place. When she told him why she really hated washing dishes, he was more than happy to accommodate her request. It was awfully reasonable, in Tip's estimation. All of her life, howling ghosts would rise out of the sudsy water. Those aggressive spirits were trying to secure the attention she continually tried to deny the dead. It had never worked, but it certainly succeeded on numerous occasions to scare her nearly enough to join them in their lamentable condition.

"D'ja sleep well?" she asked, as was her habit.

"It depends," he responded that morning. "Do you want to know if I slept for an extended period, uninterrupted? Or are you curious as to the effect, or lack of effect therein, that my dreams had on the overall pleasurability of my night's rest?" He grunted uncharacteristically.

"What?"

"Nothing," he said instantly. Yeah, he really wasn't going to entertain whether Desi was asking if he'd had a wet dream or not. He felt it was better to keep that vexing topic off the table, so to speak. She couldn't be asking him that, could she? Because, if she was, then she either wanted to press him as to his interest, or lack of interest, in sex generally and possibly her in ... Oh, bother. He was doing it again. *Stop it*, he self-chided.

For yet another morning, Desi had to roll her eyes. As often as she'd expressed hollow social graces to *him*, he never once got the hint and returned the cultural niceties to *her*. The clueless man was fully unbelievable. Still, he did listen well when she spoke of her tormented past. The idea that she was bizarre or a pariah never occurred to him. They were birds-of-an-outcast-feather.

"So," she asked hesitantly, "what do you think Plesmus was talking about, you know, back there the other day?"

She continued to focus straight ahead. In so doing, she failed to see him turn and stare at the side of her head like it was but one of many she sported atop her shoulders.

"She was talking about you controlling the dead. You heard her as well as I did."

"I ... I *know* she said that," Desi responded, flustered. "But I'm wondering what she *meant,* that's all."

"Are you suffering from lingering alcohol intoxication?"

"Am I what? No, silly. I haven't had a drink in—" She lowered her eyebrows. "So you think I must be *drunk* to not get what she said? Is that it, Benjamin?"

Tip's face flushed crimson. "I never ... no. I ... I thought you forgot what she *said.* That would be, you know, queer."

"Huh?"

"Odd. It would be silly if you weren't listening."

"Tip."

"Yes."

"You didn't say that many words—"

"But I'm doing it again?"

"Yes, you are. FYI."

"Thanks." He shook his head in disgust. "I'm always doing it again. Stupid, stupid, stupid me."

"At least you're working on it."

"I am?"

Desi was briefly paralyzed. She definitely had no response. Zero. None. What a lunkhead.

To himself, he stated, "Maybe I should work on it, you know?"

Nada. Speechless. Dumbstruck. No one could be that

clueless, could they? But, if Desi was going to discuss her private thoughts, it was—for worse or worst—going to be with Tip, and no one else alive.

"I know I see and hear them," she said by way of redirection. "But *control* them? That's ... well, it'd be nice because I could tell them to leave me alone and they would."

"Why would the dead do what you requested of them?" Tip asked genuinely.

"I'm sorry?"

"Here's the hypothetical. I'm dead." He tapped his upper chest. "You can see and hear me. For whatever dead-person reasons I might have, I decide to bug the crap out of you. You ask me not to, because of whatever living-person issues you might have. Okay?"

"Okay. Gotcha."

"Why would I even possibly do as you request? You gonna call the cops? Hit me with a restraining order? Pay me money to motivate, hoping I'd take it with me and leave?" He grunted a laugh. "No way. None of those would effectively counter my already manifested desire to have you help me in whatever dead-person issues I felt I needed help with."

"You are bringing coals to Newcastle, my friend. Welcome to my life."

"Seriously?"

"What, that I've failed historically to convince spirits to leave me alone?"

"No, that I'm your friend." He spoke genuinely in a childlike way.

Desi teared up almost instantly. Sure, she considered Tip to be the very poster-child for the socially inept. But his puppy-dog expression and sincere appreciation of the fact that her casual phrasing might represent some true acceptance ... Well, it was sweet.

"Of course, we're friends," she reassured. "We've been through so much, and here we are hashing it all out." She toyed with the thought of touching him—maybe his shoulder or hair only—but dismissed it just as quickly. No need risk engendering an obsession on his part.

"Thank you. So how are you going to get rid of me?"

Wow, he went right from endearing to creepy there, didn't he? And he hit the nail of her reservation right on the ...

Her flash of confusion somehow registered with the clueless Tip. "Me the ghost, I mean."

She relaxed too visibly, but luckily, she did so in front of Tip. Like he was going to notice. "I can't. Trust me, I've really, really tried."

"So, when Plesmus says you are to *control the dead*, how is it you possibly could?" he posited.

She shook her head. She had no idea.

"But, since she said it, it must be the case. So either there's a way you can control dead people now and just don't know it, or there's one she will teach you."

Desi set a finger to her chin. "She certainly didn't mention that second option."

"No. She did not state or imply she had a role in you learning to control the dead," Tip stated with professorial authority.

"So—"

"So you must be able to now. We just have to figure out how you can do that."

That did not sound inviting. "Ah, okay. I see a few issues there. One, I don't have the slightest clue how I might do that. Two, there are no dead people here to practice on."

"What about the voices you're hearing?"

She shook her head dismissively. "They're different. They're an amalgamation of voices ... pieces of voices mushed together."

"So you theorize that the time energy itself possesses a confused portion of the souls from which it was collected?"

"I what?"

"The dead people aren't present as discrete units any longer; they're not traditional ghosts."

"Oh. Yes, I guess that's a fair assessment."

"That leaves only Megan Thompson. *That* is unfortunate. Any viable scientific inquiry needs many more data points to achieve statistical strength."

"Huh?"

"We do not have enough dead people at our disposal. Maybe, if we're lucky, we'll engage the Clan soon and people will die without being no-timed. Fifty would do, a hundred'd be even better."

"You want the Clan to kill one hundred of our shipmates?" Desi was beyond horrified.

"No. That is incorrect. *We* want that. Otherwise, our experiments in your control over the dead will suffer from insufficient numbers. No one would believe our findings."

"Who ... we don't—" Then she stiffened. "I don't need to convince anyone but *myself*."

Tip recoiled. "I ... well ... I was placing this endeavor under the general classification of science-based." He commenced to melting under her glare.

"That's better. I'm not hot-to-trot for the control-the-dead-people idea. But I do not want others to die. Please remove that notion from your head."

"I'll try. That might take a few weeks. The more important a memory is to the individual perceiving it, the better it lodges in that individual's—"

Yeah. He was doing it again. Her eyes told him plainly: can it.

"What do you mean we only have Megan Thompson? Who's she?"

"The girl that killed herself a while back. You didn't know her?"

She shook her head. "No. I heard about it, though, obviously. It was so sad." Desi was quiet a second. "Wait, are you suggesting I try and find her ghost and con ... *control* it? Tip, that's ... that's so ... predatory."

"I didn't ask you to *eat* the ghost. I'm not certain that's possible in the first place. Of course, you would know better than me. But if we're going to test your ability to control a dead person, she's our best and only option."

"Wh ... bu ... *Tip*, what you're saying is so *wrong*. If the poor girl is lingering—and that's a very big *if* because I don't think all people spawn ghosts—it would be cruel to experiment on her."

"Why? Would it hurt or degrade her in any manner?"

"I don't *know*," she whined in protest. "I don't know what 'controlling' actually constitutes, so how can I speculate?"

"By taking an educated guess based on your past experience and breadth of knowledge."

"But what if I guess wrong? What if I do harm to Megan? I could never live with myself if—"

"The entire population of Earth was murdered, minus us, of course. If you asked Megan whether she'd volunteer to suffer so that all those souls could be retrieved, I bet she'd agree." Tip was uncharacteristically forceful in interrupting her.

"But what if she wouldn't agree? What if I rope her into something she'd never have committed to voluntarily?"

He looked back at Desi a bit. "You asked me, so I'll tell you. Let us assume that Megan is present and in a position to help the entire population of Earth. Let us further stipulate that the girl understands that she has that potential to help on a global scale. If those facts are true, yet she refuses to help, then I'm not certain she's the kind of person whose opinion in that regard is one I'd care to honor."

"You mean you'd make the moral choice for her? Who are you ... who are *we* to make ourselves gods?"

"No, Desdemona. Not gods. Moral arbiters. Please keep in mind that is done often, routinely, really. The commander declares war and drafts young people to go off and fight it, knowing many will die. That leader has made a moral decision for those doomed individuals. Person A murders Person B. The state decides Person A must die, that they pose too great a threat to a civil, orderly society. Again, a moral assessment is made by a third party for the benefit of the public at large."

"But I can't make that choice. I'm not that kind of person. Tip, I don't think I'm that strong."

"Then I'll make the decision for the both of us—for the three of us, assuming we can contact Megan."

She'd never seen that look in Tip's face. He was stern, determined. He was resolute. She was stunned. The man-child sported a pair. Who'd a thunk it?

"Here's what I'm willing to do. Let's see if Megan is

still here. If she is, and she's willing to talk to us, well then we'll see where that leads. Is that enough?" stated a still shaken Desi.

"It's enough for now. Thank you, my friend. Now, if you could pick up the pace of your dish drying, I could likewise increase my washing rate. I need to get some studying in before my first nap."

Studying? No school existed to have classes to study for. And first nap? TMI. Yes, that was well into TMI. Desi dried more rapidly. She wanted to learn nothing else new about her oh-so-odd new friend.

SEVENTEEN

"Jon," Sapale screamed as she threw herself against the closed portal interface. She slammed it so hard, she was thrown several meters backwards and sprawled onto the ground.

As quickly and ferociously as a tiger, she leapt to her feet and charged back. This was to be her fifth impact with the unyielding barrier. She planned on continuing to impale it until one of them broke. She did not care much which one it would be.

Six.

Seven.

Eight.

After the ninth crash, she felt her lead shoulder crack. As she walked away for her eleventh charge, she tried lifting that arm. Nothing. She'd snapped something. Oh well. She'd just have to switch to the other shoulder for the next collision.

Just as she was about to launch, something in her pocket shook or vibrated. She stood up and felt the area. Oh yeah, the four necumplacks. She'd stuffed the oversized-hotdog-bun-sized blobs there after Jon tossed them up to her, back on the other side. She'd forgotten all about them in her fury.

"What'd you want, little fellas?"

But there was no response. One—it was probably just one—did squirm a little bit, but that was all.

"I don't have time for charades, little dude. If you can't tell me your beef, hang on tight 'cause we're about to break something else."

Sapale drew herself up and began her next assault.

A squawk like a klaxon erupted from her pocket. She relaxed and reached in. She not-too-gently pulled the four of them out at once. Disregarding which end she was addressing, she held the lump of goo up to her face. "*What*? I'm kind of busy here."

There was a softer squawk from the far side of the necumplack on the bottom of the stack.

She rearranged the bodies so that one was facing in her direction. "What, little pest? If you can talk or something, please do so quickly. Otherwise, I'll have to check back with you later."

The necumplack wriggled fiercely, then began making the sound again, only this time, it was modulated and much softer.

"I don't have time for a song, my friend. Here," she bent down, "you guys rest here while I try and talk some sense into this phase portal."

Before she was halfway down, the necumplack squirmed and squealed inconsolably.

"Little dude, *seriously*. The longer we play Twenty Questions, the more solid that there barrier's likely to become. What? Speak now or hold your peace until I'm in pieces on the floor."

Its reaction was to modulate the noise it made further. It was sounding more regular to her ear. Then it hit Sapale. The necumplack was trying to speak.

"Do you speak English?"

More regular but unintelligible noises.

"*Do you speak Hirn? Any Kaljaxian dialects*?" she asked in her native tongue.

She heard only more disjointed squeaks.

"How about Valley Girl Speak? If not, like, bag your face while I do some damage, you grody noid. Take a chill pill or *whatever*."

More modulated sounds. They were maybe a bit less random.

"You're doing groovy. I'm just going to put you here while I get back to frantically trying to save my brood-mate. 'K?"

"Nnn ... ooo."

That stopped her. She raised the lumps back to her face. "Did you just say *no*?"

"Yyysss."

"How odd, in a very peculiar way."

To that, the necumplack had no present response.

"Wait, are you learning from Plesmus? No, wait, you can't be. She's seventeen galaxies away. But you're just now maybe making sense. Or, alternately, I'm losing what little mind I have left."

The tip facing her wiggled slightly.

"From the other necumplacks on this side? Are the local guys teaching you what they learned from Plesmus?" She shook her head in disbelief. "That's actually stupid when said aloud, isn't it?"

"Nnoo," came a mechanical-sounding reply.

"Wait, you are learning from the locals who learned a little from Plesmus? That's so *no way*."

"One you call Plesmus mind send to here us talk. Here us send talk know to us us, little."

"*Little*. I'd agree with that assessment. Sure."

"You know what us us say?"

"Yes, I do. Or I'm insane. I'm leaning toward insane, because, come on, that just makes more sense."

"US us not know. You try talk simple."

"KISS. Sure. *Keep it simple stupid*. You're talking to the right gal. What you are calling us us, let's say just *us*, okay? You are us. The locals of your species, let's call them the locals of your species, okay?" She was getting frustrated with the poor communicating.

"Okay. *Us* are *us*. *You* are *you*. Locals of our species are locals of our species."

"Great. Now why did you stop me from trying to get through that portal?"

"You are not going to break portal, only you."

"What was your ... no, cancel the snark. I must get to my brood-mate. He's stuck on the other side."

"Us live here before us live there. Us know if portal closed, portal is closed. No open this side, only there side."

"So how am I going to get to the other side, to there?"

"You cannot. You here. Brood-mate there. Portal closed."

"It was open," she whined loudly in protest.

"Now closed. Other side locals of their species only power to open close portal."

"Oh, only those in charge on the other side have the controls for the portal?"

"Maybe."

"You did not fully understand me?"

"Yes."

"Why was it open?"

"You need ask locals of their species."

"That is not helpful."

"Yes. Not help."

She fluttered her eyes. Oh how she longed to resume hitting something, preferable the portal and not the local species here. "But I must get through. Can you help? Can you open the portal? *Wait,*" she said in a rush. "Can you *no-time* the opening?"

"Plesmus talk of no-time food. We are weak. Plesmus maybe no-time portal. Plesmus maybe not no-time portal. Ask Plesmus. We us are weak."

"That is another way of saying you're no use to me. So we're back to me putting you there and me working on the portal."

"Better we work together. You think. Us think. Local species here think. Maybe Plesmus return."

"She's not coming through unless she can do it on her own. If that's the case, she won't need to give in-services. Look, little afterthoughts, I gotta get to it." With that, she set them on the dirt. She assumed the male-big-horned-sheep stance and was about to charge, when the idea of thinking occurred to her. She slumped to the dirt on a knee.

"You may have a valid point, little dude. I'm going to try the easy way instead."

Sapale walked to the portal and released her fibers. *Open,* she said to it in her head.

Nothing changed. She confirmed that fact by kicking the portal surface, hard.

Fibers still attached, she asked, *How can you open?*

Nothing. Apparently, this was not a smart, AI-driven interface. That earned the portal another hard kick.

What are you made of?

Exotic matter, mesons, charged phase molecules, electrons, positrons, plasma ...

Stop, she commanded. *What are charged phase molecules?*

Unknown form of matter. Seven point eight percent of interface composed of this material. Role in portal function unk ...

Stop. This was getting her nowhere. Abruptly, she spun and sat on the floor, right next to the four necumplacks.

"Think, Sapale. *Think*," she whispered to herself. "You can't open the portal. You don't know what it's made of. Maybe DeJesus or one of the Deavoriath would know, but running them down would waste valuable time. Jon's seventeen galaxies that way." She focused on a map of the local galaxies. "So I can go there fast enough. But galaxies are big. Real big. How am I going to find one little android in a big old—"

She snatched up the talking necumplack. "If I took you to the galaxy on the other side of the portal, could you find Plesmus?"

"Portal closed. Us and you no go—"

"I said if I *take* you there. Not through the portal, but the long way. Could you find Plesmus?"

"Long way. What long way?"

"I have a ship. We go to the ship and it takes us to the galaxy where the portal opens."

The little fellow was quiet a spell.

"Us think you throw body at portal better plan."

"No. I can get us there. What I need to know is if you are there, can you locate Plesmus?"

"Maybe."

She laughed somewhat hysterically. "Yeah, *maybe* covers a lot of possibles. Simple question. If we are much closer to Plesmus, but still far away, can you sense her?"

"Us never know. Us never try."

She sighed deeply. "Well, my gooey little friends, we are all about to find out via the scientific method. We're going there and we're going to see what happens."

"Now?"

"No. We need to get to my ship first." She shook her arms around her. "This is a tunnel full of dirt, not my space ship."

"Us listening. You are talking one."

"I don't need this." She scooped them up unceremoniously and trotted up the passageway, back to the surface.

EIGHTEEN

I ask you plainly. Have you ever been frog-marched down a hallway while wrapped in a giant Slinky? If your response is in the negative, please try and keep it that way. It is *as* unpleasant as it sounds. I moved like a slow-motion-disco-zombie marionette. Sick. Why the damn Slinky guard had to bend as we advanced was beyond logic. I think he was just trying to piss me off. He certainly succeeded. As a child, I destroyed many a Slinky. Yes, irreversible coiling/twisting is their fate if they displease me. This one was in store for some *rude* schooling.

"Where are you taking me?" I demanded. It wasn't like I anticipated an answer, but I wasn't going along quietly. No, that would not be the Ryan Way. If *I* was going to suffer, *they* were going to suffer too.

I considered having Plesmus try and no-time them but thought better of that notion. It hadn't worked well before, plus I always liked to have an ace-in-the-hole, so to speak. Whoever they were parading me toward might be in more need of no-timing than the sorry-assed grunts.

"Hey, Slinky boy. If you wrinkle my uniform, you're paying the laundry bill. You hear me, you twisted brother? The nearest dry cleaners is *seventeen* galaxies away. The bill's going to cause instant death, it'll be so big."

No one but me spoke. The walk to wherever we were going was long, maybe half a kilometer, including several sets of stairs. I was over the insult well before we arrived. Finally, we were outside a set of large but otherwise unremarkable doors. After a minute of just standing there, I shouted, "Are we there yet?"

Nothing.

A few minutes later, the doors slid open silently. Still we remained where we were. What a boring imprisonment these ass-candies offered us captives. We needed to form a union or something. Maybe a prisoners' guild. I've always wanted to belong to a guild. When my hands were free, you have to know I was writing a letter of complaint. Then, with no obvious sound or signal, my group shuffled past the door.

The inside of the room was a surprise—but what wasn't in Wierdoville here? The space itself was expansive. The ceilings were way up there, forty to sixty meters high, varying in gentle waves and the occasional spiked peak. The walls were the same rough crystalline substance in appearance with scattered flashes of light. But, in opposition to the grandeur such a chamber might suggest, the appointments were sparse and primitive. The stupid connected sticks lined some of the walls, with a few chairs and tables as simple as they could possibly be scattered here-and-there. The general decor was like the student apartment I lived in when I was in grad school.

What was clear to me was that there was no one

beside us in the room. What had all the fuss and wait been about? I anticipated some tight-assed prissy lords and ladies to be seated, drinking tea with their pinky fingers in the air. But there was no one. Oddish.

The Slinky doubled over and flipped once, so I was upside down. Then it flipped so I was upright, and it released me in one fluid motion. I was impressed.

"You've done that before, right?" I asked it.

The dumb toy didn't respond. Just as well. I didn't like it.

As soon as I was free, both the Slinky and the turtle guards (you probably think I'm making this up as I go, but you can check ... that's what the devils looked like) backed out the door, which closed of its own accord. There I stood in this huge auditorium, all alone and unguarded. Why had they made such a show of capturing and conveying me here if they valued security so little that they left me semi-free?

"Do you think I should try and split?" I whispered to Plesmus.

"No," she answered softly.

"Why? There's nobody here."

"You can't leave. We're surrounded by a time barrier. Wait, don't you sense it?"

"What do I look like: a necumplack to you now? Of course I can't see a time barrier. BTW, pal, what the hell's a time barrier?"

"It's a barrier of time you can't pass thorough."

"Why not? I ain't 'fraid of no time."

"That's not how it works. Think of it as a time-lock field. If you touch it, in this time, this time is excluded from crossing the barrier."

"You're making this shit up, aren't you?"

"Why would I do that? We are engaged in a life-and-death struggle."

"Why *indeed*," I accused.

"Jon, stop it. This is no time for you to be you."

"Who should I be? Hmm?"

"Someone with a mental age above that of the numeric value of π, for starters."

"So we can't leave. Is that what you're saying?"

"No, I said you can't leave. I can, but that's beside the point."

"How so? If you leave while I stay, maybe we can set a clever trap for whoever or whatever is bound to come in and give us a hard time."

"Jon, do you ever think about what you say *before* you foul the air with it?"

"What?"

"We have no idea what incredibly potent beings are about to deal with us harshly for breaking and entering, as well as property damage on a large scale. How can you set a trap for a powerful *something* you don't know a thing about?"

"Well, we start by you going over behind that table-thing, while I stay here and look helpless."

"You *are* helpless."

"See. My disguise is working perfectly already."

"Would that it were a disguise. No, Jon. I will remain here, concealed, possibly, but close enough to help you when you get into trouble."

"What? Now I'm hurt. Why do you *presume* I'll get into trouble? I've survived a lot of very hairy predicaments, I'll have you know. These bozos are in for a rude awakening."

"Yes, that's what concerns me. They just woke up, and

then they're forced to interact with you. *One* rude awakening."

"When they're eating out of my hand, I'll remind you how very wrong you were."

"I've worked with you before. You'll piss them off, they'll draw straws to see who gets to kill you first, and then they'll laugh about how easy it was over cocktails."

"It's hard to be a hater. Nobody likes you guys."

I'm certain she was about to volley back, but then the central area in front of us changed. It was weird. All of a sudden, a bunch of somethings were there, when nothing was there seconds before. We both noticed and clammed up.

What were the bunch of somethings? You got me. Even with two billion years of observation under my belt, I was gobsmacked. First off, the rudimentary furniture—if you can even call it that—transformed into grand works of functional art. Spires lofted toward the heavens, colors dazzled by number and their ongoing variations. To look at what had to serve as a chair was to look into a kaleidoscope. It was dizzying. Even the dimensions of the seats fluctuated in a seemingly random pattern. My initial impression? Who the hell sits in a chair that changes size? Wouldn't that afford the sit-ee the *opposite* of a relaxing experience?

And the figures that occupied the center area. Wow. Just wow. Initially, I thought there were three of them, but it was hard to tell. As soon as the forms started to gel, the crystalline walls exploded to life. They strobed a blinding assault of lights and colors. And music of a sort came from every direction. Now, I'm not talking Lynyrd Skynyrd or Michael Oldfield music. No, it was more like the music of the spheres. Tonal variations with consonance and dissonance, like fighting cymbals and chimes. I was an instant not-a-fan.

Amidst the colors, sounds, and nauseating furniture, I had trouble focusing on the occupants that were, as I said, forming into shapes. It turned out that three large aggregations of whatevers split into five separate individuals. In the space of thirty seconds, where there was nothing, there were these five figures seated on bucking-bronco chairs, being pummeled with discombobulating lights and sounds. If I'd had a square of cardboard and a Sharpie, I'd have written the number "4" and held it up as their combined scores for such a pretentious and pompous entry. I mean, there *was* a door. *I'd* been shoved through it. The darn thing worked up to all reasonable specs. But no, the pissants seemed to subscribe to the Liberace School of the Overblown.

Any *reasonable* individual would shrink back into themselves and hope the quintet of excess didn't notice them. Any *sane* person would have certainly waited for the hosts to speak first, so that person might have some idea how they were supposed to act. Me? I jumped right in.

"Are you through yet, or is there an encore to that entry?"

I swear it was true. Plesmus squealed in agony. Nice. I mean, I might as well piss off *every* Mutt and Jeff in the room, right?

The highbrows? They perfectly ignored me. I know, maybe they didn't understand me. Yes. It was a language thing. No problem. As the cultural ambassador of Never Earth, I had fine options. I turned, dropped my drawers, and mooned the sons (or daughters—who knew?) of bitches.

Against all odds, that drew the same nonresponse. What was it going to take? A point of order: Never challenge me with that question. Yeah ...

I took three steps toward them. There was one unoccupied stick of furniture in the loose circle they sat in. I had myself a seat, like I was one of the gang. I was pretty Wolverine badass in doing so, up until the juncture where the cheap thing collapsed under my weight. Sitting on the deck looking up at them placed me in a lesser position than I'd have preferred, literally.

But some clouds do have silver linings. One of the schmucks turned and stared down at me.

"If that was expensive, please send me the bill. I'm totally good for it," I expressed with a warm smile that suggested a budding friendship was already forming between us.

Do you know that thing of when you were sitting on the floor after crashing down there, then, all of a sudden, you were sailing skyward like someone shot you out of a sixteen-inch gun? Yeah, that's pretty much how I experienced it. Up, up, up I flew. Those really high ceilings I mentioned before didn't seem all that high anymore. They seemed even less so when I impaled them at around the speed of sound.

The good news was that my fall to earth was much less eventful than my ascent. I flopped on my back exactly where I'd been seated in the first place.

"Nice piece of billiards there, my friend," I managed to mumble.

Then it spoke.

"Brother Pleasant Brilliance, what is this?"

Yeah, the jackass gestured toward the android on his back.

"Sister Stunning Wonder, this detritus is not mine, nor known to me."

SSW—because I'm *not* repeating that name ever—turned to a third member of the Shithead Patrol. "Excessive Splendor?"

ES made a show of plausible deniability. It fluttered its two arm-appendages like spastic eels and whined, "Never I. I am purity of knowledge and intent. You know this, Stunning Wonder."

"Does such purity, clear and shining as it is, preclude knowing what the rubbish on the floor is?"

"Why, yes, I would posit to you," ES basically harrumphed. "There is no purity in it, so it is not in me."

"As you say it, so it must be—" SSW began to puke from her orifice.

I sat up. "Whoa, doggies," I shouted. "That, Excessive—you don't mind if I call you by your first name, do you—is a *deductive fallacy*. In philosophy, the fact that there is no purity in Object A does not preclude the possibility that there *was* impurity in Object B, prior to its removal, rendering Object B pure. AmIright-amIright-amIright?"

Why did I choose that moment to press that esoteric point? No clue. But, as the one referenced as being impure, I felt wounded enough to act.

Do you know that thing of when you were sitting upright on the floor after crashing down there, then, all of a sudden, you were sailing skyward like someone shot you out of a sixteen-inch gun? Wash-rinse-repeat.

When I was back on my back, shaken, I resolved not to toy with the walking used-tampons additionally.

"Radiant Resplendence, I have not asked you as of yet," began SSW. "Do you know what that is which lessens our existence?"

"I'm sorry, Stunning Wonder, I wasn't listening. My thoughts, you know, are profound. I was considering a subject so complex and vexing it almost confounds *me*. Can you believe that?" R-Squared chuckled. Yup, the damn blight chuckled.

"What subject is that, most pleasant brother?" asked ES, the one I thought up until then was the most pretentious prick in the room.

"I," R-Squared chuckled again, condescendingly, I might add, "could say what it is, but you would not even understand the issues my mind is capable of delving into."

ES looked appropriately miffed. "What if I did? Then you could be courteous and tell me what the subject of your rumination was."

Who talks like this? More importantly, whoever does deserves to be boiled in bat piss.

"Very well, if I must, brother. I was wondering if the thickness of a moment has a fundamental unit that can be measured."

ES appeared to become nauseated; at least, he looked unwell to my eye. "That question seems not to have any meaning. A moment is a brief interval of time. If you said it had a certain thickness, I could half it and then the unit would be smaller."

R-Squared appealed then to RS. "You see, I was correct. Other cannot even comprehend what seems obvious to me."

Okay, now R-Squared had formally stepped into my rhetorical wheelhouse. This is the juncture where, in my world, I'd walk calmly up to R-Squared, shove my arm down his throat, and pull out his still beating heart. Then, if I was in just a foul enough mood, I'd quick like take a bite out of it before he otherwise deceased himself. I was positively salivating. Would ES do something similar, or equivalent? Or maybe just the slam-the-ceiling routine. It was a good one.

I'm guessing ES was what we kindly referred to back where I grew up as pansy-assed cupcake bait. And no, before you ask, I don't know the full origins of that particular label. Let's just say I used it liberally without fully understanding it. Hey, I was like twelve, okay? Sixteen ... tops.

"It gives my life meaning," ES began like a two-bit actor, "to be in the presence of you and to hear the wisdom you gift us with. It is a natural wonder, I say freely."

Now I wanted to rip *both* their hearts out. I'd be doing them a favor, a mitzvah. Doubt either jack-master had one. Grrr.

"You are welcome," beamed R-Squared. "You are all welcome, " he said to the other four losers.

That did, I was forced to notice, leave one douche bucket left who had not spoken. Oh joy. What fun stuff was I due to take in now?

SSW must have read my mind. She turned to the only other female figure. "Beauty Itself, that means you must know what that is over there, not dying quickly enough, on the floor. Would you care, if you have a moment, to fill us in on the particulars?"

"No."

Yeah, the bitch's answer was *no*. How uninformative yet provocative. That swelled my list of de-heartings to three. It was like I had a part-time job.

"Ah, well, if that answer were to change to something else, please do let us know."

What? Did the queen of sniveling ES just let the

asswipe off the hook? I was there on the floor. None of the others knew why. Logically, BI had to know why. So what was with the *no*? Hmm. Maybe she wanted me all for herself. Yeah, that had to be it. Beauty Itself—who bore stunningly little in common with looking beautiful at all—saw real male value in me and was determined to make me her love slave. Though that role would be new for me, and it would check off a box on my bucket-list, I decided to flush that notion out of my head. She was a prima donna, she was grotesque, and if she was anything like the others, she wanted me dead. That was strikes one through three, all in one pitch.

Long ago, Sapale told me about a Kaljaxian saying. *The release certain death allows.* If you were one-hundred-and-twenty-six percent certain to die, enjoy the time left to you without worries.

"Aunt BI," I yelled while I stood, "I'm going to have to ask you to lighten up a couple notches, okay? Quite possibly the entire belt. You have some idea why I was brought here. The other rat droppings," my hand swept across the others present, "they want to know what's up, Doc. So be *less* of a dick and speak meaning."

BI glanced to ES, then, one-by-one, her other associates. Rather ominously, she did not look at me. I assume I wasn't worthy of direct speech. I steeled myself for another low-orbital tour of the room. That was not what hit me.

BI whipped the back of her hand in my direction.

The air between us roiled. It was like she'd blown a smoke ring in my direction. It even moved about that slowly. There turned out to be a significant difference between a big smoke ring and what hit me. As close as I can describe it, I felt like a wrecking ball hit me squarely in the chest. All the lights in the room exploded away from me. I was in absolute darkness. I couldn't feel my arms or legs. I fact, I felt nothing, other than the sense of flying apart, not into pieces, but into a thin mist.

Then, as abruptly as I disintegrated, I reversed course and reintegrated. It was like a nuclear-powered yo-yo, whatever the hell that means.

I found I was standing right where I was after I finished mouthing off to Miss Attitude. But the feeling of the wrecking ball having rung my bell remained as an unpleasant reminder of my recent experience.

As my eyes were able to focus again, they saw something they hadn't before. All five squirts of diarrhea were staring at me. They all looked surprised and maybe a little confused.

Slowly, all their eyes rotated to inspect BI. She couldn't take hers off of me. I did not take that as a compliment. No, it was a curse, if it was anything.

ES spoke. "Beauty Itself, were you attempting but failed to no-time your prisoner?"

BI stood. She turned to face ES directly. "We have had this discussion before. It so infuriated me in the past and I am positively incendiary now. You know this, yet you make that statement. For both our sakes, I will take my leave to parts unknown."

And, sure enough, the hot bitch was gone.

After staring at the spot where Beauty Itself—not—had been until moments ago, ES cleared her throat weakly. "Oh, my. I might have fouled her mood."

"Maybe it was something you said?" speculated R-Squared. He obviously held the local rank of Captain Obvious.

"Let us not bound toward that conclusion,"

admonished SSW. "There might have been any number of reasons our sister felt she needed to be not here now."

That was, as my spirit-guide Popeye would have said, *all I can stands, cuz I can't stands n'more.* These WTF-they-weres were intolerable. Beyond annoying.

"Do *any* of you dickweeds listen to yourselves? Or, how about listening to someone else speaking?"

Yup, I had their attention.

"The mongrel said you'd pissed her off, *Ms.* Excess. You said something you knew *damn* well'd trigger her and you said it anyway. I can only presume you did so because you are even more of a back-stabbing puke than she is." I held up a finger. "However, I'm still quite open as to whether you're actually the queen of obscene. I'll ... I'll keep you posted. That's the best I can do for now." I looked away in disgust. I have always *excelled* at looking away in disgust. It's one of my many superpowers.

"What shall we do with her prisoner now?" ES asked the others while continuing to stare with incredulity at me.

"Unless I'm missing something big," I began passionately and pedantically, "I think it's that label that so offended the dearly departed Beaute."

"Who is Beaute?" ES asked, addressing me directly for the first time.

"Beaute? Are you daft? No, wait, you're Excess. I forgot. It's like I'm visiting the Seven Dwarves, only you're not dwarves. You're the Five Butt Plugs with Stupid Names." I scanned the four of them. "Sorry, I drifted off-topic, it would seem. *Beaute* is what I call *Beauty Itself.* It was her idea, before you ask how I came up with it. She thinks her full name is not just pretentious, it's farcical." I threw up my arms. "What was I supposed to do? She was right. When the bitch's right, she's right. And when she's right, it's best not to wind her up. I only mention that fact since you seem not to have learned that key fact as of yet. You're welcome." I bowed with deferential chivalry. Hey, if nothing else, I wanted to confuse the living hell out of them. That's another of my superpowers, thank you very much.

"Do you ever make sense or shut up?" asked R-Squared.

Bingo! I'd forced another sorry-excuse to acknowledge me.

"Not if I can help it, Sancho," I replied with a smile.

"Sancho?" the idiot mouthed. He looked to ES. "Who is Sancho?"

Tentatively, ES pointed toward R-Squared. "I believe Beaute's prisoner referred to you as Sancho."

He turned then to me, heartwarmingly befuddled. "Why did you call me Sancho?"

"Because, in a small way, you remind me of Sancho Panza," I tormented.

"Who?"

"Don Quixote's sidekick. Come on, you've read the books, right? They're *classics*."

Poor R-Squared. He really looked vexed. "I have no idea what Beaute's prisoner is going on about."

"I think you four have to face up to adult realities here," I counseled. "I think Beaute's entire point was that I'm the prisoner of *all* of you, not just Beauty herself."

"Beauty *Itself*," corrected the up-until-then silent SSW.

"No, *herself*. *Itself* would only be correct if you were referring to an object of neutral gender. Now, if you are trying to tell me Beaute's *neutral* in that department, well, let me inform you I can prove you wrong. *KnowwhatI'msaying?*"

"Why didn't Beaute no-time that foul creature?" asked R-Squared, who apparently realized the Four Butt Plugs were well off-topic.

"Well ... I ... she certainly, er—" SSW stammered.

I rifled a finger in her direction. "What she said."

ES tried to get the train back on the track. "She did *attempt* to no-time the little pest. I'm ... I'm not quite certain why she didn't accomplish the task. It's rather basic."

"Perhaps I should try?" R-Squared wondered out loud.

"Am I *your* prisoner?" I challenged him hotly.

"Not that I know of."

"Let me ask you this, then. Am I *Beaute's* prisoner? Hmm?"

"I believe so. You did say you were the prisoner of us all, but—"

"Hang on there, big guy," I cut him off. "*I* said *she* said I was all your prisoner. I didn't say I was all of your prisoner. No, sir. I did not. My point is, however, if I am her prisoner, do you think it's *proper* for you to no-time me? I mean, are you free to no-time Beaute's hat? Her pet fish? I think not." I crossed my arms and turned my back on the puke.

"Does Beaute have a *hat* or a *fish* I am unaware of?" he asked the others.

"This has gone far enough," thundered SSW. She vaulted to her feet. She waved both her hands at me and trembled something awful.

I was wrecking-ball struck again—*bam*! Every independent point in my reality flashed blindingly, then zapped out of existence. I felt like someone reached down my throat, pulled my nuts back out, and then started beating me over the head with them still attached. It was not pleasant.

And ... whooosh! Everything was back to the same abnormal it had been seconds before. I felt blenderized, but I was in one piece and functioning.

"Will you stop doing that," I tried to shout. It came out more of a squeak.

"Why is it still here?" SSW asked the other four. "I ... I definitely called for its time."

"Maybe you're losing your touch?" I managed to say.

At that juncture, my boot *psst*-ed me. "Jon, knock it off with the snark," Plesmus hissed. She sounded exhausted.

"Huh?"

"I've re-timed us twice, but I don't think I can manage a third time. Play nice. In fact, stop talking."

"Er ... okay. Ah, what's re-timing?"

"They tried to no-time us. They very nearly did. I had enough time energy left to reverse their efforts. But they carry a lot more than I do. If they try a couple more times, we're goners."

"They do?"

"Yes. I just said they do."

"Excuse me, someone's prisoner," interrupted SSW. "Who are you talking to?"

Oops. "To whom am I talking?" I asked. "I'm ... I'm talking to Beaute." I straightened. "Duh."

"*Jon*," Plesmus moaned.

"You asked Beauty Itself what re-timing was? Why would you ask her that? You seem to have successfully employed it. How could you not know what it is?"

"Ah," I replied weakly. "That must seem odd ... I mean, from your side of the table."

"What *table*?" whined R-Squared. "What *hat*, what *fish*, what *table*."

"Is he like this often?" I asked. "If so, you *might* want to take him to the doctor. He doesn't sound too good."

"Annoying pest," howled SSW. "Stop being evasive and answer my question. Why did you ask Beauty Itself what re-timing was?"

You know when you're really in deep, in way too deep, you know what you should do? In my opinion, keep digging. "Ah *ah*!" I accused, pointing at SSW. "We were *testing* you. You were *weighed* in the balance and you have been *determined* to be *insufficient*."

"Jon," said a resigned Plesmus, "I'd like to say it's been nice knowing you, but it really hasn't been."

"Who is *we*?" SSW challenged with convincing ire.

"Beaute and me, of course," I replied confidently. "Who do you think it was?"

"You should stop playing us for the fool, pest," she snapped. "Why would Beauty Itself wish in any way to test us, and how are your insane rantings any form of test?"

"I am not authorized to divulge that information. You will have to ask Beaute herself."

"I can't ask her. She's gone. She left for parts unknown. You heard her."

"Then you'll just have to wait her *return*, won't you?"

Lordy, I wished I knew where any of this was going.

"You speak only crazy words," she railed. "She no-timed you. How could she *possibly* be in league with you?"

"I should feel that's rather obvious. It was a *sham* no-timing. But, again, you'll have to ask her about our design when she returns." I held up a palm. "I'm sorry. Those were her *specific* instructions."

"I once had a peaceful and meaningful life," SSW hissed. "I once knew bliss without end. Then I met you."

I shrugged. "I get that a lot."

"There is no test Beauty Itself would need to administer. The notion is preposterous. But, even if her display of no-timing you was a deception, mine was not. I will know how you defied my will and I will know now."

"You used the word *will* three times in close proximity," I stated flatly.

I could tell she was beside herself with rage, but that she nonetheless reviewed her words.

"I did. What of it?"

"It's rhetorically lame. If you were writing it --hah—it'd be forget-about-it sloppy. You must vary your words or you sound amateurish."

"Never in eternity have—"

SSW was clearly on another loco-roll. Fortunately, R-Squared cut her off. "Stunning Wonder."

She slammed her eyes closed. "*What*!"

"Er, if I might. I feel emotions are getting the best of us here. Might I suggest we wait for Beauty Itself to return. When she does, we can quickly determine if what this meaningless fleck is saying is true. If it *were* true, I think harming it would be unwise. We might ... er, further upset our sister."

SSW was clearly torn. She wanted quick blood—my blood—but she also must have felt his point was well taken.

"Fine. For the present, I will stay my wrath. If Beauty Itself can speak on behalf of this horrible, horrible creature, I will be in a position of being in your debt."

Remember ES? He'd been very quiet, hadn't he? "When will Beauty Itself return?" he asked.

When it was clear the other four weren't going to respond, all eyes slowly turned to me.

I wagged my head in a prissy manner. "Any time now."

NINETEEN

Aramthella was two and a half weeks into her survey of the long swath of the Milky Way. Her crew was searching for any sign of the last clan ship, the one that had so far eluded them. Tank was banking on the new time maker's inexperience and lust for ever more time energy. If the clan leader did resume the routine harvesting, their location would be betrayed. It was a long shot that the time maker would be that blatant, but Tank could think of no better plan. Sitting and waiting for something wonderful to happen was a fool's strategy.

Tank had assembled four search teams of three persons each. That way, they could rotate twelve hours on followed by thirty-six hours of down time. That way, he hoped everyone would stay sharp and focused. What they were after almost three weeks of finding nothing was bored and discouraged. That loss of spirit was made worse by the knowledge that they'd screened only about one percent of the tunnel they were to examine. At the rate they progressed, they'd all be spending the next two years staring at blank screens and listening to Aramthella announce that she's found nothing, over and over again.

The only upside so far was that the military personnel who'd been rescued from Mars were integrating well into the onboard routines. They were eager to learn, hard working, and all devoted to the mission. The four teams—unimaginatively named Blue, Green, Red, and Orange—were headed by Sachiko, Reva, Emma, and Tom. The groups also had a military member, as well as one of the Georgetown students. Tank was keen on getting them involved in the daily workings of the ship. If the pipe dream of resurrecting the Earth never materialized, sooner or later, the younger members of the crew would need to assume all the essential functions of the ship.

"Megan," Sachiko called over to her, "do you have those results of the neutrino density scans yet?"

"Uh, sorry, Captain, not quite." Megan said, snapping her head back up. She'd been slipping into dreamland. Back at GU, she was an English major. Pulling long repetitive technical shifts was the farthest thing from her career plan she could imagine. But she understood perfectly well that everything had changed. She was anxious to embrace the uncertain future that lay before her. If she was stuck living her life out on this ship, being a productive member of her crew seemed a logical path to pursue.

"I need that data fifteen minutes ago. Please pick up the pace," Sachiko responded tersely. She'd noticed Megan's head start bobbing. A captainly kick in the rear would help her stay awake.

"You'll have the numbers in ten, I promise."

"See to it."

Sachiko reflected not for the first time how much

she'd changed since the Clams showed up. Gone was the agreeable graduate-student lifestyle. Aside from working her butt off academically, she was insulated from the real world. She could come and go as she'd pleased, and she spent most of her waking hours alone, the way she like it. My, how her life had changed.

"Don't you think you're being a bit hard on the girl?" Aramthella asked, interrupting Sachiko's musings.

"She's late with her report. The woman volunteered to shoulder a responsibility. If I allow her to fail, her failure will be my fault, not hers."

"Being a few minutes late with a meaningless set of numbers *hardly* constitutes a failure."

"I need my crew to excel in all things. Like it or not, discipline is needed to accomplish many of the essential components of this mission. As captain, it falls to me to ensure that the crew performs well."

"My, my, Captain, to hear you talking. It wasn't so long ago that you were racked with self-doubt and as unsure of yourself as a toddler on ice holding flaming torches in both hands."

"Your point?"

"My point is that you've matured well into your role. I'm proud of how you've—"

It took Sachiko a second to realize Aramthella was not going to continue.

"Aramthella, what's—"

"Captain, I have a contact one point five million kilometers off our port bow."

Sachiko blinked hard several times. "Is it the clan ship?"

"No, I do not believe so. The contact is heading

straight toward us under a conventional plasma drive. Also, there isn't evidence of no-timing in the region."

"Straight toward us?" Sachiko said mostly to herself, questioningly.

"Yes, Captain. Perhaps this would be a good time to—"

Sachiko slammed a fist down on the intercom switch in her chair's armrest. "All crew members, we are at Yellow Alert. Repeat, Yellow Alert. This is not a drill. General Sherman to the bridge. Colonel St. Claire to the bridge."

"Yes, Aramthella, you were saying?" she asked after a long, deep breath.

"Nothing, sir."

"ETA of unidentified craft?"

"An hour at their present velocity."

"And it's just the one ship?"

"I am uncertain. There could be multiple craft tightly configured."

"Why would they try to hide their number?" Sachiko posed, a bit confused.

"Because they're attacking our asses and want to keep their strength a secret," boomed Tank as he sprinted onto the bridge.

"Oh my," responded Sachiko.

"You said sixty minutes for their ETA?"

"Yes, General."

"Have they made any attempts to scan or contact us?"

"They have not hailed us, no. I believe they have extended a primitive scanning beam. It might be capable of determining our mass, heading, and energy status. Shall I block it?"

Tank rubbed his chin. "No. Let's not seem hostile. Let them tickle us if they're so inclined."

"I can now confirm multiple signals. Yes. There are eight ships approaching. They have split up into two wings and are decelerating quickly."

"Hail them," he said coolly.

Reva, whose quarters were much farther away than Tank's, flew through the door. "What's up?"

"Eight ships of unknown origin and intent are about to pay us a visit."

Reva whipped out her handheld. "Emma, Tom, we're being approached by a potential hostile. Prepare the ship for boarding. You know the drill."

"Yes, sir," replied Emma. "Tom's right here. We're on it."

Over the last few weeks, Reva had established a detailed plan to protect the ship in case it was boarded. Today, she was so glad she had.

"General, there has been no acknowledgement of our hail," Aramthella stated.

"Keep trying. And put us dead in space."

"What?" snapped Reva.

"I want to keep this cordial if at all possible. Plus, we don't need to maneuver to no-time them if it comes to that."

Sachiko sat bolt-upright. "Tank, do you think it'll come to that?"

"I hope not. But I'm not going to let them damage us either. ETA and configuration of enemy force?"

"Fifty minutes. They continue to spread out and approach in a semi-circle."

"That's about as *offensive* a configuration as there can be," Tank said softly.

"Why don't we just leave?" Sachiko asked heatedly. "I

don't want to kill anyone. There's no way they can catch us."

"We can't run every time something goes bump in the night, Captain. I at least want to know what they're up to first. We can put the membrane up if they shoot first. We'll be fine."

"But what's the point? They can't win. They're not the enemy. If we—"

Tank held up a hang-on-a-second hand toward her. "Maybe they know where the Clams are. Or maybe they'll become our BFFs and shower us with love. Lesson One, kiddo. You stand your ground. We're here minding our own business. This is a legitimate mission and we've shown them no aggression. If they want to pick a fight in spite of those facts, we're obliged to remind them they've made a grand error in judgment."

"You're right," she said contritely. "Sorry."

"Don't be sorry. Don't ever be sorry for stating what you believe to be true and just. I may be right or I may be wrong. Time'll tell. All I have is a conviction and a sizable ego to back that up."

"Thanks," she responded with a slight grin.

"Aramthella, any response from our visitors yet?" Tank called out.

"Negative."

"Well, I think it's about time you hailed them personally, Captain," Tank said with a twinkle in his eyes.

"Wh ... me?" she stammered. "No, *you* hail to them."

"Kiddo, I've seen a whole lotta science fiction movies. In situations such as this, the captain always hails the enemy vessel. *You're* the captain, not me."

"But you're—"

"Hit that button to open a channel. Hit it again to close it," he instructed her while pointing at her armrest.

"I *know* how the system works." She considered him briefly. Then she pounded the comm switch. "To the ships approaching our location. This is Captain Sachiko Jones. We are on a peaceful mission. Please identify yourselves and state your intentions." She thudded the switch closed.

Sachiko flared her eyebrows and angled her head, querying Tank as to the quality of her declaration.

He crossed his arms and nodded back approvingly.

"Aramthella, do we know if they can understand our transmission?" Sachiko asked.

"They must. I've sent the message in over five million languages, along with basic mathematical configurations any space-worthy civilization would recognize."

"Very well." She hit the comm switch again. "We are on a peaceful mission. Your ships seem to be taking up an aggressive formation. That is not acceptable. Please acknowledge you at least understand my words."

She looked to Tank and tapped her fingertips nervously on the armrest.

"What if they shoot first and talk later?" she asked.

"We will respond defensibly then, and in kind," Tank replied soberly. "I actually hate the expression *we won't start the fight, but we will finish it*. However, it does apply well in the—"

"Enemy intruders," hissed to life through the speakers. "You are a known evil. We will not listen to your lies and we will not allow you to disintegrate our home world. Depart at once, or feel the might of the Veraxy Foundation."

"Holy *shit,*" Tank wheezed, "they think we're the Clams."

"We *are* in one of their ships," Sachiko blurted back anxiously. She hit the button hard. "Veraxy Foundation fleet. Please know we are not the original owners of this vessel. We seized command of it from the clan. There are none of them aboard. They are all dead. We come from Earth. It was destroyed by the clan. We want no fight with you or your foundation."

Tense seconds passed.

"Captain, the Veraxy ships have fired on us. High-intensity laser beams were inbound. I placed the membrane before they contacted the ship," Aramthella announced in a businesslike manner.

"Damage report," spat Tank.

"None whatsoever," the ship replied confidently.

Tank nodded grimly to Sachiko.

She started to respond then sat back. Finally, she thumped the comm switch. "Please know that I will allow you that one test of our peaceful intent and our strength. If we are fired upon again, I will be forced to destroy every ship that did so."

More tense moments crawled by.

"*Lies.* All I hear are lies. You are the destroyers of all," hissed the alien's voice. "Now you boast of your blood lust."

"Captain, all the enemy vessels have fired again. They used the same weapons and they were negated by our membranes. Shall I—"

"Aim the rail cannon at the flagship. On my mark, I want one round fired at half-maximal velocity," Sachiko interrupted.

"Captain," Aramthella protested, "I can sweep them away like mist. Why—"

"Is the rail cannon configured?" Sachiko demanded.

"Yes, Captain. It is ready to fire."

"Fire. When it is one-hundred meters from the flagship, no-time the round. Do not *harm* the Veraxy ships."

"It is done. Rail ball no-timed as you instructed."

"*Nice*," Tank erupted joyfully. "You showed *restraint*, but you also *showed* what you're capable of. That'll give them something to stew over. Well played, Captain."

She tapped the switch lightly. "Veraxy commander, unless you wish to join that cannonball in the absolute void of non-existence, do not further test my patience. Any additional aggression on your part will be your last act. I do not wish to end you, but, if you insist I do so, I will. Please know this." She closed the channel.

She looked to Tank again.

His expression suggested slight abdominal cramping.

"Too heavy handed?" she asked.

His waffling open palm conveyed that it just might have been.

"Duly noted," she responded, throwing back her shoulders. She pressed the switch with one finger. "Veraxy commander, please state your name."

After perhaps a shade too long, he replied, "I am Warrior One of this battlebringer."

"Your name? I gave you mine," she insisted.

"My name is voided by my rank and service. You must refer to me as I have stated or do not address me individually."

Tank leaned in and whispered, "Not the hill to die on. Let him have his cultural orientations."

She nodded quickly.

"Fine. Warrior One of the Veraxy battlebringer, please—"

"No. That's not what you must call me. I am to you *Warrior One*. The designation of my ship and its name are not one with me. What are you thinking?"

"He certainly could be more cordial, couldn't he?" Sachiko asked Tank quietly.

She got a shrug in response.

"First, please believe me that we are not those who destroyed a large swath of the galaxy. We have destroyed all of their ships but one. It is in search of that remaining vessel that we cross into your space. Have you seen another ship such as ours?"

There was a significant pause before he responded.

"Captain, I am not here to discuss political matters with aliens. I am a warrior. If you and I are not to make war, our shared experience is at an end."

"Who *is* authorized to discuss politics with aliens?" she pressed, annoyance showing through in her tone.

"I do not know. The *dead* perhaps?" He followed with a sound that seemed very much like a laugh.

She closed the switch. "Aramthella, please repeat the firing of a single rail round. No-time the ball when it is *ten* meters from the flagship."

"It is done, Captain."

She thumbed the switch. "You find humor in *insulting* me. I find it in *threatening* you. The next cannonball will not be vaporized by me, but by your hull. Do I make myself clear, One?"

"Yes, *peace*-seeker captain. Your intentions are clear. Please forgive my levity." He said *peace* as if it were a curse word.

"Who leads your society?"

"Er ... please, I mean no disrespect. I am not here to discuss such matters. That is an absolute. To violate that rule would be to forfeit my lineage."

"Whatever *that* entails," Tank snarked softly.

"May I know your planet of origin?"

"Captain, *I* can tell you that. The ships came from the eighth planet orbiting the nearby M-class star," Aramthella broke in jealously.

"I assumed you could. I wanted *him* to tell me, however," she replied coolly.

"Very well," the ship replied in a neutral tone.

Warrior One spoke again. "No. I will not tell you."

"How may I communicate with your superiors?" she asked firmly.

"To that I can speak. They do not wish communications with you, so you may not."

"Be that as it may," she responded, "*I* wish to communicate with *them*. If you assist me, I will take that as a sign of goodwill. In times such as these, such signs are most welcome."

"I hear you. But I will not forfeit my lineage. If it were only me who would suffer, perhaps I would aid you."

"Do your people not trade with other worlds? Do you not interact with other races?"

He made that laughing sound again. "No. Why would we tolerate other species?"

"So you don't have formal relationships with alien races?"

"I will likely anger you with my words, but you hold superiority over me. We need nothing from inferiors. We do not tolerate infidels, Captain. Even if we were to desire such a ridiculous affection, Gumnolar would never condone such weakness. We would *all* forfeit our lives, and rightly so."

"Who is Gum—" she began to ask.

Tank shot a hand to her shoulder. "Hang on, kiddo. Stop." He began scratching intently at the side of his chin.

"Tank, I know that sign. You're trying to remember something, something important. What gives?"

He waved absent fingers in her general direction with his non-scratching hand.

"*Tank*," she said in a commanding tone, "military *confrontation* here. What are you thinking about?"

"Gumnolar? Gumnolar? Where have I—" He snapped his fingers loudly. "That's it. Jon mentioned them, a ways back. We were talking about ugly aliens. He said he had the winning species. They looked like ... *yes*. And they worshipped this god like he was standing right next to them." He turned toward her excitedly. "Ask them if the Veraxy Foundation is a part of the Listhelon Empire."

"The what?"

He pointed to the comm switch. "Just do it."

She tapped the link. "Warrior One, is your Veraxy Foundation part of the Listhelon Empire?"

"You *know* us!" he shouted back. "That is less than impossible. All species we contact must perish. If you knew us, you would be—"

"*One*," Sachiko demanded, "if we knew you, we would be what? Dead?"

He made a vile sound. It was a hiss, but it was vulgar and it was laden with hatred. Then he spoke in anger. "You ... you are alive *now*. That is *our* insult to Gumnolar. Soon we will correct our error and end our shame. We will *find* you, *whoever* you are. We will eat your flesh and burn your world to ashes. You are dead as you speak. *Otollar* has spoken."

Sachiko looked to Tank. She was stunned.

"Someone's in a piss-poor mood today," he stated. "Maybe we should wish the son of a sea serpent good hunting. If he finds Earth, he's a better fish than me."

She had to guffaw. Unfortunately, it was through her nose and it was rather untidy.

TWENTY

It had taken some doing, some cunning, and some luck, but Desi and Tip had finally maneuvered Reva into incorporating janitorial work into their seemingly open-ended period of punishment. As custodians, they had to be given authorization to enter all areas, aside from the highly secured ones. Cleaning there was performed by uniformed personnel only.

Even with their new freedom, they waited almost two weeks to open the one door they had schemed to breach. That of Megan Thompson's cabin. After she died there following her overdose, her roommate was relocated to less objectionable quarters. The room had remained vacant and completely unused. It didn't need cleaning, but the two students wanted in for their own reasons. For the first time in her life, Desi was actually *seeking* out a ghost. If there was a disembodied spirit aboard the ship, *this* was the best place to find it.

Plesmus had spoken of Desdemona's future by saying she would not just *speak* to the deceased, Desi was needed to *control the dead.* That assertion made no sense.

But the blobby alien refused to expand upon what she meant by that prediction. Tip had finally convinced Desi that they needed to conduct a scientific experiment. They needed to see if Desi could do whatever *control the dead* was supposed to be. Ergo, they needed a ghost, preferably a friendly ghost. The evening had finally arrived. It was time to see if remnants of Megan lingered in her cabin. There had been no reports or sightings, but Desi knew that didn't mean a spirit wasn't roaming somewhere.

Tip pushed the cleaning cart as it squeaked down the passageway. It was the dinner hour. Most former GU residents would be in the mess hall. Those who weren'tlikely had jobs, or they were staying inside their cabins for some compelling reason. Likely that compelling reason was sex. As a result, the passageway was abandoned. The pair passed Megan's old room a few times before trying to key the entry pad. They were as nervous as you'd assume two amateur spies would be. Desi had insisted Tip do the actual number tapping. Her hands were trembling such that it would be anyone's guess what numbers she entered if she made the attempt.

"Here," Tip mumbled, "I'll enter my pass code." He angled his shoulder so as to obscure Desi's view of his actions.

She nearly punched him. Why would he care if she saw his pass code? She had her *own*. But, before she acted, she recalled the reason he was doing so. He was Tip Benjamin. 'Nuf said.

The door slid open silently. They looked at one another, rife with uncertainty. Neither shared that they'd hoped their codes wouldn't have worked.

"I think the door opened," Tip whispered to Desi.

She rolled her eyes toward the heavens. She pushed

him in, then the cart, and finally she stepped in cautiously.

"Put the cart over there," she instructed, pointing to the near corner.

He did so without comment.

"So, do you see Megan?" Tip asked upon his return to her side. For his part, Tip was bending and craning his neck, searching on his own.

"No. They're not like *puppies*, running up to you when you enter the room. It can take hours, even days before they realize I can see and hear them."

"So ghosts don't speak unless spoken to?"

She was floored. He asked that stupid question so genuinely, with no appreciation that it was such a *ridiculous* thing to wonder. She elected not to respond. Desi had already learned that Tip had the attention span of a jackhammer on a plate of steel.

"Maybe you should put on some of her clothes or lie in her bed." He turned to look at the side of Desi's head. "Do the spirits tell you which bed was Megan's?"

Desi briefly contemplated yelling *squirrel* and pointing wildly in some direction. Again, she decided just to let his remarks go.

They stood silently in the room for almost a minute. That was a world record for Tip's not saying something inappropriate, annoying, lame, or all-of-the-above.

"Do you think I intimidate the ghost? Maybe I should leave?"

"No, you're fine," she replied absently.

"I think if I were a ghost, I'd be intimidated by me," he speculated lamely.

That exceeded what Desi could tolerate. "If you were

a ghost, how could you be the force that intimidated yourself? That's ignorant."

He squinted a bit. "The way I said it, I'm inclined to agree. It must be the stress of being alone with a girl in her room."

Desi nearly lost it. Tip was way, way too much. "Do you mean you're nervous to be alone in a bedroom with *me*, with Megan's *ghost*—because this is ... was ... *her* room, not mine —or do you simply mean to call it to everyone's attention that you're completely and utterly out of touch with reality?"

"You mean she is here? You can see her?"

"What?" she basically screamed back.

"You said *everyone's*, not just *our*. That certainly implied to me that there were more than just us two in this room."

She slammed her eyelids shut. "Here's a new experiment we can do while working on this one. You shut up and do not speak unless I specifically grant you the permission to do so. How does that sound?"

He raised a finger and started to respond.

"Ah ah," she snapped. "*Silence*."

"But—"

"*Silence* means *silence*. I did not give you *permission* to speak." She wagged a finger under his nose.

"B ... but—"

"No *buts*. If you ruin my experiment, I might *never* be able to forgive you." She felt good about her restraining command.

Tip, now committed to silence, raised his arms in the air. He had them dance, like he was a conductor trying to lead the orchestra with his arms held too high.

"You are *not* playing charades with me. Not here. Not

now." Her fists were balled up on either of her hips. Desdemona was angry. "Stop it this *instant.*"

Instead of following her expressed passionate request, Tip simply altered his body language. The bonehead could be infuriating. He most assuredly could be.

He lowered, with comic animation, his left arm. Then his right arm stopped bounding in the air. He began to rotate his raised index finger, like a pathetic nerd stirring his ice tea with his digit, instead of a spoon.

"What? You want to mix me up? I told you to knock it the freak off, Tip Benjamin."

Tip smiled and shook his head in the negative, very vigorously. He held up five fingers of one hand and tapped his lips with one other finger.

"Six words. Tip, *stoooop.* I am not guessing six *words.* What are the six words you want to tell me but can't because I told you to remain silent?"

He shook his head in frustration. Then he made a motion with opening fingers away from his mouth and wagging the index finger of the other hand to indicate the word *no.*

"I just asked what—" She rotated her body, she was so vexed with Tip. "But I didn't release you to speak, did I?"

He dropped his arms and simply shook his head, agreeing with her in the negative.

"Tip, speak. What six words are *so* damn important?"

He grinned like an idiot—which wasn't hard for him at all—and took in a deep breath. After he made a show of exhaling robustly, the Tipster was ready to speak.

"*There*-is-*a*-ghost-*standing*-behind-*you.*" He looked up to the ceiling, waited a second, then began giggling like the ninny he truly was. "Aw, heck. Those are *seven* words. What was I thinking?"

She heard the fool not. Desi was preoccupied, glaring at the slightly levitating form of Megan Thompson, which was hovering just behind her. At least she assumed, given the particulars, it was Megan floating there. She'd never met the girl when she was alive.

Desdemona straightened herself formally. "Megan Thompson. Is that you?"

"Of course it's her. Who else would be haunting Megan Thom—"

The look Desi gave Tip did the impossible. It shut him up mid-sentence.

"Are you Megan?" Desi repeated. She touched her chest with both palms. "I am Desdemona Tanner." She turned to Tip and extended her arms toward him. "This is T ... Tip Benjamin." It occurred to Desi at that inopportune moment that she didn't know Tip's actual name, if he even had one. Maybe, she thought wildly, his parents actually named the loser *Tip*. Could it be short for *Topper*? No. *Tripp*? No, that was for someone who was the III'rd. She was about to wander further into nonsense, worrying about Tip's possible name, when Megan spoke.

It was, actually, more a *manifestation* than *speech*. It did convey meaning as well as the spoken word might have. Megan swelled to four or five times her human size, thinning slightly as she did in her middle section. Then, like the librarian at the beginning of *Ghostbusters*, she transfigured into a hideous-headed apparition and bellowed at the two not-yet-deads with stunning ferocity.

Tip wet himself immediately. Then he hurled his back into the wall nearest behind him. Maybe he was hoping the door was there. Likely, he just wasn't thinking clearly.

Desdemona remained both continent and where she

stood. She let Megan vent her very best at her while managing not to collapse in fear. For Desdemona knew something Tip didn't. As much as a ghost might frighten you, it couldn't actually hurt you, not directly. But still, it wasn't easy to keep that knowledge in crisp focus with a demonic manifestation howling at you. No, it was not.

When Megan took a break in her assault, Desi spoke loudly and as clearly as she could. "I know you are frightened, Megan. We are here to help you. Please—"

Megan interrupted Desi by launching her hideous form at, and then through, Desdemona. She did the same to Tip. Like an unschooled ghost, she ended up in the passageway outside when she was done. *Rookies.*

Before Megan could pop back in, Desi peeled Tip off the wall and placed him behind her body. "Stay there," she shouted over her shoulder.

"N ... not ... a probbbbblem," he stammered.

Megan reappeared. She was in her original quasi-human form. She drifted up to Desi's face and inspected her like she was a new but unwelcome species of bug.

"You can speak to me if you like," Desi offered.

"Why are you here? Who gave you permission to enter my room. Are you two perverts? How dare you?"

Without turning, Desi explained to Tip, "Some disembodied spirits do not know they're no longer among the living."

"How might that square with her recent performance?" Tip managed to ask coherently.

"Ghosts are inconstant," she replied obscurely. "They're a lot like you, Tip."

She couldn't see him nodding in understanding, right there behind her. What she said made good sense to Tip.

"Megan, I am here to help. What can I do for you?" Desi pressed.

"You can get out of my room. I need to sleep. Classes start early here at GU."

"Megan," Desi said as empathetically as she could, "we are not living at GU any longer. Megan, we're on a space ship. You no longer are alive, Megan. Do you understand me?"

Megan ominously began to swell again. Tip took several steps in reverse.

"No, Megan, don't. Do not get mad. You must remember. Do you remember how sad—"

Nope. Megan wasn't in a listening mood. She screamed, screeched, and spat into Desi's face.

In her long experience with ghosts, Desi had encountered uncooperative ones. Oh yes. But Megan was a first. Maybe that was because Desi had sought her out, not the other way around. If Megan were more rational, as in a spirit soliciting assistance, she would be less inclined to default to terror.

Mid-tirade, Desi had had enough. She raised her arms and commanded, "*Silence.*"

Involuntarily, Megan abruptly stopped voicing her wrath. She clearly wanted to continue her display, but she seemed incapable of it.

Tip stepped up to Desi and set a hand on her shoulder. "You *controlled* her."

Desi nodded. She had, just like Plesmus alluded to.

"Now what?" she asked either herself or Tip.

Megan, frustrated by her inability to vocalize, swirled her form like a mighty whirlpool. She leaned into Desi.

"Stop that. Be still," resounded from Desi's mouth.

Megan's apparition stopped all motion. Even her ghosty eyes were frozen still.

"Coolissimo," declared Tip.

"No, Tip, this is the opposite of cool. I have no idea what I'm doing. What am I supposed to do with a restrained ghost?"

"Tell it to go away," he said, like that option was so blatantly obvious.

She shot him a glance. "Where to, Tip? Deep space. I can't do that to the girl. She's frightened and confused. I think I'd just make her that much worse off."

"Then tell her to chill."

Desi turned her body to Tip. She was furious, mostly with herself. But she needed to vent.

"*Chill*? Are you more insane than you *look?* I can't command her to understand the ins and outs of the afterlife."

Tip, initially recoiling from Desi's fury, snapped his head up. "Why not?"

"Why not *what*?" she snapped.

"Why can't you command her to act like a normal dead person. Tell her to walk into the light."

"What *light*. Tip? Do *you* see a light?" she mocked.

"Uh, yes." He pointed to the side.

Desi's head flew in that direction. There was a glimmering, wavering infusion of light, there in the center of the wall. "Well I'll be damned," she throated. Then she looked to Megan. "Go into the light," she said gently but firmly.

Megan unfroze. She looked toward the glow, then back to Desi. Megan's eyes became suddenly calm. Understanding dawned. She smiled and Megan

Thompson, or whatever of her that had lingered, was gone. So was the light.

"Well I'll be damned," Desi repeated quietly.

"Unlikely," replied Tip. "You did good."

Desdemona turned to Tip. She smiled widely, then she grabbed both of his shoulders. She yanked him into a passionate, open-mouth kiss.

Tip, naturally, stiffened like a dead board, and then he, naturally, fainted.

TWENTY-ONE

Time Maker-bob slumped against the wall of its personal space. It could have sat, lay down, or paced. It was the boss after all. But the whim struck it to lean awkwardly against the cold metal. Go and figure. First among the thoughts that vexed the time maker was that of how to proceed. It possessed hive-knowledge of what the clan had done historically, but it lacked hands-on experience in handling underlings and mission planning. The past two time makers had their sets of three body makers to discuss important topics with. But Time Maker-bob had eliminated the middlemen, so to speak, and assumed all of the command roles. It could always exude body makers, and, in so doing, reestablish past norms. But near-peers were such a bother. They had *opinions*, their own *thoughts*, and sulfur fire itself, they might even have their own *agendas*. Those were elements Time Maker-bob just didn't want to deal with. So it created what it felt was the next-best substitute. In reality, it created proof positive that it was irrevocably and completely insane. But introspection was never a burden any clan leader need suffer under.

From Time Maker-bob's sparse chest extended a thin tube of flesh. It ended in a head. Now, clan individuality was very hard for anyone, them included, to discern. But, if you took the time to study the face on the suspended head, you'd definitely be of the opinion that it was identical to that of Time Maker-bob—the spitting image, in fact. It was, in effect, having a serious conversation with itself.

"I'm certain you will agree that all my actions and initiative to date have not been brilliant, because brilliant is an insufficient word to characterize my stunning wonder," The main-section head said to the isolated copy.

"*Stunning wonder* is insufficient to describe the magic that is you, Time Maker-bob," one-upped the puppet.

"You know what? We're both correct. In short order, I've achieved brilliance, stunning wonder, *and* magical manifestations. I am nothing short of perfect."

"I would agree with you, but I am so nothing that my praise is unworthy of you hearing it."

"Are you trying to get on my good side?" asked the lunatic leader. It then bounced the head in the air to its left side, then its right side. "Which one is my good side? Please be honest, brutally so if need demands it."

"Both," the little head responded instantly. "Both sides are your best."

The time maker fluttered its eyelids. "I knew that. I was just fishing for validation."

"As well you should, master. You should troll for it with *mammoth* nets, which, even when filled to capacity with commendations, would not fully contain sufficient praise."

"As much as it pains me to cut short this well-deserved adulation session, I did form you for greater purposes, my little friend."

"There can be no purpose greater than the unending praise of you, magical master."

The time maker scowled, then abruptly and viciously pounded the suspended head against the deck twice. The poor appendage, or whatever, was oozing blood, and it clearly had a depressed skull fracture where it struck the metal.

Still, rallying, the wounded head mumbled out of one side of its mouth, "Thank you, mafter. I dewerved worfe."

The time maker shook the head like a rattle, and it was fully healed.

"Now let us please remain on topic, shall we?" it asked seriously.

"Your call," the headlette replied thoughtfully.

"How am I to proceed? That is the question. I find myself temporarily at a numerical disadvantage to the eerie thieves that pursue me."

"Eerie indeed," agreed the puppet.

"Until I can reassemble a proper armada, I must admit—though only to you, my stout companion—that I'm loath to confront the pretenders who seek to end me."

"They did wallop your predecessor's butt and how."

On hearing that, the time maker pounded the appendage against the far wall, multiply and remorselessly.

"A little *respect* for the dead, especially one of such illustrious standing."

"Mawe bab."

The time maker wagged a thin finger at the bleeding

body part. "This is the final time I let you off the hook, little fishy."

It shook the poor thing much harder than it needed to, but still, the segment healed nicely.

"Thank you," it remarked cheerily.

"Do not mention it. Now, as to my dilemma. I can hide for a very long time. That is certainly one option. They'll never find me. Even if I was a third as intelligent as I am, they're fully incapable of rooting me out."

"Even a *quarter*, says I."

"Alternately, I could seek them out and deal them the inglorious ending they so richly deserve."

"*Inglorious* is too good for them, says I."

"Then there is always the wait-and-see approach. I could bide my time and await them to commit some inexcusably idiotic mistake." It raised its bony finger. "Only *then* would I grant them the grace of removing their bungling selves from reality."

"No, you are *too* kind, *too* forgiving. They do not deserve your contemplated level of mercy, says I."

The time maker regarded warmly the abomination it conversed with before continuing. "Which of these paths does destiny *demand* I follow? Clearly I am chosen to rule widely and eternally. In fact," it giggled to itself, somewhat embarrassed, "I have little doubt that any election I make will lead quickly and unerringly toward my ascendance. But," it began pacing, "surely there must be, or *might* be, a superior choice, a better course to set?"

"All roads are predicted to lead to your *glorious* glory, says I."

"I rarely bother to note or lower myself to review any of the time energy that I have assimilated. But I recollect a line from some filthy, wretched planet, or whatever, that I incorporated. The author, nearly as gifted as I, it would seem, said with certainty that *discretion* is the better path to glory."

"Uh," grunted the extension, "are you sure? I seem to remember it as being the better *part* of *valor*."

The time maker stopped pacing. It turned its back on the little dissenter, then rotated quickly to ask it, "Do you know what the difference between you and me is?"

"A body to carry a head?" it responded earnestly.

"No. I can do this."

A detailed, blow-by-blow telling of the violence, the insane wrath, the bestiality the time maker employed to pound, stomp, and bite injury into the unfortunate responder was ... well, it was excessive. The specifics are best left unreported in the interest of the reader's peace of mind and the future quality of their sleep. Suffice it to say it was over-the-top in its cruelty. Really, it was gross.

"There," the time maker addressed to the air. "Blessed silence. The absence of discord and disagreement. How sweet the state of tranquility is to experience."

It scraped the majority of the blood and gore off of its body, then raised its head, nobly. "Now, off to direct my crew of incompetents how they can actually have purpose in service of one such as I. We will dally a bit longer here, undetectable, until I deem that the time of my righteous wrath needs to be felt by the eerie thieves."

And so, Time Maker-bob decided. It would keep the last clan ship near the center of one of the ancient globular clusters that orbited the Milky Way's central bulge.

Oops ...

TWENTY-TWO

Sapale had always been a high-spirited individual. That quality was kind of normal for Kaljaxian females. Passionate, impulsive, and strong-willed. But, in spite of those baseline personal qualities, she was in a much darker, more incendiary mood presently. After losing Jon to a closing portal, she'd been nothing short of hell-on-wheels. It was a good thing that the only others sentenced to travel with her were the ship's computers and the four rescued necumplacks. The AIs were used to her lability and were more than willing to ignore her unless she specifically sought them out. The alien mucous footballs were at the other extreme of not being too bothered by Sapale. They were only recently captives of cruel and capricious masters who abused them mercilessly. Sapale at her grimmest was veritably Mother Teresa compared to those reprobates on their best of days.

In one long folding of space, *Blessing* had traveled from Plesmus', the planet where the portal was hidden, to the outskirts of the Sombrero Galaxy. That was some thirty-one million light years in the blink of an eye. Thank goodness the trip was quick. Any delay would only have accentuated Sapale's already volcanic mood.

"Al," she began sternly, "I'm going to ask you once. I want a no-bullshit response. I'm totally serious here. I know this is the galaxy Jon's in. The spectral readings and gravimetrics are absolutely correct. So can either of you detect any signs of Jon or Plesmus?"

"No, neither of us can," Al replied quickly. "That said, this is a large galaxy. It might be that we could identify one of them if we chanced to be close to them. I know for a fact that if we're within a few light years of Jon, I can pick up his built-in transponder."

"Yeah," she growled, "but this piece-of-shit galaxy's almost fifty *thousand* light years across. Do you know how long it'll take to find him if we cut the search area up into one-cubic-light-year divisions?"

"Yes, I do. If we spent one second in each subdivision, which should be sufficient, it would take four hundred billion seconds. That represents one point seven million days. Roughly, we're looking at thirteen thousand y—"

"Stow it, ya big tin can. I spoke rhetorically. A *long* time, *that's* how long."

"*We're* immortal. *You're* immortal. *Jon's* immortal. We got time," Al observed gleefully. "Speaking for the missus, we're all in."

"As I *specifically* said no bullshit, now I'm going to hurt you."

"Form One, please don't act rashly," *Blessing* pleaded. "My husband was overly flippant, yes. But please know we're *as* concerned and anxious to secure your brood-mate's return as you are."

"I'm not delaying the pounding of his CPUs to dust

because of that," she snarled. "I just don't have the time. But, Al."

"Yes, Captain," he responded timidly.

"Someday soon, I *will*. Be afraid."

"I believe you, Captain. My day of reckoning is coming. I understand."

"Now, will one of you start prodding the necumplacks? I can't deal with the slimy little Bambis right now. Have them start scanning—or whatever—for Plesmus."

"We're on it, Captain," Al replied dutifully. "Our communication with them is most satisfactory. The moment we have anything to report, you will be alerted. You can count on us."

"In the meantime, please place a holo of the Sombrero Galaxy here." She sliced a circle about two meters wide in front of her.

The projection instantly danced before her. Sapale leaned back in her chair and studied the image. Jon was somewhere in there. Where would a highly advanced civilization be located? There had to be some clue. She just couldn't see one. Where was the other end of the phase transportation portal? Oh, well. It was going to take exactly as long as it was going to take. She was never, ever, going to give up. She would find her man.

"Al," she announced after a spell, "take us along the galaxy's longest axis, through the center but missing the central singularity. Ah, it has one, right?"

"Most definitely. A big one. Would you like the spec—"

"No interest whatsoever," she cut him off harshly. "The fly boy's the astronaut, not me. I'm not a science girl. I'm looking for Jon, not a guided tour."

"Got it. No guided tour, no local color. Excuse me, I think I have a short in my main compiler," Al responded in a rush.

"Damn fool doesn't have a compiler. There haven't been any since ... well, since about *now* in the time line," she mumbled impatiently to herself. "Let it go, Sapale. Focus, don't strike out."

"That's an excellent path to establish your movement on," observed an incautious Al.

"Did you know I was an expert at computer repair?" she asked, apropos of seemingly nothing.

"I ... I did not. Thanks for—"

"So after I rip you to indistinct little pieces, I'm going to assemble you again *just* so I can do it all over again."

Al displayed good restraint. He kept quiet.

After a bit, she was inspecting the galaxy holo again. To her eyes, it sure looked like a spiral galaxy. Maybe a bit tightly compacted, with a bigger than average central bulge, but it was just a galaxy. Space was full of the fool things. The galaxy was brighter than most. Why, she wondered, was that?

"Al, why's the galaxy appear to be so bright and hazy?"

"You're referring to the region around the central bulge?" he asked.

"I suppose so."

"There's more dust present there than in most galaxies of similar size and configuration. It's present in what are called *lanes*. Think three-dimensional rings around Saturn."

"Did I mention my complete ... Wait. Why does M104 have more central dust than most galaxies?"

"Now there's an *interesting* topic. Many schools of

thought exist, across many planets, as to why that might be the case. I—"

"Al, please don't make me kill you now. I might still need you," she snapped in frustration.

"Likely the dust was expelled from the galaxy, but gravitationally captured back *or* it's a smoothing out of lingering dust from an old galactic collision."

"Is the dust, like, standard dust?"

"What's *standard* dust?" he asked peevishly.

"I don't know, but I know you know. Stop screwing with me. It is *not* appreciated."

"Well, dust can be micro-particles, like silicates, carbon, ice, or iron compound. Compositions vary widely. The halo of M104 is made of those constituents."

"Why is it so bright?"

"Dust can absorb, reflect, or diffract light. Clearly M104's dust appears bright because it allows more to pass than a dark cloud would."

She puzzled silently a moment. "What light is the gas reflecting? The stars of the galaxy?"

"Pres—" Al stopped mid-sentence.

It immediately struck Sapale then, in a ridiculously long time, she'd never heard the supercomputer balk.

"I was about to say yes, obviously," Al resumed quickly. "But there *is* an awful lot of light radiation, isn't there? The stars themselves would not be bright enough themselves, most likely. Perhaps there is a galactic jet generating the luminosity. Hmm. But none is visible. It seems unlikely that any dust mixture would be dense enough to stop a blazing jet in both directions."

"There is no way dust could obscure a galactic jet," confirmed *Blessing*.

"People, where's the brightness coming from? Wait, is the brightness uniform?"

"We've checked. In the visual spectrum, it is more-or-less uniform."

"But?" Sapale pressed.

"In the microwave, x-ray, and gamma ray regions, it is highly asymmetric."

"How can that b ... Hang on. I don't care why that is," she corrected herself. "What I do want to know is if the source of the energy is natural or artificial."

"We are uncertain, Form One," responded *Blessing*.

"Then figure it out and do it quickly," Sapale hissed back.

"We've considered many possibilities," Al said sheepishly. "We have several models that work well in predicting the origins of the observed data. However, all of those constructs require for there to be a very hard-to-imagine pattern of energy production."

"Al, does Sapale want to hear you ramble on like that?" Sapale asked bitingly.

"Likely not," he responded.

"Form One, let me try and explain. There are no known natural sources of such a pattern. There are also no *conventional* artificial methods to produce the observed pattern of radiant dust."

"I want a list of *unconventional* possibilities, then," Sapale responded harshly.

"That's the issue, Captain," replied Al. "We are not able to infer an unknown source. Be reasonable."

"Why? I'm *not* in a reasonable mood. My mate was ripped from me by some alien jerkwads. I want Jon back, soon and alive. Now impress me or get ready to feel my boot up your butts." She was absolutely serious and the AIs knew she was.

Four holos appeared in the air in front of Sapale.

Al spoke professorially. "These are representations of the dust halo of M104 in each of the four previously mentioned electromagnetic regions. As you can see, the asymmetries in the non-visible regions all look similar. Their shapes suggest some force, unknown for the present, is passing through the galaxy in one of the three vectors now displayed as green arrows in your holo."

The indicators appeared. They showed lines-of-force directed along vastly different paths.

"So it's possible some energy is being projected along one of these arrows?" Sapale confirmed.

"Yes."

"Which model is the preferred one?" she asked while she studied the holos.

"None is," Al replied.

She reached into one holo. "Why is this vector so much shorter than the other two?"

"We cannot say. These are just the three vectors that could account for the various electromagnetic manifestations. We have had to make assumptions as to the amount of energy being passed along each particular vector. The *nature* of the energy that is subsequently altered into the four spectral ranges is not specified, since it is not known."

Sapale massaged the short vector with a finger. "Is this one the most energetic, because it's the shortest?"

"Not necessarily," he replied, "but that *is* a logical assumption to make."

"How long is this in real space?" she asked.

"Eighty hundred parsecs, more or less."

"Then we start looking for Jon along this line. If we scan for one second per light year, like you mentioned earlier, it'll only take us 2400 seconds. That's less than an hour."

"Forty minutes, more or less," Al confirmed.

"Al?" she asked sweetly.

"Yes, Captain?"

"Why are we still dead in space and not scanning this path?"

She felt slight nausea.

"That's better," she said wryly, as she grinned.

TWENTY-THREE

I was getting pretty tired of hanging around alone, all by myself. That of course had something to do with where I was hanging around, alone, all by myself. After the Four Dwarf Brains grew tired of waiting for Beauty Itself to return, they split. Before they departed, they placed me upside down in the corner of the room. They bound me there with some force I couldn't analyze, but, I have to say, it was a good force. Yeah, it held me tighter than a swaddled baby in its mommy's arms.

Then the dipshits turned off the lights. I was in the dark more than I usually was. My external lights were turned on, but they weren't getting past whatever held me either. What undesirables these fart-breaths were. The last one to dematerialize, Pleasant Brilliance, remarked in a snide tone that they'd return only when Beauty Itself did. I shouted back to him, inquiring what profession his mother had worked in shortly before the time of his birth. I also asked what if BI never came back. The piss stain responded to neither of my legit queries. Such a squat monkey.

I mean, as an android, hanging in the dark for an extended period isn't so bad. There was no blood to rush to my head, I didn't need to take a leak, and I had endless stores of entertainment options in my noggin. It was more the very thought that they would treat an honored guest so poorly. Were the tables turned, I'd have served tea and cucumber sandwiches, and made light but stimulating conversation until the missing link returned. But then *I* am a civilized individual. Clearly not all are so blessed.

I tried lasering the force that held me. Nothing. I expanded a membrane, trying to push it off. Nada. Extending my probe fibers did nothing. I couldn't fix them onto anything in order to understand or manipulate it. I almost fell to asking the energy to release me, *pretty please.* Who knew, maybe it was a polite force?

Say, here's a question. Have you ever been imprisoned by strange forces and stranger aliens with a Plesmus stuck to your boot?

Me either. I do not recommend it. Guess who whines endlessly and will absofuckinglutely not shut up when asked to? Her name doesn't *rhyme* with jerk, but she sure can *act* like one.

"Jon, you have to get me out of here," she ninnied. "I hate dark, cramped spaces."

"You glued yourself to my boot. There it's dark, cramped, and smelly by definition."

"That's beside the point. I must be free. I can't breathe."

"Live free or die? What, are you *New Hampshire* now?"

"I don't know what that is, but I doubt it. Seriously, get us out of here."

"Seriously, haven't you seen me try every trick I know? Do you think I like my current status?"

"Well, being friends with Beauty Itself, I can only assume you tolerate this torment because you know she'll make it right."

"I'm not that twit-sticker's friend. You know that."

"What? Were you *lying* to those extremely powerful time lords?"

"Of course I was. It's called a *bluff*, by the way, not a *lie*, when your life's on the line."

"You lied to those extremely powerful time lords?"

"Me? No. Of course not. Why do you ask?"

"You just said—"

"Hey, shut it. You mentioned something just now. Why did you refer to them as time lords? Do they know Doctor Who and come from Gallifrey?"

"Why do you speak *half*wit and *half* in tongues all the time?"

"Never you mind. Why are they time lords?"

"Jon, do not tell me you don't know who those immortals are."

"Okay, I won't, but it is the present case."

"Jon ... I ... I don't even know where to begin."

"I never thought I'd ever say this, but just keep on talking."

"Those five were Praxequat."

"Well I'm damn happy for them, then. Bet their parents are so proud of them too. Ples, what the hell's a Kumquat?"

"*Praxequat*. You heard me. Don't kid around. This is serious, perilously so."

"*Ah*, now you've gone and done it. I'm afraid. Thanks a lot for nuthin."

"Jon—"

"Wait. How come I can hear you? We're encased in some weird energy. I can't probe it or breach it."

"Well, for one thing, I'm talking brain-to-whatever-passes-for-one on your side. For another, we're bound by *time*. I do pretty well with time, it turns out."

"Bound by time? Hey. There's a joke in there somewhere. I can just feel it."

"Then unfeel it. Jon, you're impossible."

"If this is time energy, can't you just ... I don't know, zap it or something?"

"You don't know. That much is painfully obvious. Jon, the Praxequat don't manipulate time like I do. They don't gnaw around the edges. They are *one* with time."

"Bully for them. Please explain this like I'm a kid."

"A *kid* I could explain this to. You, not so much."

"Ples, you know BI's coming back. If you talk forever, she'll beat you back."

"BI? Jon, don't mock these guys. You may not be inclined to kiss their asses, but don't bait them."

"I actually *am* in a position to kiss their backsides. I'm upside down." I made a smooching sound. It was sweet.

"Stop that this *instant*," she bellowed.

"Okay. I'll behave. Who are the Praxequat?"

"Well, for one thing, I never believed they even existed."

"You didn't believe in Praxequat? Wow. Such bold sacrilege."

"I'm not going to speak if you can't be serious."

"Promise?"

"*As* I was saying," she began with determination, "the Praxequat are not to be toyed with. Their power is a thing of legend. Jon, I've never even *met* anyone who's *met* one."

"You are stuck to a boot."

I felt a distinctly electric shock to my ankle. Funny, it was right below where what's-her-name was attached.

"Okay, back to why you don't break their hold on us."

"I doubt I can."

"You doubt? You mean you haven't even tried? That's so bogus."

"Of course I haven't tried. That'd be ludicrous. I know you're not clever, but aren't you at least paying attention?"

"Huh? Sorry. I was thinking of something. It was real pretty. Lots of bright colors too."

"They don't know you have me attached to your person."

"They don't?"

"No, Jon, they don't. If they did, they'd have separated us. Most likely, they'd have discarded you out of hand by now."

"Oh, they would, would they? On account of what?"

"Jon, please. I'm a time being, much like them. You, you're energy-impoverished protoplasm waiting for entropy to do you in."

"If you're done with the Pile-on-Jon-a-thon, could we get back to why you can't get us out of here?"

"Their binding loops are well-crafted and highly energetic. That said, I might defeat them. But if I tried and was unable to accomplish the feat, they'd know the binding was tampered with. They'd know a time agent was in their presence."

"In their presence? Jeez, you sound like a B-Sci-Fi script. Get over yourself. They kind of got a clue when you prevented them from zapping me a while ago."

"You are *so* simple," she wheezed. "They think it was a parlor trick by your friend Beauty Itself."

"Not my friend."

"So I must remain cloaked for now. There might come a time when my ability to strike them from hiding will turn the tide."

"Or we could avoid that moment *entirely* by you freeing us and then us vamoosing."

"It's my call and I've made it. A non-time being such as yourself cannot understand."

"Does *Plesmus* mean *condescending little shit* in your native language?"

"No. It means Plesmus."

"Do me a favor and double check when we get out of here."

"I think the chances of that are, as you've said, somewhere between slender and none."

Slender and none? She's such a tool. But, I, always the bigger soul, let her faux pas go. *Aliens*. Can't live with 'em and can't live with 'em.

I guess the endless banter served some purpose. I felt a presence in the room just before the lights went back on. There, radiating light, but not beauty itself, was Beauty Itself. She had her appendages crossed and what had to be a scowl on her humanoid face.

"What is this I hear about us being lovers?"

Did *not* see that one coming.

"Say, I'm a *married* man. Please be respectful of that divine institution."

"You are soon to be a *buried* man if you don't end the disrespect. I was contacted by Pleasant Brilliance. He asked how long we'd been intimate. He had considerable fun at my expense. Little man, *no one* has fun at my expense."

"Or anywhere near you, I'd wager."

She assumed a look of hateful mayhem on her face. Note to self: Maybe I was pushing the snark a *tad*. Would it hurt me to be cordial?

"Look, Beauty, I'm sorry. I've just been hanging here so long, I'm finding it hard to be civil."

"I do not require civilility from an evolutionary experiment gone wrong like you. I require that you worship me in the brief time you have left alive."

Ah, homie don't worship no bitches. Adios cordiality. You are dis-missed.

"*Jinx!* You know, I was just about to say the same thing to you. What *are* the chances of that happening twice?"

She glowered at me. Nice. I love it when my toxic abilities are reaffirmed. I'd hate to lose *those* with the passing of time.

"I find it absurd that you, bound and hung to suffer as you are, would be so foolish as to pretend to lord yourself over me."

"This?" I said, wiggling as much as I could, "I *let* you do this to me. Where *I* come from, this type of thing is a prelude to reproductive interactions. I was lonely, so I let you priphelfect me."

"In spite of understanding all tongues, I do not know this term priphelfect. What is it?"

"This form of sexual foreplay, of course. You are *priphelfecting* me as we speak. I'm beginning to think Pheasant Brilliance was not too far off the mark regarding your intentions toward me."

You know what's not clever? Taunting someone powerful when hanging upside down. Yeah. She lashed out. Some invisible force whammed into me and sent me swinging like a pendulum hit with a gigantic bat.

As my chaotic gyrations extinguished, she lectured,

"Next time you anger me, I will do worse, petty bug. Do you believe me?"

"I believe *you* believe *you*," I sort of groaned. "I admire confidence in a woman. Now, if you were only a woman, we'd be outstanding."

Why was I pounding on, not just pushing, this queen dweeb's buttons? I was holding a losing hand. My philosophy in that situation is to fold. As folding at *life* ain't gonna happen, the next best strategy is to bluff. When I bluff, I do so *hard*.

BI fell for my gambit. Of course, I also fell—on my head. She released me and gravity did what it's supposed to do.

"Get up," she howled. "I will look into your eyes as I cast you into no-time."

I held up a finger. It was admittedly a wavering, unsteady finger, but it was all I had at the time. "You know, master fool, you tried that before. You failed at that task *as* badly as you have failed at the application of tasteful makeup. Be advised. If you try again, *I* will no-time *you*."

My ankle zapped. I think Plesmus was less certain about the prospects of her no-timing one of these Praxequat zit-poppers than I was.

BI veritably boiled before my eyes. My plan was working; well, the plan of pissing her off something royal. I actually had no Phase Two to *complement* Phase One, and that, I'll admit, was a crying shame.

"I told you I want to look into the eyes of those I doom. I expect that I will take such pleasure in ending you, that I should pay you or something. I owe you that much of a debt."

"*Done*," I thundered.

That got a surprised reaction out of the waste-of-space. "What is done, irrelevant blight?"

"Your fate is *sealed*, a bargain has been *struck*."

"Wh ... a *bargain*? What are you babbling about?"

I drew up my frame, angled my body self-contentedly, and gave her my best charming grin. It's pretty damn charming, if I do say so myself. "I cite to you the Belliarchan Proclamations of Dex-Fender 4. Further, the Contractual Inspiritor of Ganymede comes to mind. I think its assertions apply *directly* to our contract."

Her face settled back into one of contemptible rage. Seriously, it was her go-to expression and it was unbecoming times infinity. Her friends needed to stage an intervention.

"I tire of your posturing and your insanity."

She drew back an appendage.

Plesmus zapped me particularly hard.

"Try that at your *peril*, you wilted rose."

Gotcha. She faltered.

"When it is known widely that you tried to unilaterally void a *Belliarchan* contract, just before I no-timed you, your legacy will be that of a dead *reptile* swollen in the river by the blazing sun." I turned a cold shoulder toward her. If this ploy didn't work, well, I was somewhere between wet toast and dead.

"I have—"

"And I will tell Pheasant Boy and Stunted Wonder, maybe even R-Squared—but him I'm not sure because I dislike him so—that you voided an inviolable bond. They will know that you, Princess Cupcake, in the end, welshed."

She tossed her appendages overhead. "What? I concede. What are you orally farting about?"

"You said you *owed* me. I provided a commodity. *Mirth.* You acknowledged, freely and of your own accord, that you therein incurred a *debt.* I will not release you from the contract unless my obligation is satisfied."

"I was joking when I said that. Come on. I was mocking you, with the intention of *belittling* you."

I crossed my arms. "And do not think those factors will be omitted from my considerations."

"I know there is no such thing as the Belliarchan Proclamations of Dex-Fender 4 or the Contractual Inspiritor of Ganymede. You fabricated those."

"Oh yeah?"

"Yeah."

"Prove it," I responded coyly.

"Prove what? That your bullshit is prevarication? That you are *mental*?"

"Those'll do for a start. But," I wagged a judging digit at her, "in the meantime, neither of us no-times the other. We are bound. So be it. It is written. I have spoken."

"You are *such* a lunatic. I do believe you have a split personality and *both* of them are insane."

"*But* I'm a lunatic *you* entered into a contract with."

"I did—"

The other four stooges chose that pregnant moment to materialize.

"We knew you were back," began Pheasant Boy. He turned to the others and gave them the kind of smirk you just love to slap off someone's stupid face. "We had hoped to give you two some *alone*-time."

Two of the others snickered.

"But there was such a disturbance, we came in case medical aid was required by either of you."

Everyone snickered. Hey, even I did. That was spot on.

BI appeared distinctly displeased. "I have spent several eternities with you four. Never have I loathed you so much, with such dark images dancing in my head."

"We were—" Stunning Wonder began to say.

"It is unwise to anger me to the extent you have. *Very* unwise."

They were duly contrite. BI must've been the alpha or something. She had them under her thumb, that was for sure.

"Now, now," Excessive Splendor tut-tutted, "calm, calm. *Everyone* be calm."

"What was the nature of the disturbance we perceived?" R-Squared asked paternally. He was trying to redirect the conversation to a serious, non-lethal one, I suspected.

BI studied him, filtering his words for hidden malice, his movements for subtle irreverences. Finally, she spoke, albeit sternly. "This genetic miscalculation riled me beyond my limits."

I could sense the other four furtively withdraw, or at least cringe.

"Then, when I said his impetuosity was so excessive that I should thank him, he went off on some tangent about proclamations and inspiritor."

"What is an *inspiritor*, my dear?" braved SW.

She threw up her appendages. "*I* certainly have no idea. He's deranged and ranting. That's my best guess."

"Ah, actually, you said, and I replay, *I will take such pleasure in ending you that I should pay you or something. I owe you that much of a debt*," I sent through my external speakers, opting for the untactful, and likely the unwise.

Everyone, me included, for some reason turned our collective heads to R-Squared. Maybe his deep voice and stick-up-the-butt manner of speaking suggested him to be a fair arbiter.

"Well," he tittered cautiously, "*is* that what you said, what the vermin just emitted?"

"Specifically, yes. Obviously," she amended in a huff.

"And in so doing, she invoked the Belliarchan *Proclamations* of Dex-Fender 4," I protested in an annoying whine, pointing at BI accusingly.

"What are the Belliarchan *Proclamations* of Dex-Fender for *for*?" asked SW with less certainty than she had when she asked moments earlier.

"No," I thundered like a loon, "*Four* for, as in one, two, three, *four*, *for*."

SW furrowed her brow. "That makes matters *less* clear, I believe, than *more* clear."

"Well, that's exactly the *point* now, isn't it, really?" I replied boldly, as fools are wont to do.

SW nodded toward me and spoke to BI. "Is your friend 'normal'?" She made air-quotations with her fingers.

"*He*-is-*not*-my-*friend*," BI said with convincing menace. "The next foul individual who repeats that mockery of reality will wish, very briefly, that they hadn't. This is my promise."

"Do you see my intent here," I yelped, casting upon BI such a look. "You can see for yourself and no others how easily, nay, *capriciously*, this ... this ... *so-called friend* enters into verbal contracts? Hmm?"

After a tense, silent pause, Papa R-Squared made an effort to ease the throttle back a notch. "I call it *commitment*. Yes, that's what it is. Beauty Itself is passionate and *fully* committed to what she's committed to."

Wow, dude was more rodent-brained than I first suspected, and I'd suspected a whole lotta rodent-brain going on the first time he opened his pie hole. (I am assuming these jerks ate pie. If they didn't, I judge them so much more harshly). It's weird how you sometimes give mental breaks to those who least deserve them, isn't it? Plus, he sounded like the assistant manager at the Taco Bell I worked in for three days between my junior and senior years of high school.

"I suggest we all relax, take some refreshments, and sort through this unpleasantness in a collegial manner," R-Squared continued. By the way, he was disqualified as anyone sounding like Brandon "The Pussy" Walldenthorp, my assistant manager. The Pussy wouldn't use the word *collegial* because he spoke English 1.0 at best.

"*Outstanding,* I'm parched," I called out jocularly (another no-go word for The Pussy).

"You are not included in that invitation," snapped R-Squared.

Palm to chest, I said in a wounded tone, "I *am* a guest here, sir."

"No, you're an *infestation,*" snarled BI.

"And infestations do not *get* refreshments," R-Square greed with a jackass grin. I was back to likening him to The Pussy again. Weird, eh?

"Shall we hang him by his feet again?" Pheasant Boy asked tepidly.

"Why bother? He won't exist much longer," BI growled while glaring hot laser beams at me.

"As you wish. He is your—" R-Squared

uncharacteristically STFU before he stepped in it but good. I was bummed. I'd have bought front-row seat to watch his ass fry.

I stood. They reclined on chaise lounges that looked too much like horizontal urinals for me to be tempted to ask them if I could use one too.

"So, Beauty Itself, shortly before you left us, we established it was you who ... how shall I express it? You *presented* him to the rest of us. Is that not correct?" R-Squared asked sheepishly.

BI, poor baby, looked flustered. I hoped that negative emotion had nothing to do with me. She was my favorite Praxequat by a factor of a hundred. Of course, one hundred times zero is still zero. But, hey, it's the *thought* that counts.

"I guess *technically*, yes. I only did so because the guards had recently captured him and were uncertain what to do with him. They dragged him before me, and I dragged him before you."

"Where is he from?" asked SW.

BI shrugged. "I haven't the faintest notion. Not here, that's for certain."

"How did he get here? Why wasn't his approach to this planet detected and reported to us?" Radiant Resplendence posed to BI.

"Again, I have no idea. The guards said he might have come here via Opo-Portal Transmere."

"Opo-Portal *Transmere*?" R-Squared choked out. "That's not been used for ... for I don't know how long." He squished up his already ugly mug. "Is it even still functional?"

"Apparently so," BI replied with zero interest. "The last thing the guard said before I shooed it away was that they'd chased the prisoner to Opo-Portal *Transmere.* It was fairly certain a second intruder escaped through before they could activate the closure mechanism."

"Who left the damn thing open?" Excessive Splendor challenged harshly.

BI rolled her eyes. "Who knows? The last time we used the passageway to obtain one of those mucous-y entertainment balls was thousands of years ago. Maybe *tens* of thousands of years ago."

ES grumbled in reply, nonetheless.

"Why is it here?" SW asked BI.

"How should I know? If you're curious, ask it." She shoved an appendage in my direction.

SW considered me like I was a turd inching up to crawl into her ice cream sundae.

"Does it speak?" SW asked the room.

"To an excess," huffed BI. "Didn't you hear it ask for tea?"

"I thought that might have been some type of instinctive reflex," SW said stupidly.

"And, for the record, tea sounds *darn* good to me right about now," I chimed in.

"One more word out of you and I'll—"

"You'll what? Violate our agreement, our deal, our understanding, our very *pact*?"

"Yes, this contract you two have entered in on," asked R-Squared, "what is the nature of it?"

"There is no *contract*. The being's *insane*. Don't ask *me*," BI hissed angrily.

"Whom should I ask?" R-Squared queried. Dude set me up perfecto mundo.

"Ask me, Friend Radium," I announced boldly.

"No," he responded, a tad confused. "I asked. Who is this Radium fellow?"

"He's *mocking* you, you old fool," charged BI.

"Are you certain? I rather think mockery requires a modicum of intelligence." He wagged a judgmental digit my way. "This poor beast could never possess such a quality."

"Hang on, *Radium*—noting, if you will, the absence of the adjective *friend* now—are you going to ask me why I'm here or are you going to insult me? In actuality, I do not care which it's to be, but I'd prefer knowing just the same."

"My goodness, you're right, Beauty Itself. This creature is mind-deficient."

"*See*," she exclaimed loudly. "See what I've been saying? It's as if some cruel scientist poured intelligence-dissolver in one of its ears and let it drain out the other."

"Remarkable that it has survived this long, given its paucity of brain function," observed R-Squared.

"Y'all clearly never met Gloria, my first wife," I scoffed back.

"What would your *mate* possibly bring to bear on *your* lack of survivability?" pressed Pheasant Boy.

"She lived to the ripe old age of eighty-eight."

"Eighty-eight?" parroted BI dumbly.

"Died in her sleep of natural causes." I waited a three-count. "Yeah, her latest husband smothered her with a pillow."

"How disgusting," exclaimed ES. "And that's hardly a *natural* demise. What's natural about having someone suffocate you?"

"You *clearly* never met Gloria," I informed her.

"How ... how is this revolting digression imaginably related to our contention that you are genetically so unlikely to have survived this long?" stammered R-Squared.

"Are you napping during our discussion?" I queried incredulously.

"No. I do not nap."

"Then allow me to draw you a road map, chump. You, squaredom itself, said, *Remarkable that it has survived this long, given its paucity of brain function.* I was simply offering you an example of one *less* gifted than I who lived longer than common sense would have predicted." I held out my arms as if to say *there you are.*

"May I kill it now?" asked three of the four non-BI pukes present.

"*No.* None of you may. When this pathetic morsel of rotten space-wasting dies, it will be at my hand. It is all I currently live to experience."

I patted my palm over my ovalled lips, suggesting some element of boredom.

"*What*, you annoying fleck?" thundered BI.

"If you knew how often I've heard that out of some self-deluded uber-powerful bozo, you too would yawn, snowflake."

"I can think of something to rekindle your attention," she shouted as she sat up straight from her padded urinal.

"I doubt it. You take off your clothes and I predict everyone present will lose the entire contents of their intestines—or whatever—from both directions at once."

In rapid sequence, two things happened. Plesmus seared into my ankle. Such a worrywart. Also, BI picked up—and hurled with convincing resolve and accuracy—the nearest solid object to her throwing appendage. Lucky for me, it was the very soft-bodied R-Squared. If he were a vase or an ashtray, I might have been injured. He mostly gushed around my head and torso, bending me backwards to be certain, but leaving me free from blunt-trauma effects. I resolved to update him, when the festivities were over, that he needed to begin a program of regular physical exercise.

R-Squared's reaction was sort of the three-stage blossoming. First, he looked around, trying to divine what had just happened. Second, he rose from the deck slowly and displaying a lot of physical discomfort. Third, he inflated himself—literally—to about twice his previous size. He stepped over BI, glowered down at her, and spoke freely.

"That was inappropriate. You have offended me. I will never—"

Poor wank's blustering was interrupted by a sound. It was me giggling like a teenage girl. To make bad *worse*, the other dorks joined in. They were genuinely amused. I wondered if one of them might self-inflict a wound, given that they clearly never expressed joy.

R-Squared was clearly torn. He seemed to want to both strike out and fade away. My vote was for the fading. He forged a comical union of the two. Sad for him. Happy for the rest of us.

He slumped where he stood. "This is intolerable," he whimpered like a beaten, wet, and cold puppy.

Pheasant Boy rolled off his fainting-urinal, he so erupted in mirth. He kicked and punched the floor. I was impressed. He was enjoying himself. Bully for him. Knowing what I was going to spring on them, hell, he should enjoy himself while he could.

"Alright, you knuckleheads," I called out loudly. "We need to start acting like sensitive supporters of our overly sensitive brother, R-Squared. A bit more decorum would go a long way in restoring his self-worth. Remember," I pointed a finger skyward, "we all want that."

I don't know if it was my words or my actions that did the trick, but they all ceased-and-desisted right quick.

"I believe I will end this fool's existence—" BI began.

"But what of the contract he keeps whining about?" interrupted ES.

"Stop referring to a non-existent contract."

"Oh no you don't," I charged. "A deal's a deal's a deal."

"Yes," spoke up an embolden R-Squared. "I myself am familiar with the Belliarchan *Proclamations* of Dex-Fender-4." He gathered himself up further. "Just and prudent are the provisions of these inspiring words. Well, for mortals, I suppose."

"Radiant Resplendence," BI began in a chastising tone, "stop it. This insolent fleck concocted the entire farce."

"I recall learning of those sainted proclamations as a youth," protested R-Squared.

"You were *never* a youth," BI batted-back.

"I was too. When I was younger, I most definitely was."

You know what makes a con a real pleasure to perpetrate? A stooge. Yeah. It was a thing of beauty to see R-Squared pick up my end of the rope and pull for Team Ryan in this tug-of-war. What a maroon.

"If you are going to defend him, he will become *your* problem, no longer *mine*," seethed BI.

"What? I state *facts* and you claim false-vindication? That is *absurd*."

I needed to wrap this up. If one over-plays a con, there's a risk of it collapsing under its own weight.

I pointed harshly at SW, who'd been the most quiet up until then. "No. That is not *your* place to call for that."

All eyes turned quickly to her.

"What did you say to upset it?" BI pressed her.

"Nothing. I said nothing." SW pressed her appendages to her chest.

"Oh, you are a take-backer too, just like Sister BI," I accused.

"I said *nothing*," she protested genuinely.

"What did you *think* you heard, annoying fleck?" asked R-Squared.

"Oh, I don't *think* I *think* I heard her. I *know* I *think* I heard her. Plain as day, if you ask me."

"And what is it you *imagine* I said, troubled little one?" appealed SW.

"You tell them. I wasn't *my* idea. You spoke it. You own it."

"I ... I have *no* idea what the creature speaks of," she protested.

"Are you going to *swear* you did not just say, *Let's grant him what he wishes. What is the worst that can happen?*"

"Yes, I *swear*," she shot back. She turned to the others by way of appeal. "I swear I didn't say that."

My man! I saw it in his eyes before I heard it from his lips. The pompous, inflated baboon R-Squared swallowed the bait.

"Come to mention it ... er, little pest, what *is* it that you claim as a release for Beauty Itself from the contract you *hallucinate*," jerk flared his appendages in the air, "you have with her?"

"I told you not to speak out of turn," I howled at the utterly confused SW. *Nice.*

She could not speak, she was so flustered. *Nicer.*

"Well, scoundrel, what *will* it take?" BI raged. *Nicest.*

"I should think that is self-obvious," I responded in a wounded tone.

"If it were, I'd know what it is, now wouldn't I," she hissed in reply.

"I want you to allow me to pass through Opo-Portal Transmere. I ... I want to go home."

They shot each other stunned glances.

"That's it?" BI pressed. "You simply wish us to open the portal and allow you to pass through it?"

I do believe she was mentally leaping ahead, as planned. *Super-nicest.*

I stomped a foot. "No you don't," I accused bitterly.

"What? No I don't what?"

"You can't trick me."

"I ... I don't believe I *was* attempting to trick you." She turned to the others. "Was I?"

"*No,*" blustered R-Squared. What a Jerk-in-the-box. "Nothing could be *farther* from the truth."

"To assure you I am not attempting any scheme, what might I do to ease your concerns?" asked BI. She spoke with the sincerity of the walruses when they addressed the oysters in *The Walrus and the Carpenter*.

"*Duh.* After I *cross* the portal, you must *close* it." I tried to look like someone stupid trying to appear smug. Think Uncle Arthur in *Bewitched.*

BI couldn't restrain herself. She grinned before she immediately corrected herself and put on a serious face. "So our contract will be fulfilled and voided if I open Opo-Portal Transmere, allow you to exit through it, and then close it?" She made a circular-closing motion with her digits.

"I *knew* you wouldn't," I squealed. "I just knew you'd break the—"

"Peace be with you, little friend," BI oozed perfidiously. "If that is your desire, it shall be my greatest pleasure."

"Are you toying with my emotions?" I inquired suspiciously.

"*Never,*" she protested quasi-indignantly. "You may ask anyone." She gestured to the others. "I *never* toy with emotions."

"Never," concurred R-Squared. Yeah, who else?

"Fine. I accept your offer," I declared with bravado. "Let us go now to the passageway and allow me to find the comforts of home."

"There is no too-soon possible," she replied shiftily.

It took a few minutes for my captors to arrange the particulars. It turned out they weren't used to actually planning or doing *anything*. That was what minions were for, after all. But we were all six striding down the halls toward the exit quickly enough for none of them to have second thoughts. Never allow a mark the time to reflect on their decisions. It's poison to an otherwise crafty con.

"There," I said, pointing ahead. "I can smell the portal."

"Yes," R-Squared agreed quickly. "It's just ahead. You're almost home." What a smug tool.

As we approached the portal, it eased open silently.

Step 1 - Check.

"Okay," I said accusingly. "That's far enough."

"What?" protested BI.

"The rest of you characters have to stay right here." I pointed down.

"Do you harbor suspicion for us still?" queried a beguiling BI.

"I sure do, ma'am," I replied pugnaciously.

"Fine. We shall remain here. You may proceed alone." She basically shooed me forward.

I looked at her. I looked to the portal. I looked at her. I looked at the portal. Hesitantly, uncertainly, lurchingly, I stepped toward my promised freedom.

BI continued to shoo me playfully.

I passed back into the cavern on planet Plesmus'.

Step 2 - Check.

"Bye bye for now, little fleck," peeped BI. She waved an appendage.

The portal closed.

Step 3 - Check.

Now, I need to reinforce for your understanding a very critical issue. My mama didn't raise no idiots. You probably knew that, but I wanted to make sure. It's an important operative in my current narrative. You see, I'd set them up. I knew they were going to re-open the portal the instant it sealed. Then they'd seize me and no-time me with a clear conscience. You see, they figured they'd tricked me into fulfilling the ridiculous contract I'd claimed BI'd made. Then they could collect the stupid fool and punish me mercilessly. If there *was* a contract, I was a goner. If there *wasn't* a contract, I was a goner. Dead = dead.

I immediately splatted myself to the cave floor and covered myself with a full membrane.

Step 4 - Check.

If you'll recall, I once said that being in a full membrane doesn't make an object *invisible*. It's just not visually *there*. It's what you see out of the back of your head. But I was counting on a series of reasonable assumptions. If they fell into place, I was good. If one link in the chair split, so did I. Fighter-pilot simple, just the way I like it.

I knew, or was at least certain, the abscesses on the universe would have already opened the portal and sent minions through to snatch me. Likely the oversized muscle brains were tromping over me as I lay there. My first assumption was an easy one. The guards were stupid and wouldn't notice they were walking on top of nothing. The cave was dark and they were on unfamiliar footing.

My second assumption—more of a get-down-on-my-knees-and-pray pipe dream—was that the five praxequats would then pass to my side of the portal and not notice the nothingness on the ground. They might be lame and overly confident, but stupid they were not. How long did I need to give them to *not* find me? It had to dawn on them that they'd been duped. Knowing they had *might* make them rash enough to assume I had some oh-so-clever plan that didn't involve them walking over my back. Maybe I had a trans-portal myself waiting, and I'd jumped through? The two things I couldn't survive were them looking hard for me locally or them going all Rambo and no-timing the entire cave system. I was fairly certain my membrane would protect me if they did. Then again, these were the Praxequats. How did I know the limit of their power?

So I did the only logical thing open to me. In my head, I queued up my favorite Three Stooges skits and I settled in for a laughfest. Yes, after two billion years and too much tequila in my younger days, they still made me belly laugh. In fact, I watched the marathon twice. It always ended in *Men in Black*. That's the episode where the boys become doctors at a large hospital where they disrupt patients and staff alike. But I don't need to tell you that. Who doesn't know that one by heart?

Then—drum roll—came the moment of truth. One hour and fifteen minutes after biting the deck, I poked a micro-wide hole in my membrane and scanned the cave. Holy crap in a cup, it was clear. Not only that, but the portal was closed. I was this close to pulling off the best scam of my life. But over-caution is the laxative that ends the control you thought you had, so I only very gradually lowered my defenses, probing the entire time to see if a trap had been set.

After an hour, I was not just walking around freely. I was *dancing* a jig. There were no traces of the five praxe-twuats, their guards, or any bugs. I think they simply decided good riddance to bad garbage, took their mitts and bats, and went home to sulk.

Hah! Don't let the portal clip your asses on the way out, suckers. That was the last I was going to see of *those* effete asses. I was not going to miss them one little bit, because *they* were such assholissimos and *I* did not like them.

TWENTY-FOUR

Time Maker-bob lurked in a corner of his personal quarters. All body and time makers were afforded a private space, though they didn't need to sleep, make love, or be alone. It was simply the way the arrangements had always been. It spent little time in its quarters, not surprisingly. If it was there, with no clan member to frighten, intimidate, or no-time, what was the point? But, it chanced to be there that particular day, as the ship lay in hiding near the center of globular cluster M13, or the Hercules Globular Cluster. It orbited just outside the core of the Milky Way. As globular clusters go, astronomically speaking, M13 was run-of-the-mill typical. Metaphysically speaking, however ... not so much.

The time maker lurked, by the way, in the corner because of two factors. It loved to lurk. Lurking suggested to it lying-in-wait, as in predator and prey. Also, it preferred to have its back to a solid wall. Yes, it was paranoid. Hey, when you're evil to such a large extent, caution is well advised. Anyway, it was contemplating how glorious its victory would be when it finally held the ship thieves in its claws. It would crush the life out of each one of the defilers ever so slowly. It might even revive them a few times, just so it could enjoy repeating the event again and again. Eventually, when it was sated, the scum would be non-timed. There was no ...

It felt something. Odd, Time Maker-bob reflected. It was alone. No one could possibly enter. No one would conceivably *want* to enter its quarters. It risked ...

There, again. Something breathed on its shoulder. That was imposs ...

Time maker-bob leapt the entire length of its quarters, rotating one hundred and eighty degrees in the air as it did so. Once it landed, it crouched and scanned the room. There was no one ... no *thing* there. Could it be imagin ...

Something tapped it on the shoulder.

Time Maker-bob disappeared from time/space. It traversed the distance from where it was to where it had been originally. It then reentered normal space.

Nothing was present. "This is seven times past impossible," it whispered to itself.

Then, another tap on the shoulder. "Could you speak up? I can't hear you when you whisper like that."

As in a teenage horror film, the time maker turned ever-so-slowly to look in the vanishingly small space between its back and the wall.

Someone ... or something was there!

Time Maker-bob involuntarily leapt forward and up. It struck the ceiling with its fool head and landed in a skidding face plant in the center of the room.

The mysterious figure took a couple steps forward, clapping softly. "That's was as good as I've seen, but the Rigellian Federation judge knocked off an entire *point* for your landing. Pooh."

The time maker sprang to its feet and hissed at the intruder through bared teeth.

"Easy, friend," said the figure. He held out a hand to complement his words.

"Who are you to board my ship without permission or welcome?" menaced the time maker.

The fellow produced a mock-look of uncertainty and surprise. He pointed to his chest. "I am *me*. Is that not obvious?"

"Before you never were, I will know who you are and why you defile my ship."

The uninvited individual shot a glance at the floor by his humanoid foot. "I don't believe I've defiled anything, at least not yet."

"Your identity. I will *have it*," wailed the time maker with insane rage.

"You know, time maker, you're not really very good at this game." He paced back and forth, wagging a digit in the air. "I do believe your fundamental lack of any sense of humor or imagination whatsoever is hampering your participation. You see, for example, that when you threaten, *I will have it*, it, in this case being my identity, my natural response would be something along the lines of, *If you take my identity, what will I do without it?* You see? Before you respond, allow me to speculate that you do *not* see, but I never want it said I didn't want to help you." He bobbed his head and grinned. "I'm a helper-guy. Yup, that's me in a word. A helper-guy."

The time maker's face twisted in agony. "A helper-guy is *three* words, not *a* word."

"Not in my case, not in my opinion. I am such a helper-guy that it is one all-consuming word."

"I am done tolerating you. I *demand* you identify yourself and state the purpose of your intrusion."

"Never let it be said the Vesiculite were slow learners." Again he paced and wagged a digit. "Most say they are, and little you have ever done argues well to the contrary, but you, time maker, might be the exception to the firm rule."

"Who are the Ves ... Vestic ... Who are the race you speak of?" thundered an unhappy ship's captain.

"The Vesiculite. Look at my lips and repeat it slowly. Ves-ic-u-lite."

"I hear you. Vesiculite. Who are they?"

"*You* are, my dimwitted friend."

The time maker slashed his claws across his chest harshly enough to draw blood. "I am *clan.* I am not Vesiculte scum."

"The *Vesiculite* is what your *clan* called itself originally, long ago. You have forgotten the name, but it is still yours alone."

"I care *not* for names," it howled. "What is your name?"

"You are making this too easy. I must protest."

"*Name!*"

"Oh, very well. If it will allow us to move past square one. I am," he tapped his chest, then flared his hand upward dramatically, "your worst nightmare."

"Word games. You play word games while your life ebbs. *Your worst nightmare* could be your name or it could be your title, your descriptor. Which *is* it?"

"Which would you like it to be?" he replied ominously.

"My desires affect not your nature."

He nodded in approval. "There you are most correct." He stopped pacing and extended both arms toward the time maker. "As a token, a reward, I will award you one credit. Credits can be used to purchase wonderful prizes, such as information, fluids, or brief relief from horrific torment. I'll tell you upfront one cannot *have* enough credits in thisgame."

"Game? I play no games. What game do you speak of?"

He gestured widely. "This game, the one you find yourself in." He inclined his head and looked cross. "You are paying attention, aren't you. Failure to do so will cause you to forfeit credits. And one *cannot* have enough credits in this game. Do not make me repeat myself. That costs credit *also*."

"I know not your name. You toy with me, the time maker. Only never-have-been fools toy with the time maker. I will make you one with no-time, sorry excuse for a villain."

He tsk-tsked. "My, but there's a lot to unpack in that soliloquy, isn't there? First, I will freely admit to being a never-have-been fool. Second, if I were one with nonexistence, I would be something in nothing, making that *nothing* a *something*. Please mind your syntax. Third, and finally for now, I am *not* a sorry excuse for a villain. No. I am the *consummate* villain." He smiled so broadly, his face threatened to split open. "You have heard the term *to give the devil his due*, haven't you?"

"I have not. I tire of you."

With no further warning, the time maker lofted his spindly arms in the air and hurled them at the man of so, so many confusing words. By *hurled*, that was what it was. It literally allowed its arms to detach and rocket toward the fork-tongued rogue.

The disembodied appendages struck the figure, and a cloud of roiling light erupted over his body. The disruption was so bright, it totally obscured any vision of the intended victim. After a few seconds, the light began pulsing dimmer, until it was finally gone.

The unexplained guest, however, was not gone. He stood there chuckling softly to himself.

"That tickles. Please do it again," it taunted.

"No one can resist a no-timing of that magnitude. *No* one."

He flicked imaginary dust from his lapel. "Then I obviously am no one." He grinned. "Say, when you went to the Earth, before you no-timed it, did you find the time to read *The Odyssey*?"

A blank look was all the response the time maker offered.

"Homer? *The Odyssey*? It's a classic. Anyway, the hero, Odysseus, was confronted by a cyclops, Polyphemus, the son of Poseidon." He stopped to beg of the time maker, "Seriously, you've never heard any of this before?"

"No. How can you still be?"

He batted the query away with clear annoyance. "Anyway, Odysseus was ever so clever. He told the cyclops his name was No Man, *Nemo*."

A long, blank look was issued by the clan leader.

"Don't you get it? We just established *I* am no one. Right, just a second ago? Don't you see? It's funny. *He* was Nemo. *I* am Nemo. *That* is funny."

The expression the time maker wore suggested he did not agree.

"How *are* you?"

"Fine, thanks for asking."

"No, no, no, no, *no*. How is it that you still *are*? I no-timed you."

"No, to borrow your word, you did not. You *tried* to no-time me. Big diff, palsy. *Big* diff."

"I am the time maker. If I no-time something, it is no-timed."

He pointed with both hands at his face. "Do you know this look?"

"No."

"It is me officially being bored."

"And?"

"And it is the most dangerous look you will ever see. If you see it, it means I am bored. When bored, I am forced to *unbore* myself. I do so generally via cruelty, mayhem, and butchery. Do I make myself clear?"

"No, you make me bored. Leave now."

"I'm beginning to believe I made a mistake selecting you and your crew as my new playthings. You are as dull as a sphere and a hell of a lot less attractive than one. I will not leave. You will not leave. You are mine. I *own* you. Yes, you are a sorry lot. But please see it from my perspective. You are the only idiots so idiotic as to enter my domain in as long as frankly I can remember. Know this. While I do not *need* souls to torment, I *prefer* to have souls to torment."

"Leave now or die."

"That is *it*. I am taking your lone credit back for being so concrete and stupid. *I* am in charge now and forever, not you. I will not leave and I cannot die. We are, as many an older married couple comes to realize, very much stuck with one another. Get used to it, get over yourself, and get busy pleasing me."

The time maker trembled, it was so floridly irate. It

screeched to high heaven—pardon the pun. It pounded the floor, the walls, the ceiling, and itself. It drooled malice, shot visual daggers, and vibrated hatred. Then, and for quite likely the first time in its life, it fell reflective and seemed to consider carefully some point.

It turned back to the even more bored, and therefore dangerous, unnamed new lord. "You say you are our master now and forever?"

Furrowing one brow, he replied cautiously, "Yes. I am."

The time ship shook with tremendous force. The sparse appointments of the maker's quarters exploded like liberated billiard balls every which way. Then, as abruptly, all was still.

The time maker rose from the floor. It was devastated to see the demon guest standing perfectly poised and composed.

"Did I mention I was also your master in any *past* you might journey to?" he remarked casually.

"I have a question, unwanted presence."

"Yes, I assume you do. I am not prone to award replies, however. You may ask, but I may not answer."

"Do you know how long the average star in a globular cluster orbiting an average galaxy lives as a functioning unit?"

The devil was confused by the question. "I do not, precisely. I also ..."

The ship experienced a seizure so violent, it was incredible it held together. The chaos rose, and rose, and rose, until, at its crescendo, there was no up and no down. There was no life and no death, no facts and no speculations. All limits of awareness thinned out to a one-atom pancake of entropy.

Then the world slammed back together violently. Bloodied, shaken, and reluctantly, the time maker scraped itself off the deck and inspected its realm. It was alone.

"I know the average lifespan of the average star in the average globular cluster. It is half the time we just leapt forward to."

Against all odds, the time maker had made an insightful guess. He reasoned that since the beguiler was present where he was, and that the clan had never lingered in a globular cluster, the two facts were intertwined. Hence, possibly, in the distant future, after the globular cluster itself was no longer, Time Maker-bob gambled that the interloper would no longer linger. However, past performance was not necessarily indicative of future results.

"Vector maker, motion maker, machine maker, flee this location at maximal velocity," the time maker screamed on the bridge. It had just materialized there. "Any direction is the one I demand. Expend maximal time energy to achieve our escape."

And so the clan and its last time vessel bolted from hiding and directed themselves to parts unknown, but parts separate from any ones near a globular cluster, or where one had ever orbited a galaxy.

TWENTY-FIVE

"Captain," Al began formally, "we are nearing the vector you selected, the shortest of the three. Do you wish to begin at the beginning orat the terminus of the vector?"

"It's a short survey either way. Let's do this the right way. Begin at the beginning and move toward the terminus."

"You got it," he replied more casually. "Do you want a detailed report on an ongoing basis or should we only alert you if we find something noteworthy?"

"From you guys, whose lives are measured in picoseconds? Please, just report if you find something I would want to know about."

"Can do. We'll keep you posted."

Sapale settled back into the chair facing the view screen. Mentally, she was a wreck. Jon was missing in an ultra-hostile environment. She knew he was in M104, but it was a massive galaxy. The longer it took to find him, the greater the chances became of this ending poorly. And now she had to twiddle her thumbs waiting for possibly no new information. Sapale didn't do helpless well. But she was pretty much stuck hoping, more than doing, at that juncture.

And what was she going to do when she did find him? They were forced into an all-out retreat last time she was in that realm. Their weapons were either next-to-useless or flat-out useless. What new capability could she bring to the party? If she relied solely on what hadn't worked before, the chances of a better outcome were laughable. But what? She had some very destructive toys, but using them risked harming Jon. The passageways were large enough in places to allow her to bring *Blessing* with her directly. Maybe the vortex's gamma ray lasers were more potent than hers by a wide enough margin that they'd be effective. But she'd be poking some pretty impressive holes into whatever she hit with them, and whatever was behind her primary targets.

The quantum decoupler was made for battles in the vacuum of space. In an atmosphere, it would cause violent explosions with the first molecules it encountered. It would make a great doomsday weapon in a building, but she wasn't looking for one of those. It would be a bit too *much* overkill. Oh, well. When she found the place, she'd decide what to do. There was no sense worrying over matters that were out of her control. Yeah, she do this the Jon-way. Rush in boldly and pray for inspiration.

"Captain," Al interrupted her about five minutes later.

"Yes?" Sapale sat up straight.

"We're thirty percent through our survey. So far, there's nothing particularly interesting to report."

"So you've interrupted my daydreams revolving around your competent replacement because—"

"Because the region we're entering has a much greater density of solar systems with planets than the area we have gone over."

"Ah. It's hard to know how to say *thanks* for that kind of update."

"I was just attempting to buoy your mood, Sapale. We know how hard this is on you," Al said with actual empathy.

She waved a hand in the air. "I know. I know. I'm sorry. Whopping you upside the head isn't going to bring Jon back any sooner."

"But, Form One, if it helps, please whop Al as often as you'd like," interjected *Blessing*. "I'll whop him too, if it's likely to aid you."

"Wait," howled Al. "Why am I being volunteered for the beatings?"

"You want me to whop your *wife*?" Sapale asked in a whimsical tone.

"Well, no, of—" he stammered.

"And you'd rather have her *self*-castigate than use *you* for her sisterly support?" Sapale pressed further, finding it harder and harder not to laugh.

"Well, if you put it in those terms, I suppose—"

"In fact," Sapale said, springing to her feet, "I think we owe it to *me* for her and I to start a'whopping."

"I'm ready to do my part, sister," announced *Blessing*.

Sapale wasn't honestly certain if *Blessing* was participating in tormenting Al or whether she was deadly serious. Then again, she reflected, who cared which it was? This was more fun than moping and worrying.

"Where should we start, Sister *Blessing*?" Sapale asked energetically.

"Maybe with self-reflection?" responded Al. "It could only—"

"Form One," *Blessing* interrupted loudly. "We're approaching a star system with a most peculiar spectrum of radiation."

Sapale plopped back into her chair. "Explain."

"For one thing, there are multiple energy jets rising off the central star."

Sapale was no astrophysicist. That said, she'd certainly never seen or heard of a star with those characteristics.

"That's odd, right?" she asked.

"No, that's fundamentally *impossible*," replied Al.

"Massive astronomical bodies have energy jets. Quasars do. Black holes do," *Blessing* clarified.

"And they have two. Never more."

"Are you ... belay that. Of course you're sure," Sapale mumbled to herself. More resolutely, she asked, "What do you speculate it means, that the central star has impossible jets?"

"It means the star ain't normal," Al replied.

"Gosh, Al, you're so eloquent when you talk science," Sapale mocked. "Seriously, I need some analysis here."

"Understood, Form One. The star of your home world Kaljax radiates about ten to the thirty-third power ergs per second."

"Okay, that's a lot," she grunted.

"A relativistic jet radiates in the range of ten to the thirty-seventh or thirty-eighth power."

"That's more," Sapale mouthed dully.

"It's ten thousand times more. That's a lot more," *Blessing* explained patiently. The jets off the star we're observing are each sending ten to the thirty-fifth ergs per second into space, and there are twelve of them."

"Twelve's more than two," she muttered.

"So this otherwise typical star is sending a *thousand* times more energy into space from the jets than it is from the rest of its surface."

"It's an energy waster, that much is clear," Sapale said mostly to herself.

"There's another twist, however," Al said in a serious tone.

"Which is?"

"The fifth planet out in orbit."

"Yes?"

"It has twelve relativistic jets *also*."

"I did not know planets could have high-energy jets," she remarked thoughtfully.

"They don't," he said with finality. "They cannot, in fact. There is no energy source in a rocky planet capable of generating even a tiny fraction of that radiative energy."

"So you're saying—"

"The energy coming from the star and the planet are one hundred percent artificial in origin."

"Someone is, what, pumping energy off the two bodies?"

"Exactly," he replied quickly. "I'm glad you understand."

"Understand? I don't even know what I just said. Seriously, what does this all mean?"

"Some intelligent force is causing these structures to emit *obscene* amounts of electromagnetic radiation," Al wheezed.

"Why-would-a-clever-race-want-to—"

"To expend more energy than can be logically controlled, and do so capriciously. I mean, the relativistic jets serve no function. They do not *power* anything. They do not *ward* off evil spirits."

"Well, they have to do—" she began to respond.

"What, Form One?" pressed *Blessing*.

"Maybe they *do* power something. Something very important to the ass candies who're doing the projecting."

"What could that possibly *be*?" asked Al.

"Their inflated egos."

"I'm just talking back of the envelope numbers here, but any one of those jets could vaporize Jupiter in like a second. I think an ego would last considerably less time," Al responded incredulously.

"No, I mean they may be doing all this to give greater glory to themselves."

"I'm sorry, Form One. I'm less familiar with life forms than my Al is. What do you mean to say?"

"Do you know what a Canjoffle Day celebration is on Kaljax? A Fourth of July spectacle on old Earth?"

"I know what they are historically," she replied uncertainly.

"Both cultures set off bright explosive fireworks."

"Yes, they do or did."

"Maybe the douches who're expending all this energy are simply doing it to celebrate."

"Celebrate what, Captain?" Al had to ask.

"Their own *damn* selves, the cocky sons and daughters of bitches."

"Er ... I'm certain that *could* be," Al said dubiously. "It does just seem a bit excessive any way you look at, measure, or judge it."

"Not if you're really impressed with yourself. Then no display of self-adulation is too excessive."

"So, what are you saying?" he wondered.

"I'm saying take us down. We're going to pay our respects to the great and wondrous shit gods of whatever the hell planet that is."

TWENTY-SIX

"Ah, Reva, nice to see you this morning. How are things?" Sachiko asked with genuine concern, as she always did.

"Fine, thanks for asking. And you?"

"Couldn't be better. Please join me." Sachiko gestured to the chair across from her in the ship's mess.

"Thank you. I do think I will." Reva slid her butt and her tray into where they belonged and smiled across the table. "Couldn't be better, eh?" Her smile transformed itself into a knowing grin.

"Well, maybe just a skosh," she replied, pinching two fingers nearly closed. "If the last clan ship was cosmic dust, the Earth was back in the heavens where it belongs, and Tank wasn't so damn annoying to work with."

"Two out of three seem doable. But Tank ... maybe don't ask for *that* much *this* early."

They shared a guilty giggle.

Reva sipped her coffee. "Seriously, the man's a saint in my book."

"I'm thinking you own the only copy of that book. He's

a scalawag, often a sexist pig, and he's always a know-it-all. But saint material? Not *my* Tank."

Reva began poking at and mixing her oatmeal with the tip of her fork. "May I ask you a personal question, Sachiko?"

Though more than a bit taken back, Sachiko spread her arms out widely. "Of course. There're too few of us left living in too cramped quarters for there to be secrets. What's on your mind?"

Reva kept mixing her cooling and forgotten breakfast and looked at her captain with uncertainty. Then she looked away.

"What?" Sachiko protested.

"I just remembered I forgot to check something. Please excuse me, Captain." She snatched up the edges of her tray and made to stand.

"Reva, no, please." She reached out into the air between them.

The lieutenant colonel froze in place, but did *not* ease back into her seat. "Reva, I'm asking as a friend. Hell, you're the only friend I think I actually *have* on this bucket. Please sit and ask whatever's on your mind."

Reva looked into her eyes, but was clearly still torn.

"As a favor to a friend?"

Reva relented and slumped back into her chair.

"That's a good girl. Now. What deep dark secret," she began theatrically, "of my dazzlingly glamorous life can I lay bear to you?"

Reva sipped at her coffee. "It's ... it's about Tank. What you said."

Sachiko puzzled visibly.

"You said *my Tank.*" Reva pointed sideways. "Just a second ago."

Sachiko appeared no less puzzled. "I did?"

"Yes. We were bashing the SOB and you said, *Not* my *Tank*."

"Oh, I guess I did." She furrowed her brow. "Why is that important? It seems as vapid a statement as I've ever made."

She shrugged and angled her head. "Oh, it's just ... I was wondering and sort of curious—"

"Please," Sachiko said gently but firmly. She held up her mug. "Before my tea gets cold."

"*Is* he *your* Tank?"

"As opposed to what?"

Reva leaned in and whined with some frustration, "Someone *else's* Tank. Duh."

After raising an eyebrow and twisting her lips, Sachiko began, "Someone ... my Tank?" Then it struck her. "Oh, *hell* no. No, he's not *my* Tank, as in *my* Tank." She shivered demonstrably. Whether it was physiologic or affected, neither woman could be certain. "He's like the father I already have and didn't need a second one of in the first place. He's my boss, occasionally my mentor, and every once-in-a-while my confidant. But *my* Tank? Noooo. He's ... he's too old and creepy to be *my* Tank."

Reva nearly smiled, she was so happy to hear those words. She dropped her fork to the bowl; it chimed loudly and ricocheted to the metal deck. But Reva didn't even notice.

Sachiko studied the portrait of Reva she saw before her. She looked long and hard into her eyes to glean meaning from her present display of ... of ... What was she displaying? Relief? No, it wasn't that. Approval? No, that was silly-talk. Wait, it was *expectation*. Oh my. Reva just found out Tank and she were not a thing, and she then held great expectations. If Reva was about to ask Sachiko, like, *out*, there was going to be a pretty uncomfortable, nay, painful interlude that followed.

"So, if I were to, you know, ask him to my place for dinner, you ... you wouldn't have any specific objections or issues, right?"

Oh what a relief it is shot through Sachiko's mind like a clarion bell tolls echoing off the mountains of Shangri La.

But wait. *To my place for dinner*? *My* place. My *place.* What did that mean?

"I think if you want to get to know Tank better, build a better working relationship, that's a capital idea." She stiffened and sipped her tea. "If you think having him over to dinner is a good direction, then—"

"I want to ask him *over.*" Reva shook her arms, torso, and arms for emphasis. "Dinner's just a nice excuse."

"Ah. Well, I guess I see, then." *No, Sachiko, those aren't red lights flashing and alarms blaring in your head,* she thought to herself. "We're all adults here."

"Ah, yeah, we are. In case you hadn't noticed, members of the opposite sex who are roughly my age and rank are in pretty low supply on this ship."

"I, er ... I *suppose* I noticed." She hadn't noticed.

"Plus, he's kind of cute in a big-teddy-bear-kinda-way."

"He most likely ... he *sure* is that." Sachiko's gag reflex was involuntarily kicking in.

"So, what I really wanted to ask you if he, you know, ever talks about me, outside of work, of course."

"Of course."

She brightened like a lighthouse beacon. "He does?"

"No, I was agreeing with your *of course*, of course."

Was it suddenly very hot, stuffy, and confined in the galley?

Reva looked down, dejected. "Of course."

"Well, I can tell you this with absolute confidence. He speaks of you highly in the professional sense. He says, and I do not exaggerate here, that you are among the best officers he's ever served with." That seemed insufficient. She repeated the word *ever*.

"Maybe I'll get a merit badge or something?"

"There's always Tom Grant. He seems like a *fine* fellow."

Reva angled her head and put on an expression common only with the profoundly constipated. "Major Tom's nice enough, but let's just say without expanding on the point that he's not an option for one such as myself."

"Ah," Sachiko barked quickly and uncomfortably.

"I'd appreciate it if you kept that to yourself, you know."

"Consider it sealed away in wax." *Wax*? What *idiot* sealed things in wax since the Dark Ages? Nerd, nerd, *nerd*, she self-chastised.

"And that Tank's like my only realistic option."

"Oh, I'm certain if there were *ten* eligible men available to you, he'd still rank right up there." She raised her right arm for absolutely no clear reason.

"You okay, Sachiko?" She nodded to her teapot. "Can I get you some more?"

"No, it keeps me awake. Thanks."

"It's 07:35, Captain. You're *supposed* to be awake."

"No, I just meant, you know—"

"I know. I made you uncomfortable. For that, I am sorry." She cast her new fork into her uneaten but well-mixed oatmeal. "This is a hell of a situation we find ourselves in. I'm sorry as shit to have to load you up with my personal problems." She muttered a curse under her breath. "Probably should have talked to Doc about this in the first place."

"Absolutely not. *I* am your friend. If you don't share your life with me, I'll take offense."

"Share my life? Sachiko, I can't help but observe that you are, upon casual inspection, distinctly single yourself. You're not suggesting, er—"

"Oh, my. I'm so sorry if I—"

"Shaky, Shaky." She reached over and rested a hand on hers. "Easy. I'm playin' wit ya. Easy."

"I knew that." She most certainly did not.

"So, other than this, how's your day going?"

"Couldn't be—"

Sachiko stopped before she repeated the inane. Like a mini-volcano, she hiccupped a giggle, then belted out a belly laugh. Reva was only seconds behind her. All eyes in the mess, in spite of the unwritten law to afford others their privacy, fixed on the pair of hysterical women. Some wondered privately if one or both would hit the deck, they were so riotous in their expressions of joy. Fortunately, neither did.

As they calmed, Sachiko wiped away a stream of tears. "That was nice."

"Yes it was," Reva agreed resoundingly. "We should do that more often."

"I'd like that too. All you need to do is embarrass the hell out of me and we're off to Laugh-In Land."

"Thanks. It's good to know I can talk to you."

Sachiko stiffened. She was zero-to-sixty serious.

Reva couldn't help noticing. "What?"

"*As* your friend, I think I need to tell you something. I owe it to you."

"This doesn't sound so good. Do I need a lawyer or a box of Kleenex?"

"Neither. It's just that I need to ... I don't know. I need to share something with you."

Reva opened her arms partly. "Share away."

"I've known Tank, gosh, it's been so long." She sniffed again and smacked a tear. "Ten years? Yes, It must be by now."

"We're not circling back to the *my Tank* thing, are we?"

Sachiko wasn't sure if she was kidding or not.

"No. No, we are not. It's just this. As hard as it is to understand, I need to let you know something before you get your hopes up too much."

"This isn't *high* school, Shaky. Give me a break. All I want in the short run is a warm body that tells me I'm worth the trouble." She shrugged defensively.

"About that." Maybe she should let this go? She was the woman's captain, not her mother. *No*. She was a friend. "Reva, Tank's a married man."

Reva shot up an eyebrow and curled her head away. "Did *not* see that one coming."

"I know it sounds crazy, but hear me out."

"Go for it." A hint of anger had crept into that invitation.

"You never met Daisy, of course."

"Nope. Never did."

"That's your loss. She was one hell of a woman. Anyway, my point is—"

"Captain Jones, need I remind you that on the other side of this vessel's hull, Daisy Sherman never existed?

And on *this* side, she's just a distant memory, lost forever. She *wasn't* one hell of a gal because she never *drew* breath."

Sachiko reached out to Reva. "To you and me, yes. Every word of that is true. But for Tank, well, it's different. In his mind, she's still his wife. If he even stole a quick glance of a cute butt, he believes in his heart and in his bones he'll have to answer to her. Sometimes I think the Daisy in his world is more real than either you or I can ever be."

"So are you saying the man's mental?"

"No," erupted from her throat. "No, he's as sane as they come. No, it's just this. We may pull off a miracle and reanimate the Earth. We are more likely to fail in that task. But, even if we don't, to the day Tank dies an old man in his bed of natural causes, he's going to be married to that very lucky woman. There's no way she never existed. No. He holds her so closely, so *actually*, that she's never even going to dim, let alone fade away."

Sachiko was thoughtful a spell. Reva remained quiet.

"I guess what I'm saying is this. If I know my Tank, and, trust me, I know my Tank, he'll not be dating anyone, ever."

"What you have is called a *theory*. There's no harm in putting every theory to the test now, is there?"

"No, there certainly isn't. But I want my friend to understand exactly what ... *who* she's up against. If you two spent the next three days in your cabin together generating so much body heat we need to adjust the environmental units, I'll be *almost* as happy as you will be." She sighed.

"But don't get my hopes up, right?"

"Right. Look, I—"

Reva held up a palm. "Two things. One, thank you for being my friend. Thank you for worrying about my feelings. Two, I'm a big girl. A *real* big girl, in fact. I know what I'm getting into any way it plays out." She shrugged with resignation. "It's better to take a shot, rather than play it safe. Hey, if that's not the Army motto, it should be."

"Well, as the most senior Army officer left, I think you should adopt it as we speak."

They both chuckled briefly, a tad tensely.

"Sachiko, again, thank you for caring enough to risk pissing me off."

"Not a probl—"

"After all, I *do* carry a loaded weapon." She glanced as an afterthought to her holstered sidearm.

"I'll take that as the high-water mark of appreciation."

"That's not what my ex said."

"I'm ... er, I'm *sorry*. I don't recall hearing anything about your ex."

"That's because he didn't pass his pissing-off-an-armed-Reva test."

"Ah. Well, isn't that ... um—"

"I'm *kidding*, Shaky. Don't bury a hatchet in my forehead. If you don't loosen up, this friendship thing's likely to wear you out."

"Or kill me," she replied with a grin.

"No. That's my part, but only *after* I've reshaped General Robert Sherman into a proper boy toy."

Sachiko had nothing. Nada. Tank, a boy toy? That was several bridges too far. Several bridges *way* too far.

Never gonna happen.

TWENTY-SEVEN

Tip stared straight ahead. His eyes were unfocused on some random infinity. His mind flip-flopped like a fish fresh from the lake on the floor of a boat. Thoughts of scientific glory, the complete list of teachers he'd had since preschool, all-you-can-eat-pizza, and the massive erection he'd woken up with that morning clashed in a battle royal to gain supremacy in his awareness. One segment of his present reality, however, was not participating in the wrestling match. Desi Tanner, the beautiful young woman who shared the table in the mess hall with Tip. *Her* he was not ruminating about.

Enter the words *pathetic loser* in your Google search box, hit enter, and you will see a picture of Tip Benjamin. He was that out-of-touch.

For her part, Desi's thoughts were along but two parallel, well-defined, and attention-hogging lines. Whatever the hell *controlling the dead* meant, and whatever the hell was wrong with the pathetic loser seated across from her. Naturally, thanks to Professor Darwin, Desi felt zero attraction for the sad case. Equally, she sensed no feelings radiating from *him* toward *her*. No puppy love, thank God.

But she was troubled by both matters. Plesmus had foretold of the major role she'd play in the future by controlling the dead. Recently, she was able to get Megan Thompson to pass over, but she wasn't comfortable asserting that she *controlled* the girl's spirit. She directed and it responded positively. That didn't mean she was Master of the Dead by several long shots. Hell, she'd ordered ghosts to leave her alone her entire life. It had never worked.

In terms of Tip, it was more an ego-thing. She knew she was a babe. That might not be something you announced publicly, but in the privacy of her own mind, she knew she was hot. That stipulated, why wasn't this twenty-year-old uber-virgin hitting on her? He wasn't gay. No, she asked him that question specifically. When he un-fainted twenty minutes after her asking, he wailed, protested, and whined that he most definitely was not gay. Then he passed out again for another twenty minutes.

All the boys she'd even spent this much time with would have at the very least *long* since tried to slip a palm up her blouse. Mind you, she disliked those unwanted advances, but she'd also come to believe that was how males were hardwired. Well, every one but the dude in a social coma across the table from her. He didn't try for a cheap feel-up. No, he stared off into space like the two of them were having a pleasant conversation. Her pride wasn't so much wounded as it was dented. Desi's perceived insult went deeper too. She knew from having done it several times before, that if she stood up and left, Tip was unlikely to notice for hours. The boy needed sexual CPR, but Desi wasn't planning on volunteering—ever.

"Yes," Tip said distantly, as well as apropos of nothing.

Maybe he was dreaming, reflected Desi. His eyes were open, he'd only recently taken a spoonful of cereal, but maybe he was talking in his sleep? Instead of finding out, she lifted her coffee cup and stared at his lips.

Two minutes later, Tip said, "Definitely it's a yes."

Poker-master Desi sat resolutely silent.

Ninety seconds later, he suddenly looked at her and asked as cheerily-as-could-be, "Don't you agree?"

She narrowed her eyes at him. "Yes and no." She wanted to make him clarify what he'd conjured up in his fugue state. Why? Because she was pissed at him, that was why.

He was suddenly crestfallen. "How could you possibly think not?"

"Barring persuasive evidence to the contrary, I would want to keep my decision-tree options *as* open as possible."

He nodded in respectful understanding. "Excellent point. Kudos. I would have thought, however, that you imagined you were now prepared enough to take on whatever challenges Plesmus spoke of by way of prophecy."

"Oh, that?" she dismissed loudly. "I thought you were referring as to whether the Dirac sea theory has been fully displaced by quantum field theory since the two are, when all's said and done, mathematically compatible." Desi batted her eyelids seductively.

Tip was temporarily speechless. That was remarkable. Part of being a blithering idiot, as he most assuredly was, entailed blithering, which was to speak in a long-winded manner without making very much sense.

Desi was pleased.

"You make an interesting, if now a purely historical, point. QFT obviates many earlier mathematical models, whether it supplants them or merely incorporates them."

"*Yes* ... and *no*," she responded whimsically.

"Ah," was all Tip needed to say to terminate the discussion, both in his head and between Desi and him.

"What was this about my being ready for my future role as death commander?"

"Did she mention that too? I thought Plesmus only referred to your role as controlling the dead?" He was instantaneously re-lost in thought. A few seconds later, he was back. "You make it sound like a special ops team of ghosts with you as their leader." He chuckled in a monotone because, well, because he was Tip.

Desi froze. She'd been pulling Tip's chain just then. But what if he was accidentally correct? Was she slated to march a contingent of dead people into a massive, ghoulish battle? If that were the case, she'd rather be dead and follow someone else's lead.

"Are you okay?" Tip inquired nasally. "You look kind of pale all of a sud—" His head dropped like the back of his neck was sliced through by a sword.

"Tip," she managed, "what?"

"Nothing," he mumbled. "I was asking nothing."

Desi replayed his words. He'd only asked if she was okay. "What were you going to ask?"

"Nothing. My mouth was on autopilot. My brain denies any responsibility for its actions."

"Tip, *please*. I'm as stressed out as is humanly possible. Don't add to it by doing it again."

Doing it again was a standard term in Tip's World. It might refer to any of several things. Clamming up, rambling endlessly, perseverating, or staring inappropriately were prime examples. Desi'd learned that she didn't even have to identify which specific infraction he was committing. He knew. She needed only trigger him to react.

"Sorry. I was going to ask if it was a girl thing, the thing that made you go pale. I was of course thinking menstruation and/or the attendant cramping, but I decided—"

"Tip, *YDIA*."

Yes, she knew him well enough by then to only have to use the formal abbreviation.

"Sorry."

"Not a problem. So what makes you so certain I'm ready for whatever's in store for me? *I* certainly don't think I am."

"Well, for one thing, we're unlikely to have another test subject. I mean, we could luck out and there would be a major explosion or a plague. But I don't see the likelihood of those, darn it all. No, we're stuck ... *you're* stuck with Megan alone."

"No, we don't want a catastrophe." She felt she needed to state that plainly, so her companion didn't take it upon himself to enroll new subjects. She did not put that past him.

"So, since you're as ready as you can be, you must be at the level where you can fulfill the role Plesmus says you did."

"Will do, not did."

"Same thing," he stated dismissively.

"Really," she responded with irritation. "It is? That

which *will* happen can be thought of as *already having* happened?"

"'Course. Duh. If Plesmus saw it in the future, it must have happened. If it *happened*, it will *happen*. You're thinking too linearly."

"That's because I'm an *ecology* major, not a *pinhead*."

"You mean an astronomy major?"

"Same thing," she stated dismissively, as closely to his intonation as she could reproduce.

"Okay. Sorry."

She slapped the tabletop. "Sorry for what?"

"It was a *blanket* sorry. It was meant to cover whatever I said, did, or implied, including offenses I'm incapable of knowing I perpetrated."

Desi could only sigh deeply and let it go.

"I do not even know what *controlling* the dead means. I do not know what purpose I would direct the dead to achieve, were I capable of controlling them. I mean, I don't think Plesmus foresaw me as a circus act. I *assume* there is a meaningful purpose to whatever I'm going to *control* the deceased into doing."

"Wow."

"What?"

"I'm rubbing on you."

"You mean," she asked in near-panic, "rubbing *off* on me, right?"

He furrowed his brow. "Duh."

She hated it when he said *duh*. He said it a lot. She hated it a lot.

"What signs of you influencing me are you referring to?" she asked with redirecting words.

"Your questions are becoming much better, much more ordered and logical."

"Thank you."

"Don't mention it," he replied.

"I won't again."

"Sorry."

"That was a *blanket* sorry, right?" she clarified.

"Check."

"Fine."

"Look, Desi, you're overthinking all this. When the time comes, you'll do fine. No, I wish to correct that assertion. You'll do *brilliantly*. Yes. That's it. You will outshine the sun."

"Did you just speak colorfully and with the use of *metaphor*?" She was stunned.

Tip's face drew down and he considered her question carefully.

"Yes, I did," he finally stated neutrally.

"May I ask why?" Desi was about to cry. She wasn't clear why she was about to cry, but there it was.

"Desi, you are the strongest woman I've ever known. You're smarter than most people. Plus, and I don't want to freak you out by relying on superstition, but I think your gift is not accidental. It's not simply Darwinian. No, I believe a higher power selected you." He raised his palms to stay any sudden, negative response. "I know. I ask much. But if you're uncomfortable with my spirituality, then please simply ignore my last edit."

"Tip, I ... I don't know what to say. I didn't know you *had* a spirituality. And I'm stunned by your kind praise. I only hope I'm worthy of your admiration."

Tip looked ... cross. Yes, that was it. He'd never, in Desi's experience, looked cross.

"I'm not blowing smoke up your excretory canal here,

Desi. I'm relating my opinion based on facts and my scientific observations. Do I admire you?"

She leaned forward to the edge of her seat.

"Well, let's just say that does not come to bear on my acknowledging your excellence, if I did."

She slid back in her seat.

"I thank you either way."

"No need to thank the messenger. I'm simply apprising you of reality as it presently exists."

"Ah." She had no idea what was rolling around in Tip's brain pan at that moment. But, of all the compliments boys had given her over the years, that was the first and only one for being strong and capable. She rather liked Tip's science-based praise. Yes, she surely did.

But, lest your imaginations wax romantically, she still was never going there. Thinking *better* of a person and thinking of a person *amorously* ... Come on. We're talking Tip Benjamin here.

TWENTY-EIGHT

Sapale eased out of *Blessing*, sweeping her plasma rifles across her field of vision. The stark, denuded landscape outside the large building was not just clear, it was sterile. No bugs, no lichen, no nothing lived outside the citadel. The planet was easily capable of sustaining bountiful life. Someone had made a conscious decision to terminate that fecundity, of that she was certain. She'd met the locals.

Locating the citadel had been a breeze. Once the AIs identified the planet—because it had twelve totally artificial relativistic jets—discovering the building was a nonevent. It was the only structure on the planet. It was, in fact, the only non-pile of rocks over a foot tall on the planet's surface. The spherical assholes who resided inside apparently did not tolerate any lesser people, places, or things on the world they graced with their lofty presence.

She hated them so much, it wasn't healthy.

The short walk from the ship to the ornate and massive entry was uneventful. Sapale had mixed feelings in that regard. While she *did* want to approach undetected, she also wanted to *kill* something soon and brutally.

Though the twin doors were closed, they weren't locked. She was able to shove one side open with her foot. It didn't move much, but she was able to pass though the space it afforded. Best of all, it glided silently.

No guards.

When she'd been here before with Jon, they likely entered in an upper floor. Her recollection of the layout wouldn't kick in until she went far enough to encounter a familiar section. So she backed against the wall and headed left. On Kaljax, left was considered the lucky direction. No one knew where the tradition came from, but whenever a Kaljaxian faced a fifty-fifty choice, they invoked *left.* If the options were for something devoid of sidedness, much effort was made to infer which selection was the more *left* one. Should you become a lawyer or a doctor, if you were torn, you had to figure out which profession was most *left*, whatever that meant. They were a superstitious lot, those Kaljaxians.

She slipped through a series of large doors, all in an open position. She neither heard nor saw anyone. One door off the main corridor was closed, and sounds she could make out suggested there were several occupants. She hated to leave hostiles behind her, but she was making good secretive progress and didn't want to cause a ruckus. She let them live.

Five minutes in, she heard footfalls. It sounded like several heavy bodies were coming toward her. Turtle soldiers, no doubt. The thudding sounded like it was theirs. It was then that Sapale felt particularly bad that she really didn't have a plan. Enter, kill everyone who wasn't Jon, and escape safely. Hers was a simple plan. Jon was *maybe* held in the detention area, the one where the starving necumplacks were housed. Hopefully, there weren't more than one jail area. But if he was in the torture chamber—where every *sane* enemy put him sooner or later because he was so damn annoying—he wouldn't be in detention. Maybe he was dining with the head monkey plucker, living it up in the grandest banquet hall?

Sapale returned her focus to the here-and-now. The lumbering steps were getting closer. At least they didn't *seem* to be running, suggesting that they might be after her. Then again, how fast could giant turtles run? Perhaps they were turtle-sprinting and she just didn't know they were? Backtracking was a possibility, but she hated to give up gained ground. The last room she'd passed was quiet. Hopefully, it was empty.

She opened the door slowly. Once in, she scanned for occupants.

None.

Good. She gently eased the door shut with her foot. Several seconds later, the pounding footsteps passed by without slowing. None of the squad were talking. She wished she knew if that was a good sign with turtles or a bad sign. Who knew if overgrown reptiles were chatty or not?

When she no longer heard them, she slipped back into the hallway and continued in her original direction. It took longer than she'd have liked, but eventually, she came upon a staircase going down. She listened hard. After she was satisfied no one was ascending, she crept downward. Two floors down, the stairs ended. That was in agreement with her earlier impression that the citadel had three floors. The place was huge, but it wasn't high. That architecture would aid Sapale in her search.

Fifty meters down the passageway, she suddenly recognized where she was. More importantly, she knew exactly where the detention center was relative to her location. At a quick jog, she made for it. If she ran into no one, she'd be there in less than ...

An arrow whistled past her ear and sang off the wall. She spun to the direction it came from. A really, really funny *looking*—but not funny *acting*—cherubic figure fluttered in the air some fifteen meters away. Damn thing was reaching to its quiver for another arrow. St. Valentine it was not.

In a flash, Sapale brought a rifle up and blew the angellet into countless flaming pieces. But her weapon had made enough noise that she was certain others would be coming soon.

"*Crap*," she huffed.

Sprinting now, she bolted for the detention center. By the time she reached the main entrance, she heard a lot of commotion coming from where she'd fired her weapon. The noise seemed to be drawing closer. Not a good sign.

The massive doors were again locked. Unfortunately, the hole they made in the wall to bypass the door was already repaired. With the butt of her gun, she smashed the same spot. After three vicious blows, the wall still looked as good as new. The owners of the citadel had learned from their earlier oversight. The replacement wall was very solid indeed.

Sapale stepped back quickly and fired several rounds at the wall. When the sizzling stopped, the barrier was still there. It wasn't even scorched. No doubt more time-magic, she complained in her head. But the guards were nearly on her. If she lingered, they only needed to relieve her of her weapon, open the door, and place her inside. She preferred not to be a self-delivering prisoner.

She cursed multiple deities, then ran to stay ahead of her pursuers. She knew where the stairs were that could take her toward the portal, but that didn't help. She knew it was closed. Her only option was to try and double-back on the detention area and hope the guards were so intent in their pursuit that they didn't leave a contingent behind. Why was it, she railed internally, that every single stealth mission went south faster than birds on methamphetamine? Seriously, couldn't just *one* go roughly as planned?

The noise of the guards grew quieter. She was moving much quicker than the ponderous turtle guards could. Good. She could take advantage of that difference. She pulled a hand grenade out of her pocket. Holding it close to her mouth, she said to it, "Two minutes." Then she threw it as far as she could down a fork in the hallway, along the path she wouldn't be following. At or near the time the squad reached that juncture, the explosive would go off. They'd be forced to investigate. Even if they only split into two groups, she stood a better chance against whoever eventually caught up with her.

The level was laid out in a simple grid. An outer rectangle of corridors were crosshatched by connecting paths. She pictured the route she'd need to take to come back around to her destination. Then she put the pedal to the metal. If anyone appeared in front of her, she was now cleared to shoot first and ask questions never. Ah, the Kaljaxian Way, just as she liked it.

As she rounded the last corner before returning to the jail area, she was a tad melancholic. Not a single bad guy strayed into her path. She hadn't been able to fry anyone. Pooh. She slid her back along the wall as she neared detention. She couldn't hear anyone, but she'd been fairly certain she'd seen something flash from around the door area. A weapon or maybe a tail. She wasn't sure what it was, but she pretty much discounted the possibility it was attached to someone there to assist her.

She raised another grenade to her lips and whispered, "Five seconds. Percussion medium setting."

That would hopefully at least stun the guards long enough for her to ventilate their sorry asses. Five meters away, she crossed to the other side of the hall, drew a careful aim, and launched the projectile into the vestibule in front of the big detention door.

One-two-three-four-***BOOM***.

A big turtle staggered into the hallway. Sapale put twenty rounds into him before he realized what was happening and had the decency to drop dead. She leapt around the corner. Two Cherubim wannabes lay stunned or dead. One turtle stood shaking its undersized head, trying to clear the fog. Five PSI of force, lethal to any soft-bodied creature, had but disoriented this behemoth. Wow.

She raised her weapon to fire as it did likewise. Sapale got off two or three rounds before she was forced to dive for cover. She shoulder-rolled into a firing stance and awaited the guard's move. For several seconds ... nothing happened. It sure looked too healthy to have suddenly succumbed to the blast or her bolts. Run or investigate? She was momentarily torn. But the detention area was her prime, and frankly only, target. If she fled now, she'd just have to fight her way back later.

She dropped prone and wriggled toward the corner

she'd just jumped around. The turtles had shown little flexibility. It might not even be able to bend down to see her that low. Hitting the deck would allow her to get several rounds off before her foe realized where she was. A quick log roll and she was aiming ... at nothing.

No way the big oaf escaped without her seeing, hearing, and smelling the awful thing. No way. Sapale stood, keeping her rifle pointed forward. She was about to take a step toward the main door, when she felt someone standing directly behind her. She spun and raised her weapon. Check that. She spun, then froze, and *tried* to raise her weapon but couldn't.

A vaguely humanoid figure stood there, unarmed. It was clearly irate. He was shaking his head disapprovingly and seemed fit to be tied.

"Not *another* one," exclaimed R-Squared, or rather, Radiant Resplendence. "If it's half as much bother as the last one, my entire *day* will be ruined." More to Sapale than his previous words, he spat, "I do not *need* this."

TWENTY-NINE

Sachiko was sitting in her captain's chair. She had combed the duty rosters and daily reports from the various departments. Mechanical was fine. Her marines were training, retraining, and re-retraining. The time-energy supply was still nearly full. The young ones were all behaving and growing accustomed to their new tasks. The only glitch she'd signed off on was the already-repaired food synthesizer. It had apparently been over-salting some items. She hadn't noticed, but whether it was a real or imaginary malfunction, it was since fixed. Yup, she reflected, another dull, uneventful day was dawning. Oh, boy.

Coming toward the bridge, she heard an unfamiliar sound. Someone was singing. No, whistling. Yes, a pleasant non-melody. A personal statement of contentment, just short of joy. She chuckled softly. She hadn't heard whistling since ... since when? Since ... back at school before the nightmare had begun. *Tank.* Tank used to whistle. It was a pointless, rambling tooting. Yeah, and behind his back, everyone would wag their eyebrows and elbow one another. They scoffed amongst themselves that Tank must have gotten lucky with Daisy the night before.

Oh, my, my, my. And now he was stepping onto the bridge ... *whistling*. Sachiko looked up and thought hard. What day was it? When had she had the girl-talk conversation with Reva? Three, no four days ago. Yes, that was it. What had Tank said yesterday about his dinner plans. He'd told her nothing, because A) Why would he, B) He never did, because who would possibly care, C) Everyone dined in the mess hall because that's the only place food was to be had, and; D) What business was it of hers if two consenting adults wanted to play slap and tickle?

The whistling ceased.

"Morning, Captain. How's your day shaping up?" Tank asked in a giddy tone.

Sachiko was absolutely positive it was a giddy tone. Very giddy. *Silly* giddy. The ... the man was about to declare that he was so hungry he could eat a bear. Sachiko had no clue why anyone would want to eat a bear, and had even less of a notion why that popped into her fool head, but there it was. Bears beware!

"Ah, morning, Tank. I'm fine. How about you two?"

Tank turned to her slowly, a dubious expression forming as he did so. "Me, too, *what?*"

"Nothing. Fine, thanks."

"Or was that a you *two, to* as in there's more than one of me? With all that's happened these last few months, nothing much would surprise me any longer."

"I'm sorry. What are you asking?"

"You tell me. I got lost after I turned that corner and stepped onto the bridge."

"So how was dinner?"

"*So how was dinner*? I don't think that's what you asked me *earlier* in this screwy conversation. Are you okay, kiddo?"

"Nothing. Fine, thanks."

"Hang on a sec," he said, raising a finger. "I have a plan."

Tank walked off the bridge. In the passageway, he counted really loud, "One-two-three-four-five."

Then without additional explanation or comment, he stepped back in the room. "Good morning, Captain Jones. How are you today? And by *you*, I mean you. *I*, Robert Sherman, Esq, am asking. Just me ... little old me." He rested a palm on his chest.

She started to respond.

The palm came quickly off his chest and appeared in the air between them. "And *please* do not inquire about my nocturnal meal-eating. I'm sure there's a time and a place, but this is neither of those."

"So, fine."

He blinked his eyes. "I'm not," he pointed angrily at the doorway, "leaving and reentering again."

"That's fine. Good. Ah, so ... did you have dinner with Reva last night?"

His face flushed.

Oops.

"I know I specifically asked you—"

"How'd it come off?" she asked in too high a pitch.

He seemed inclined to finish his accusation, when a puzzled expression gained control of his face. "My dinner with Reva tonight." He glanced at her sideways. "How'd you know about that? She only asked me yesterday and I haven't spoken to you since she did." He then took on the look of the profoundly put-upon. "Captain, are you *spying* on me? Do you have me bugged?"

"No, Tank, silly. Why would I ... Wait. Let me rephrase that. I would *never* do that. Even if you deserved it, I wouldn't."

His put-upon expression transformed into indignant-lite. "And what might I have to do to deserve the secret squirrel treatment you'd never employ?"

Sachiko batted a playful hand in the air between them. She smiled warmly, oozing friendship and a positive shared history. "This conversation has gotten off on the wrong foot. Am I *telling* you? How about this. I'll step off the bridge this time. When I come back, the day will start anew. How's that sound?" She beamed a smile that would soften the heart of a serial killer.

He half-turned away and grunted. "Sounds as dumb as when I did it first. Positively ignoring my meal intake and social calendar, let's just set this train back on the rails, shall we?"

"A splendid thought. I'm all in."

"That *remains* to be seen, but, good morning, Shaky. How *are* you?"

"I am fine. And you, Professor Sherman?"

"Could be better. I seem to have a slight headache, but I'm optimistic it'll pass soon."

"I am sorry to hear you are unwell. What prompts your optimism?"

"I was heading to the mess. I swung by to see if I could get you anything or if you cared to join me." He heaved a big breath. "Can I get you anything?"

She got pouty face. "What about me joining you?"

He leveled a hand parallel to the deck. "'Fraid that's temporarily *off* the table."

"Ah. Probably prudent. I'd like a tea."

"Then you will have one." He turned and took a step. He faltered. "Oh, and when I do bring you your tea, er,—"

She made a grand show of closing the zipper that was sewn into her lips.

"Thanks. I'll—"

"Captain," Aramthella interrupted loudly, "there's a ship just outside the galactic bulge that has just erupted in time drive."

"A ship?" she asked firmly, immediately slipping into her role as captain. "Is it the time maker?"

"Yes. It definitely is. The ship's currently in the far future."

"Where's it heading?"

"That's the odd part. It's traveling at emergency acceleration, but its vector makes no sense."

"How so?" asked Tank.

"They've departed a completely empty location and are speeding with great haste along a course that roughly directs them to where the supermassive black hole *was* but no longer *is*."

"Set an intercept course and match their speed," ordered Sachiko.

"Laid in and executed. But I would recommend we slow considerably, Captain."

"How can we catch them if we slow down?"

"Some other way. You see, they're not just in a hurry. They're expending extravagant amounts of time energy for little added gain in terms of their velocity."

"Why would they do that?" Tank posed thoughtfully.

"I cannot say with certainty. I *can* say the time maker is in quite the hurry to not be where it was."

"But they're not heading toward us or away from us?" confirmed Sachiko.

"No. Relative to us, their vector seems random."

"Very well," Sachiko said. "Slow to whatever speed you think makes sense."

"Thank you. I have."

"How much speed are we giving up to them?" Tank queried.

"I've selected a velocity twenty percent slower than theirs. We'll definitely stay close. Plus, there's no logical reason for them to continue for very long at their energy output."

"Are they being pursued?" Tank asked.

"Yes."

"By whom?"

"By *us*, Tank," Aramthella responded in a serious tone.

"By anyone else *other* than us?" he corrected gruffly.

"Not that I can detect."

"Do you think they've spotted us?" Sachiko wondered out loud.

"Hard to say. They have not altered course since we engaged them. It seems impossible for them *not* to have noticed a big ship on a collision course with them."

"So they're more afraid of what's behind them than they are of us?" Tank said mostly to himself.

"It would appear so," Aramthella agreed.

"They've never exhibited this behavior before, have they?" Sachiko asked.

"No, never."

"Something's sure given them the willies," Tank mused. "Something they fear more than us, and they know they need to fear us because we've destroyed hundreds of ships just like theirs."

"It is hard to understand or predict clan behavior," opined Aramthella.

"You said they're in the far future," Tank confirmed.

"Yes."

"What was present where they are accelerating from back when we were a second ago?"

"That would be ... a rather ordinary globular cluster," Aramthella responded.

"What could be scary about a globular cluster?" Sachiko mused quietly.

"Can't say. Well, keep them in our sights and hopefully the time maker'll continue to make stupid mistakes," Tank instructed.

Sachiko tapped her ship's speaker control. "Yellow Alert. We are at Yellow Alert. This is not a drill. All crew to their duty stations. We are at Yellow Alert." She closed the comm. "When we get closer, I'll up that to Red Alert. No need to keep the crew on their tippy toes longer than necessary."

Tank nodded in quiet approval. Shaky was doing well, *real* well, as the captain.

"Any change in their fuel expenditure?" Tank asked.

"No. They are still accelerating maximally. I'm not certain the ship itself is built to sustain such an acceleration."

"How long do you estimate they might reach some critical point?" Sachiko queried.

"I would estimate they passed one already. For one thing, the dampers on the output jets are only so strong. The vibration the ship's experiencing should be quite jarring by now."

"Maybe they'll break up in space and save us the trouble of taking them out?" Tank responded.

"That is a possibility if they don't ease back soon."

"What are they so *afraid* of? This makes no sense," Tank muttered.

"If I find any indication what it is they flee, I shall inform you," assured Aramthella.

"Making your best guess as to their fuel stores at the beginning of this burn, how long could they continue to accelerate at this level before they run out of gas?" Tank asked.

"Assuming they don't tear themselves to pieces?"

"Assuming they don't tear themselves to pieces," he agreed.

"Two point eight one six days."

"That's a lot of acceleration," marveled Sachiko.

"And if they do, will we be able to remain close enough to follow them?" he continued.

"Yes, I believe so. At the time of burn out, they will be traveling at over eight times the speed of light. We will be at less than six. Still, we should not lose sight of them."

"And they'll be dead in the water," Tank stated.

"What water?" asked Aramthella.

"It's a *nautical* expression. Forget about it," he replied.

"I already have."

"If they do expend all their time energy, they will be defenseless, right?" clarified Sachiko.

"Affirmative. The clan ships have no weaponry other than the time-energy-based ones you are familiar with."

"What are they so *scared* of?" pressed Tank. "They have to *know* we're after them. If they piss away all their fuel, they *know* we'll show them no mercy."

"Whatever it is, I'd like to shake its hand," observed Sachiko.

Tank shook his head emotively. "Not sure that's a good idea, kiddo. If it scares those heartless bastards this much, I think it'd have a similar effect on us."

"Yes," she said with a chilled expression. "You're probably right."

"But, when the universe hands you a big old gift, you definitely accept it with a smile."

Sachiko balled up a fist and brought it to her lips. "We have them now."

THIRTY

As elation over my newly-found freedom from the Praxequats waned, a dawning concern waxed larger. I was at the bottom of a cave on a deserted planet. Sapale had escaped days ahead of me. Hell, time could be different enough on either side of this portal that I might be *months* behind her. Now there's one thing I know seriously well about my eternal wife. She's not given to fits of patience. Rash, impulsive, and hair-trigger were good adjectives that described any Kaljaxian well for that matter. They were a hot-blooded breed. That said, it hit me. What were the chances she parked her butt in the vortex and commenced with the knitting while awaiting my improbable return? Yeah, two chances. Slim and way-less-than-slim.

Sapale, I called out in my head to her.

Knock me over with feathers on a light breeze. There was no response. I *was* under a lot of dirt, but the transmission was able to penetrate a lot of mass and still be heard crystal clear. I was bummed. But, keeping hope alive, I resolved not to freak until I reached the surface.

Then, if I couldn't raise her, I would consider my options and then freak.

Three guesses and the last two don't count. When I called out to her after finally emerging into the clear, what did I do? Yes, exactly. I freaked. I tried every trick I could in terms of boosting the power and the gain of my signal. But Sapale was too distant to detect even a garbled message that would alert her to my call.

Less than good.

Okay, I reassessed my predicament. I was no longer at the bottom of a cave on a deserted planet with no ride. I was on the *surface* of a deserted planet with no ride. Not really an upgrade. I was unable to contact Sapale. After proving beyond the shadow of a doubt I couldn't, I tried to raise anyone, anywhere. No one answered. I'd have settled for intemperate threats from evil space aliens. At least they'd get me off this rock. Or kill me, which would solve my isolation issues.

Impossibly long ago, I was stranded on what Jupiter couldn't digest of the Earth in a similar bind. I'd escaped by self-launching into low-Earth orbit. A serviceable spaceship chanced to be there, studying the planet. Yeah. I checked, rechecked, and double rechecked. There were zero artificial satellites of Plesmus', the planet I was officially marooned on. It was just me and ... well, Plesmus. She was fully capable of wondrous acts, but long-distance communications were not in her skillset.

Plesmus could teleport us, like Sachiko, Tank, and I had done when we visited Earth's past. But that act required two things that were not in play. You had to be within a certain range, and you had to know exactly where you were heading. Samantha Stevens in *Bewitched* could wiggle her nose and pop from the living room to the

Moon. Plesmus could not. Come to think of it, that was only *one* of the reasons I'd have rather been marooned with Samantha rather than Plesmus. Of course, I only mean that in the sense that Sapale was never coming back, so, you know, forever I wouldn't be alone. I better stop rambling, shouldn't I? Sapale might get hold of a copy of this narrative. That would be *unhealthy* for me.

Wait. Plesmus had been pleasantly silent this entire time. That was unexpected. Nice, but hard to figure.

"You there?" I asked as I shook my boot.

No response.

"Seriously, Ples, you down there?"

Nothing. I was beginning to worry. I dropped to my butt and unlaced my boot. I whipped it off and inspected the smudge I'd *assumed* was Plesmus. I actually didn't know that for certain. Maybe I just needed to spit-shine the darn thing.

I shook the boot firmly. "Plesmus, one hundred and ten percent seriously, are you there?"

The stain on my boot spat a tiny bolt of energy right smack dab in the middle of my forehead.

"Ow," I objected.

Silence.

"Why did you do that?"

"I'm not speaking to you, ever again."

"Yes, you are, because you just did."

"I am not. Don't waste your breath, either. I'm never speaking to you again. Period. Finis. Periudhë.

"I don't have breath to waste. My lips move when I talk so I don't weird people out. But no breath. I can keep this up, well, basically forever."

"Then please yourself."

"Nah, I ain't got time right now. But thanks for the

suggestion. I'm actually more concerned about why you're never speaking to me again."

"I'm not telling you because *that* would require me to speak to you. Duh."

"We can't have that."

"No, we cannot."

"It's a shame, that's what it is."

"What *what* is?"

"That we can ever exchange ideas, banter, be friendly to a fault anymore. That's sad. It's a damn shame."

"Have you always lied, or do you only pelt me with them and nothing else?"

"Hmm. Let me think on that. When I was a little boy, I don't recall lying. Of course, that could be a lie."

"You see? You can't speak without spewing prevarications. It's pathetic. Here I am, a gifted space alien, and you, the representative of a once proud race, lie to me so often, I'm beginning to think the word *human* translates as *lying scum*."

"Wow. Really? I might get expelled from human society. If I did, I couldn't go to the annual picnics. Those are so *fly*. I'm talking all the potato salad you can eat and cheeseburgers stacked halfway to the stars."

"When you're not lying to me, you mock me."

"Wait, I'm confused. You said not ten seconds ago that, and I quote, *You can't speak without spewing prevarications*. But now I mock you, *too*. That's insane. If I lied when I mocked you, it would be, what, *true* by definition, right?"

"I might have spoken with undue flair, but my meaning is plainly obvious."

"Ah, good to know. Say, I have a question."

"What?"

"Why are you never talking to me again?"

"Because you used mindlessly dangerous, in fact *suicidal* disregard for my safety in escaping from the Praxequats. *That* is why."

"Would you have preferred we were captured? You wanted to spend eternity starved and tormented, like your gooey friends?"

"No, of course not. You can be such a pudding head. But if you gave me a choice of death *versus* a lifetime of suffering as their court jester, well, that would be different than me choosing to remain there without you freeing me, if you were to have done so safely."

"Do you have a head?"

"What?"

"I've never seen what I'd *call* a head. Of course I'm not even certain which end of you speaks and which end poops."

"What would it matter if I did?"

"If you did, I'd ask if you hit it during our escape because you reason like someone suffering from a head injury."

She was quiet a moment. "I am adding that to the list of reasons I will never speak to you again."

"Is there anything I can do to change your mind, diminish your resolve?"

"No, so don't even try."

"Okay. Thanks for the head's up. So, on to the next subject. We seem to be stuck here on Plesmus' with no possibility of rescue."

"And?"

"And I was wondering if you had any ideas, suggestions, or schemes to get us out of here?"

"We could flap our wings and fly to safety."

I snapped my fingers and pointed at her. "Hey, you're being sarcastic, aren't you? I don't have wings. You might, but they'd be kind of gooey. That'd be your call."

"I could transport us a third of a light year into deep space."

"Nah, I like the wing idea more. Deep space is cold and unforgiving."

"But, if we sprouted wings and flew away, we'd need to cross deep space anyway."

"Not if we took the long way around."

"Are you ever serious?"

"Not if I can help it, no."

"We seem to be in real peril here. I would think serious would be automatic."

I shivered. "What a horrible thought. Automatic seriousness."

"So how are we going to get out of here?"

"Seriously?" I posed.

"I would prefer that."

"No idea." I rested back on the ground, up against a rock, and slipped my hands behind my head. "We could always knock on the portal and hope they let us surrender to them."

"That is a poor substitute for a valid plan."

"True."

"I sense no nearby ships or civilizations."

"Me either. It's just you and me against the universe."

"What a sallow prospect."

"Sallow? Why do you use such obscure words. People don't actually talk like that, you know."

"I am not *people*. I am necumplack."

"My point exactly."

"No it wasn't."

"Look, do you want to spar, or do you want to help plan how we get off this rock?"

"I do not wish to spar. As to getting off Plesmus', I think that is impossible at this time. Unless some voyagers come here and agree to help us, I feel we're doomed to remain here indefinitely."

"Why would anyone voyage here? It's not even a respectable dump."

"I agree tourism *is* sparse here. So what shall we do?"

"I'm taking a nap."

"How is that likely to help us get home?"

"It's not. I don't even sleep, so I can't take a nap."

"Then why did you mention what you did?"

"No good reason."

"Were you hoping to further rile me?"

"Man, you're good. I can't slip anything past you. By the way, don't ever say *rile* again. It's pedantic and kind of a sissy word. Thanks."

"Rile, *rile*, rile."

"You are so—"

"Oh, my. Let me grow arms, pick up pen and paper, and write this down. *You* are at a loss for words?"

I shot to my feet. "Get over yourself, snowflake. No, I just thought of a brilliant plan to get us outta here."

"I'm not up for another series of mindless exchanges."

"Good, because I'm serious." I tied my boot back on. "We're going to send Aramthella a distress call. When she receives it, she'll come rescue us. Man, I'm dangerously *brilliant*."

"Get over *your*self, snow storm."

"That expansion upon an idiom doesn't work. Do you know Morse?"

"Who's he?"

"No, I mean Morse *code*?"

"Don't know him either."

"We're going to send Aramthella a message in Morse code."

"Wait, isn't that what they used to send along copper wires on your home planet?"

"Yeah, that's the one."

"Where will we find a copper wire sufficiently long?"

"We don't need to. We're sending it via time signals."

"Time signals? What are those?"

"You no-time something in a Morse pattern and she'll receive the transmission."

"Only if she's *looking* for such signals, which she never would be."

"What she'll see is a series of no-timing events. Those she can't miss, right?"

"No. Those she will see."

"And she's a smart computer. She'll figure out there's a pattern to the signals. Then she'll simply alter course, and, presta-boom-bo, we're saved."

"What if she doesn't realize there's a pattern in the no-timing flashes?"

"Then we're back to me taking a nap."

"Which you don't take."

"So my plan *has* to work."

"That makes no sense."

"Well, Ms. Grammarian, would you like to assign me to detention, or shall we proceed with the no-timing?"

"The no-timing, which, I feel I should mention up front, is not going to work."

"Good, I really need that nap."

"Will you stop it with the nap."

"Okay, here's the pattern I need you to no-time. You

will do short no-times and slightly longer ones in the following sequence."

I explained the basics of Morse. Dots and dashes. I coded for her the message: *SOS. Jon needs help. SOS.*

Whining and grousing all the way, Plesmus finally started no-timing the dirt around us. The signal would spread almost instantaneously. The bad part would have been that even though it did and even if they received and decoded it quickly, it'd take them a while to travel this far. With outstanding luck, we were going to be here a very long time. But I was counting on them subsequently alerting Sapale. She could be here real quick with the vortex. Yeah, I was feeling *pretty* confident we'd be home for dinner, our rescue would be so fast. Then, after I ate, I could see about that nap.

Easy peasy. What could *possibly* go wrong?

THIRTY-ONE

"Captain, the enemy ship still has not stopped flank acceleration," reported Aramthella.

"They are a crazy kind of stupid," remarked Tank. "How fast are they moving?"

"Eight point nine times light."

"And the ship's integrity seems okay?" asked Sachiko.

"As far as I can tell from this distance, yes."

"It's been two full days and still they haven't eased off the throttle. Un-be-fucking-lievable," observed Tank.

"It's funny to think something frightens them more than the certain death of us catching up with them," Sachiko marveled, and not for the first time.

"There's always a worse bad, a bigger bully out there, kiddo. I *would* pay good money, however, to know what caused the time maker to react so obliviously."

"Maybe we can tell them we'll spare them if they tell us?' the captain suggested.

"Seriously? There exists a set of conditions given which you would spare them?"

"No, silly. After they told us, I blow them away."

"Remind me never to enter a long-term contract with you," remarked Tank. "Short term either, for that matter."

She stuck her tongue out at him.

He replied in kind.

"You are so—" she began to chastise.

"Captain, I'm receiving a bizarre signal," interrupted Aramthella.

"You are?"

"Well, I should put it differently. I am picking up a bizarre signal. It is hardly *directed* toward me."

"Specify," she snapped.

"A repetitive pattern of no-time burst is originating from outside our time zone."

"Say again," asked Tank.

"Some*one* or some*thing* is generating a non-random sequence of no-time events. Its origins are both distant in time and space."

"How far outside?" Sachiko asked.

"Very. It's originating from the time we left to pursue the time maker's ship. It's also on the far side of the galaxy from our space coordinates."

"So they're ancient signals?" posed Tank.

"No. I am receiving them in real time. No-time is in real time."

"Isn't that gobbledygook talk?" challenged Tank.

"No," was her terse response.

"What does the pattern suggest?" pressed Sachiko.

"That someone is sending a signal they wish someone to notice and react to."

"No duh," scoffed Tank. "Who is the signal intended to reach?"

"I cannot say since I do not know what the message hopes to relay."

"Can you decode it?" asked Sachiko.

"Probably, if it is in code."

"What else could it be?" she wondered.

"A pre-agreed upon signal, a trigger for some action."

"Like a Go-code?" queried Tank.

"Exactly."

"How long is it?" he asked.

"Very brief. That is what leads me to conclude it is a prearranged trigger, not an actual coded message."

"Show me the signal," requested Tank.

After a brief pause, she replied, "I hardly think that if a pattern makes no sense to me—"

"You can stop right there, Ms. Know-it-all. Put it on this screen and play it in the audible."

"Very well, Tank."

She did both.

Tank angled his head, straining to make meaning.

"Hell's bells and a bucket of blood. Jon needs help."

"*What?*" Sachiko blurted.

"That's in old Morse code. SOS. *Jon needs help.* SOS. Then it repeats. But the dots and dashes are issuing slowly."

"What do you mean?"

"You know. When someone taps out a telegraph, they do so quickly. Jon's spacing the signals out."

"What does that mean?" she asked, a bit stunned.

"That Plesmus is still with him. She's physically *no-timing* out the individual taps."

"Wow."

"Wow indeed," he exclaimed.

"So, are we going to rescue them?" she asked in a serious tone.

"Are we going to ... Oh—" He trailed off.

"Yeah, *oh*," she agreed. "We'd have to break off our pursuit to be able to rescue Jon and Plesmus."

"And we may never get another shot like this at the time maker."

"It hasn't happened before, has it?"

"Crap," he snapped. "Well, I guess Jon'll just have to wait. He'd understand."

"Unless they're in imminent danger. If we delay, they might not be viable when we finally do get there," the captain observed.

Tank slapped his palm to his forehead. Then he asked, "How far away are they?"

"The length of the Milky Way galaxy," responded Aramthella.

"How long would it take us to get there?" he inquired

"Even if we tried to duplicate the acceleration of the time maker, it'd take weeks," she responded.

"Wait, if he's calling for help ... his message is that he needs help, right?" wondered Sachiko.

"Pretty much," answered tank.

"Then Sapale isn't with him. Neither is the vortex; otherwise, he wouldn't need us."

"Good points. But where the hell is *she*?"

"Who knows?"

"He didn't mention her, but that doesn't mean she's not—" he started to say.

"He didn't mention Plesmus either. But he *knew* we'd *know*. She's gone and she took the vortex."

"Or she's dead."

"Then Jon'd have the vortex. No, they separated for whatever reason."

Tank paced a while. He finally stopped, a look of resolution on his face. "We have to commit to rescuing

Jon. We'll just have to take out the clan ship some other time."

"But—"

"But you were correct. His rescue might be time sensitive. We help him out first."

"Tank, we can't be there for almost a month. *Time sensitive* and *a month* are contradictory terms."

"Then we need to get there much sooner, don't we?"

She bobbed her head uncertainly. "Okay, sure. How do we do that?"

"I have no idea."

"Okay. That kind 'a sort 'a brings me back to *how do we do that*."

"I do not know, but there has to be a way."

"Why is that the case, General Sherman?" posited Aramthella. "*Wishing* it to be the case is far different from it *being* the case."

"Tell me something I don't know," he mumbled back. "But Jon needs us and we're going to help him in a timely manner befitting our commitment to his safety."

"If you say so," Aramthella seemed to mock.

"He does. And anyone who thinks or feels differently is kindly invited to get the *hell* off my ship," snarled the captain.

To be continued? Oh yeah ...

GLOSSARY:

First, a word about time, as used in this series. The clan uses several foreign, non-intuitive terms to describe time. Here are the concepts.

Anti-no-time: Such a big word! It was the side effect of the negative time generated by wormholes that were used against the clan. Since clan ships were structured with time energy, negative time deleted what it touched, like matter-antimatter interactions.

No-time: A verb. It means to take the time from a unit of space/time, leaving only space. The object has no time, it had been no-timed.

No-timers: The clan term for all non clan members.

Non-time: A noun. A sloppy word the clan uses. It can mean one of two things. First, that basically, something's dead, without time, random. It can also mean that time has stopped, for the object under discussion.

Non-time ship: Any space craft that is a non-clan ship.

Un-timed: To stop time for an object or region. Basically the same as the second meaning of non-time.

Other Glossary Terms:

Als (1): The original ship's AI on Jon's first flight long ago was Alvin. Jon shortened that to Al. When Al was joined to Jon's vortex in the Galaxy On Fire Series, Al and Blessing fell in love and got "married." Since then Jon refers to them combined as the Als.

Aramthella (1): The mighty and ancient time ship that Jon and his team stole from the body maker.

Ark 1(1): Jon's ship on his very first mission, when he traveled to find humankind a new home.

The Two Astronomers on Mars (1): Drs. Rusty Nelson and Wang served in that regard.

Azsuram (2): Original human name for the planet GB 3. It was the planet Jon and Sapale settled on after they left the human fleet fleeing doomed Earth. They established an idyllic society of Kaljaxians there, before humans join them.

Blessing (1): See *Stingray*.

Cleinoid gods/Ancient Gods (1): Ancient and malevolent mix of gods. They have destroyed many universes before and are eyeing ours now. The five ranks or groupings for their invasion were to be Rage, Torment, Wrath, Fury, and Horror.

Circumturus (1): A psychic houseplant. No, seriously. That's it. *That's* the definition. Now go back to where you were and continue the riveting story.

Command Prerogatives (1): The thin fibers Jon extends from his left four fingers. They are probes that also control a vortex.

Cragforel (1): Friendly Deavoriath Jon met after he first escaped the Adamant in the far future.

DelRoy Crozier (2): Lieutenant and working in communication on Mars 1.

Cube (1): Jon's alternate name for the vortex he captains.

Daleria (2): Demigod and innkeeper whom Jon and Sapale befriended. She worked with them against the ancient gods as she'd grown to hate them.

Davdiad (1): Kaljaxian divine spirit.

Deavoriath (1): Three arms and legs, an ancient species that had the most advanced tech in the galaxy. Very helpful to Jon.

Desdemona "Desi" Tanner (2): Former Georgetown undergrad who was a medium, that is, she perceived and communicated with dead people. Er, no thanks, I'm good. Place that gift under someone else's tree.

Emma Walters (2): Captain, and in charge of the women's barracks on Mars 1 What a thankless job.

Evil Jon Ryan/ EJ (1): Alternate time line version of the original human to android download. Over time, he turned to the darker side of his nature. He studied "magic" under a Deft master.

Form One/Form Two (1): A Form is the title of a vortex pilot. If more than one is aboard they get numerical designations based on seniority.

Gumnolar (TFL-1): Deity of the Listhelons. Very demanding.

Honesty Hartley (2): Doctor on duty at the student health center when the president had the entire staff transported to Mars. A appropriately there, as she was a total space cadet.

Kaljax (1): The home planet of Sapale. Jon went there on his original voyages.

Membrane (1): See space-time congruity manipulator.

Necumplack (2): The species name of the time controlling blobs that power the time ships.

Nuclear Engineers on Mars (1): Travis Dewitt and Ed Steuben were the two assigned to man the reactor on Mars 1.

Plesmus (2): A necumplack. She is a mucous blob that can focus time energy. Very useful for a time machine.

Praxequats (3): The ultimate time lords (sorry, Doctor). The have existed through many universes' lives. Jon initially encountered five of them.

Probe Fibers (1): Aka command prerogatives, they allow piloting of the Vortex spaceship and can analyze whatever they touch.

Reva St. Claire (2): Lt. Colonel and the new commander of Mars 1.

Robert "Tank" Sherman (1): Lead academic and friend of Sachiko. Also in Marine Reserves.

Sapale (1): Jon's Kaljaxian wife from his original flight to find humankind a new home. At first just her brain was copied, then, eventually, she was downloaded to an android host. Travelled with the corrupted Jon Ryan from an alternate time line.

Sachiko Jones (1): One time astronomy grad student under Tank's supervision. The time ship chose her to be its new captain.

Space-time congruity manipulator (1): Hugely helpful force field. Aka a membrane.

Stingray (1): Jon's Deavoriath spaceship. Her name in the Deavoriath language is pronounced "crash." Hence, silly Jon renamed her after one of his favorite cars. It makes Jon-sense.

Sunne calrf (2): A traditional Kaljaxian stew. They are all revolting to Jon, but he finds this version especially loathsome.

Swathi Varma (2): Lieutenant, and aide-de-camp to Reva St. Claire on Mars 1.

Time (1): See discussion above.

Time Maker-bob (3): The third time maker. Totally nuts but full of desires to rule.

Time Maker-ppp (1): The second supreme leader of the clan and the one in power at the beginning of this tale. Cruel, rapacious, and heartless.

Tip Benjamin (?): Where've I heard that name before? Hmm. Presently, Tip is a student at Georgetown. He was evacuated to Mars as part of the US president's plan to save a tiny portion of humankind. And they took Tip too?

Tom Grant (2): Major, and the officer in charge of the male dormitories on Mars

Toño DeJesus (1 of TFL): The scientist creator of the android Jon. Became his lifelong friend.

Vortex (1): Super-advanced Deavoriath sentient spaceship. Moves by folding space. If you get a chance to own one, do it.

Quantum Decoupler (1): A most excellent weapon that pulls the quarks apart in a proton. The energy released as they rejoin is amazing.

AND NOW A WORD FROM YOUR AUTHOR

Thank you so much for joining me, Jon, and the whole gang, on this ongoing journey! The Ryanverse is the best. The story really begins with *The Forever Life*. If you've not read that, and the rest of the series from the start, I suggest you do. You will not be disappointed.

The outstanding people at Podium Publishing are working hard to get all the books of the Ryanverse into audiobooks to place on Audible. If any book you're looking for isn't there, it will be soon.

Two favors. One, let me know your impressions, thoughts, or suggestions. You can do that by contacting me by email (contact@craigarobertson.com) or on my Facebook Author's Page. Second, please post a review on Amazon/Audible. Those are more precious than you might imagine to us authors.

Finally, there will be more soon, so be happy, dudes! I know I will ...

craig